TREASURE LUST

TREASURE LUST
THE TRIANGLE OF DEATH

Bury yourself in the pages of
Mystery, suspense and romance
That forms a triangle around
The Beale Treasure of Bedford County, Va.

RICHARD L. STOCKDALE

Author of
MANA - A Loved one's Bipolar Mania
And
REDRUM - Murder in D.C.

iUniverse, Inc.
Bloomington

Treasure Lust
The Triangle of Death

iUniverse books may be ordered through booksellers or by contacting:

iUniverse
1663 Liberty Drive
Bloomington, IN 47403
www.iuniverse.com
1-800-Authors (1-800-288-4677)

ISBN: 978-1-4620-6045-0 (sc)
ISBN: 978-1-4620-6046-7 (e)

Printed in the United States of America

iUniverse rev. date: 10/17/2011

Introduction

In 1822, a tall dark man named Thomas J. Beale left three coded ciphers with a hotel manager in Lynchburg, Virginia. A metal box contained a note telling what the ciphers would reveal once they were decoded. The first cipher was decoded 1845, and it read:

> *"I have deposited in the county of Bedford, about four miles from Buford's Inn an excavation or vault, six feet below the surface of the ground, the following articles; the deposit consists of two thousand nine hundred and twenty-one pounds of gold and five thousand one hundred pounds of silver; also jewels, obtained in St. Louis in exchange for silver to save transportation. The above is securely packed in iron pots, with iron covers. The vault is roughly lined with stone, and the vessels rest on solid stone, and are covered with others...."*

This was the beginning of a tidal wave of treasure hunters who sought the vast treasure promised in the ciphers. The lust for gold and riches drew people from all lifestyles, each one thinking they had the key to where the treasure rested.

This heavily desired fortune is now better known as the Beale Treasure. For well over a hundred years, many people have tried to decipher the other two coded messages. Many have spent their lives and fortunes seeking this treasure. Some have even died for it.

One hundred and seventy years after its deposit, three groups of people formed a triangle of intrigue around the Beale Treasure. One group was comprised of wealthy and prominent executives who were out to gain fame and to line their pockets with more wealth. Since they did not really need the money, the hunt for the Beale Treasure was more of a game to them. It was an escape from the monotony of their day-to-day money making ventures.

The second group included couples in love. Each person in this group was innocently and inadvertently been drawn into the search for different reasons. One of those reasons was not to seek material wealth, though. Each couple had their own treasure in their love for one another.

The third and more ominous group had no wealth and felt they had a claim to the treasure. They would stop at nothing to assure that the treasure ended up in what they thought were the rightful hands, their hands. Murder became their method of operation. Secrecy and deception were the founding principles of their code of honor. There was no price too great to pay for the rights to the treasure, as long as it was not them paying the price.

Chapter 1

There are many advantages to living on a mountain overlooking a beautiful valley. When you awaken on a bright spring morning to find a low fog in the valley covering up everything but the highest hilltops, resembling islands in a vast sea, and the mountain range in the distance looks like a giant tidal wave about to sweep over them. One can sit on his deck drinking his morning coffee and admire the wondrous sight of the sun slowly creeping over the mountains, shining down on the fog and giving it a golden glow.

In minutes, the sun will bake away the fog and reveal the ugly truth; which is, temporarily, hidden from view. As one looks over the valley, he can see it as it must have been before the first white man put his dirty footprint on it. He can see it as the Indians must have seen it three hundred years ago- natural and beautiful, wild and free. No factories, towns, streets, or houses were there to mar its natural beauty.

I guess I look at things a little differently than most people do. My work exposes me to a life filled with mans atrocities to one another, murder, greed, and deception. It no longer surprises me how ugly and cruel one human can be to another. Yes, soon the sun will cook away the fog, revealing the world I live in and work in, the ugly world of crime. I will face once again with the rising sun. The many nightmares which man perpetrates on one another, while under the concealment of the night. As the sun climbs into the sky and the fog lifts, the city becomes visible, and the ugliness of the night will soon become news.

To most people, it is a relatively quiet and peaceful city, clean and beautiful as far as cities go. They read about the crimes, but it is just a story to the majority of them. Most crimes are just a blurb in the newspaper that most people are unaffected by. I am one of the few who is affected more so than others because it is my job; a job that I love and am proud of, I am a cop.

As I drink my second cup of coffee, I gaze out over a valley that has now lost a great deal of its charm and appeal as the last of the fog disappears. My dog, Ranger, sits beside me as I wonder what problems the day might hold for me. What crimes will I be faced with this morning? Will it be burglary or assault? Maybe it will be robbery or domestic abuse. Of course, there is also rape or possibly even a homicide. The good thing is that I was not, called out during the night and my pager had not beeped. Maybe, just maybe, crime took a holiday last night. What a joke. I have been a cop for a long time, and not one single day in all that time did crime ever take a holiday.

Nobody forced me to join the police department, and nobody has forced me to stay. I do it because I love the work. I feel that I help a lot more people than I harm and that the people I do harm deserve it. They commit crimes that hurt other people, sometimes many people. Sure, I see the bad side of many people, but I also see the good side of a great many more people. That is one of the things that make's my job more worthwhile and important to me. It takes a special kind of person to be a cop, and I like to feel that I am one of those special people.

It is a dirty job, but it can be very rewarding. That feeling you get when you put a criminal away makes the bad times worth it. I like getting the bad ones off the street so they cannot hurt anyone else, at least for a while. There are those few that do conform. They do their time and come out of prison rehabilitated. They become good citizens. They are the people, along with the citizens that I have protected, that really put a nice warm fuzzy feeling in my gut.

It was time for me to finish my coffee and pat Ranger on the head before beginning the ritual of dressing for work. The need to leave the comfort and safety of my mountain top hideaway to head into the city was rapidly approaching. As I put on my Teflon bulletproof vest and holstered my gun, a nine-millimeter semi-automatic, I say a little prayer that both would prove themselves useless today. One thing about being a cop is that every day I walk out of my front door, I never know if I am going to walk back through it again. Even if I do come home tonight, will I still be the same man that walked out of it earlier today? Does every day on the job change me? I think so. Some change me for the better, and some change me for the worse. Not knowing which of the two changes today will bring is what I face every day in this job, and the change begins when I get in that car and turn on the police radio.

As I head for the city, some people are heading for bed, but the majority of them are waking up and starting a new day. Like me, they are heading out for work. If any crimes happened during the night, they would soon be discovered and then reported. Then my job would begin.

Reaching the highway to town, I heard a siren coming from the direction of the city, so I waited until after it passed before pulling out. It was an ambulance. There may have been an accident down the road, but my radio remained silent except for the normal morning chatter. I switched bands to pick up the county traffic and listen for any details there, but again, just normal morning chatter ran through the airwaves.

When I reached City Hall, I pulled into the police lot and parked in my regular spot. I saw the Mayor's secretary, Lora Jean Coffey, heading to work. As I watched her walking toward the employee entrance, I thought to myself, *"Now there's something I would like to spend some time investigating."* I had gone to school with Lora Jean. She was so popular that I never had the nerve to ask her out. I wanted to, but I was too afraid of the possibility that she may reject my interest in her. It would have crushed my ego at that time in my life. When I came back from the Army and a couple of tours in Vietnam, I was a different person, but she was married by then. Now, we are both divorced, and I have been thinking more and more about asking her out.

When she saw me getting out of my car, she waved at me, and I waved back. To her, it was just a friendly gesture, but to me, it was an indication that she knew I was alive. I went into police headquarters and straight to the coffee room to grab a cup of Joe and a donut before they were all gone. Then, it was off to my office. After so many years of pounding a beat and then patrol, I had finally made detective. I had spent a couple of years in the squad room before making sergeant. Now, I have my own office with my name on the door, "Lieutenant Damon Carter."

I had only made lieutenant a couple of weeks earlier, so I was still getting my feet wet and getting used to the fine people I worked with for so long treating me differently than they had in the past. I was lucky, though. I had some very fine detectives working under me, like Sergeant Mike Dorsey and Kelly Williams. Dorsey was a decorated officer and a bronze star recipient from the Army. Kelly was a second-generation police officer, which allowed her to think outside the box. She was a very good detective and had solved some very difficult cases. Even though she was younger than most of the others, she was up for promotion to sergeant.

The rest of the squad could not have been much better if I had hand picked them myself. I trusted almost every one of them completely, not only as fine honest officers, also as men and women that I would and did trust with my life. No, I had no doubts about most of the officers under my command, but I did question some of the decisions that came down from one or two of my superiors.

I had five men whom I got my orders from, Captain Mirant the Section Commander, Major Taylor the Division Commander, Chief Lewis the Chief of Police, Scott Barker the Police Commissioner, and Mayor Caldwell. Chief Lewis I trusted completely. Captain Mirant seemed upright, but I still had a few reservations about him due to an incident in 1985 that involved a good friend of mine. The rest would sell their mothers to get ahead, or so I felt anyway.

It was almost ten in the morning, and so far, it was a quiet day. There had not been any new crimes reported, but then I saw Detective Williams heading toward my office. By the look on her face, I could tell that she was not just coming to wish me a good morning.

"Lieutenant, Captain Mirant wants to see you in his office right away."

"So much for a quiet morning," I thought to myself.

"Okay, Kelly, tell him I'll be right there."

Stopping by the coffee room for a refill on the way, I headed over to Mirant's office.

"Good morning, Captain, what's up?"

"Morning, Damon. This isn't a homicide, but I don't know whom else to give it to."

"What do you mean? What do you have for me?" I asked.

"Well, we had two graves dug up at the City Cemetery last night. The grave sites were the resting places of a husband and wife who were killed in an automobile accident a little over a year ago in April of 1989."

"Really, Wow? That is different! Bodies removed or what?"

"No, nothing was bothered as near as we can tell. The coffins were opened and closed but not fastened down, just plain morbid."

"Think it was vandals or kids that did it?"

"No, Damon, I don't think so. It was done much too neatly, as if they would have covered the graves back up if they'd had the time. The sod was in neat rolls so it could be replaced once they had filled the grave in."

"Captain, I hate to sound dumb, but what can we do? Was anything, in the way of evidence, left behind?"

"No, not a thing. Put some people on it. Get them to question relatives of the couple. See if they can come up with anything."

"Right, Captain, consider it done. Anything else you might have in mind?"

"No, Lieutenant, that's my best and only suggestion, I'm afraid. There are the tarps that they used to pile the dirt on, but they are available in many stores in town. They weren't new, either."

"Well, that's something. We can have the lab boys look them over. They might just come up with something. It's a start anyway."

As I walked back through the squad room, Kelly was watching me, so I said, "Kelly, you and Bill Austin come to my office. I have a job for you two."

Kelly just smiled, grabbed a pad of paper, and yelled at Bill, "Come on, Bill. The boss wants us."

I explained what was going on to Kelly and Bill. They then headed out to the cemetery to see what they could find. We had a stack of cases that we were working on, and even though this was not our cup of tea, it was important. We cannot have people just going around and digging up our dear departed loved ones. This sort of thing can cause a great deal of public unrest.

That evening, I stayed late, waiting for Kelly and Bill to come back. When they arrived, I had them come into my office and report their findings.

"Lieutenant, the family members we questioned have no idea why anyone would have dug up these graves, but everyone we questioned was very upset that it happened," Kelly reported.

Then Bill added, "I took the tarps to the lab, but they haven't come back with anything on them yet."

"What about the graves and the bodies? Was there anything there?"

"We had the funeral director, who handled their services and burials, come out. He seemed to think that both bodies had been moved from their original positions in the coffins. Not taken out but moved around as if someone had checked or looked for something under the bodies," Kelly replied.

"That's it? You have nothing else?"

"No, Lieutenant, except we told them it would be okay to reseal the coffins and cover them up again," Kelly said, not seeming too confident that she had done the right thing, by allowing them to recover the graves.

"Kelly and Bill, you did just fine. I don't know what else you could have done. Maybe the lab will come up with something on those tarps."

The next day was a little busier. There had been a shooting during the night in a trailer park near the city limits. An abused wife had decided that she had enough of her husband beating her up every time he got together with his friends and got drunk, so she shot him. Unfortunately, she did not kill him. She simply ruined his sex life permanently. She was already under arrest for felonious assault.

Then Kelly came to my office, "Lieutenant, we have another one."

"What do you mean another one, another one what, Kelly?"

"Someone dug up another body in the last couple nights, but this time they covered it back up and put the sod back over the dirt. The attendant just happened to notice the fresh looking appearance of the grave and thought that it was odd since the date of death was a year ago, April 1989. Upon closer examination, it was evident that the grave had been dug up."

"We have a court order to dig up the grave and check it. Bill and I are about to leave to go over there."

"Okay, Kelly, I think I'll join you."

Then Kelly informed me "This one is at Diamond Hill Cemetery, not the City Cemetery. I am having Bill check to see what funeral home handled the services. When we find out we'll request that they send someone to the cemetery to meet with us and examine the grave."

"Is there any connection between the grave that was discovered today and the graves the night before last?"

"No Sir, not that we have found. Well that is other than the date of death being only one day apart. An automobile accident had killed the couple on April 27, 1989 and the woman at Diamond Hill died on April 26, 1989. She died of heart failure at the hospital."

"That's interesting. Start calling every cemetery in the area, and have them physically check every grave that was dug in April 1989."

"Of course we can do that, Lieutenant, but there are a lot of cemeteries. It might take a couple of days. You really think that's necessary?"

"It's just a hunch and could turn out to be a waste of time, but do what you can, Kelly. I will give you Jack and Leonard to give you a hand. Go back to the families and see if there is any connection between these two incidents. "

"You're the boss. We'll take care of it right away."

A couple more days passed before the cemeteries started reporting their finding. Two more graves had been disturbed recently, and the only apparent connection was the dates of the deaths. They had all died between the 26th and 29th of April in 1989. Kelly and the other detectives questioned all of the families involved and the funeral homes that handled each service and burial. They compared the funeral records and lists of people who attended each funeral.

After reviewing all of the information, Kelly put her finger on a narrower commonality. While they had all died on different days, they where all buried on the same day, April 30, 1989. She then began pulling the obituaries from the newspaper for that date. She found that on April 30, 1989, there were nine funerals. Kelly and Bill went to each cemetery where a funeral had taken place that day, and they were able to locate all nine graves. It was evident that all nine had been disturbed within the last two to three weeks.

The news media had gotten wind of the investigation and were playing it up big, so when we contacted the cemeteries to check all of the graves that funerals were between the twenty-fifth and thirty-first of April in1989. The cooperation was overwhelming. We found that the only graves that had been disturbed were the ones at which funerals and burials were on April 30.

The media attention had also gotten the public concerned and involved, so, naturally, we started getting tips on everything from UFO sightings over the cemeteries to descriptions of suspicious vehicles and people seen in the areas near and around the different cemeteries.

We had gotten several reports of a black van in the vicinities of the cemeteries. Out of twelve sightings, seven witnesses said that the van had a ladder rack on top. The remaining five were not sure about that detail, but three people reported that it had diamond shaped windows on the sides near the rear and fancy hubcaps.

Upon reviewing the case, we knew that we had discovered a date of some significance and a fair description of a van that was most likely involved. It was not a bad start, but we needed more.

We started going through newspapers from a week prior to the thirtieth of April in1989. We also checked police records for the same period but turned up little. We did find that there had been six burglaries, three armed robberies, two missing persons and two murders reported during that time. Out of the two missing person cases, both reported on the thirty-first but both went missing on the twenty-ninth. Out of the two murder cases, one was solved and the other case was still open and under investigation.

One of the people reported missing at that time was Adam Knight, a reporter for one of the local newspapers. The other person was Ellen Christian; she was a server at a diner. This diner was a hang out for the employees that worked for the same newspaper as Knight did. Christian was a divorcee who had been dating Knight for a couple of months. Adam Knight's roommate reported them missing after not hearing from them for more than a day. They had Christian's ex-husband brought in for questioning. He had an airtight alibi for the entire week they were first reported missing. There has never been a trace of either one since.

I decided to check with Missing Persons to find out if there had been any new developments in the case. The investigating officer, Lieutenant Charley Gant, informed me that the case was still under investigation and that Adam Knight's brother, Tom Knight called him at least twice a month to see if there was any progress to report in the case. His answer was always negative. Because no trace of the couple or the car that Adam Knight had been driving had showed up.

On a hunch, I asked Lieutenant Gant, "Lieutenant, do you happen to know what kind of vehicle Tom Knight drives?"

"Yes, we met a couple of times at the diner that Ellen Christian had worked at. He always came in a black Chevy van. He had customized it and used it to carry a kayak. He said that he likes to run a river down state."

"So he had a rack on top of his van, like a ladder rack?"

"No, it wasn't a ladder rack. It was a rack specifically used for canoes or kayaks, Lieutenant."

"Do you have a current address on Tom Knight?"

"No, I don't. He moved about nine months ago from the motel, he was staying in, and he always did the contacting. I don't even have a phone number for him."

"That's alright, Lieutenant. Just give me the name of the motel and any other information you have on him. I need to know everything you know about his brother and Ellen."

"What's going on? Do you have a lead? I have sort of a personal interest in this case. This case has been a thorn in my side for over a year."

"Not really, that is nothing for sure. I am just following up on a hunch. It may have nothing to do with your missing person."

I went back to my office to check on what type of vehicles that Tom Knight had registered in his name through the Division of Motor Vehicles. He had a 1987 Chevy van registered to him, but the address was the same as the one Lieutenant Gant had given me. He had bought the van a few months ago from a local dealer. I called the dealer and found that he had paid cash for it. I drove to the motel, but they had no forwarding address on Knight. The clerk did say that Tom came around and picked up his mail for a couple of months after he had moved out, but they had not seen or heard from him in months. They also said he paid cash for the room and always a month in advance.

When I got back to the office, I called Kelly and Bill in and told them about Tom Knight. I explained that he has a black van registered in his name. That he was driving one that had a rack on top of it. I gave them all the information I had gathered on Knight and the info that Gant had given me on his brother and his girlfriend.

"Lieutenant, if you're going to solve all of our cases for us, why are you keeping us around?" Kelly asked.

"Kelly, this case is a long way from being solved. I played a hunch, and it may have paid off. Believe me; you both have your work cut out for you on this one. Something tells me we haven't scratched the surface on this case yet."

"My gut tells me that it seems pretty logical that this Tom Knight might very well be our grave robber. All we have to do is find him."

"Finding him might not be so easy. I haven't been able to locate anything on him since he moved from the motel where he was staying. There is also the why. Why was he digging up those graves? What did he hope to find?"

"Well, Lieutenant, we'll ask him that when we find him, and we will find him." Kelly said as she left my office.

It was about time for lunch, and I thought I might try a new place for lunch today, like the diner that Ellen Christian worked at before she disappeared. When I walked into the diner, to my surprise, I saw Lora Jean seated in a booth alone, reading a book.

I walked up to her and said, "Hi, Lora, you alone?"

She looked up at me, "Hello, Damon. Yes, I am alone. Would you like to join me?"

"Thanks, Lora, I would love to join you, if it's no bother."

"Congratulations on your promotion, Damon. I saw where you made Lieutenant a couple of weeks ago. Your career with the police department has been impressive, along with your military service."

"Thank you. I'm just getting used to the new job. I expect it will take a while for me to feel comfortable with it. This is wonderful having lunch with you. We really haven't spoken much since high school."

"We didn't speak much in high school, either. You never seemed very interested in talking to me," Lora said to my surprise.

"Are you kidding? I wanted to talk to you in the worst kind of way, but I was a little shy back in those days. In fact, I'm still a little shy, especially when it comes to you. I wanted to ask you out to a movie or something but just couldn't muster the nerve."

"I wish you had asked me out, Damon. I would have gone. I just can't believe you lacked the nerve. You were quarterback on the football team. Then in the Army, you won some very impressive metals and became a hero. Doesn't sound like a man that lacks having nerve to me, not at all."

"Lora, I'm no hero. I have a couple of minor decorations, but I am not a hero. You come here for lunch often? This is a good distance from your office. I'm sort of surprised to see you here."

"Yes, I do. I meet a friend here for lunch a couple of times a week."

"Oh, I'm sorry. Maybe I should not be sitting here when he arrives. He might not like it."

"Damon, relax. 'He' happens to be a woman, and she is not coming today. Even if she did show, I would still want you to stay. You know her. She went to school with us, Norma Christian. Her younger sister used to work as a waitress here before disappearing a little over a year ago."

"I remember her from school. So, she's Ellen Christian's sister?"

"Yes, that's correct. How do you know Ellen? I wouldn't have thought you would have known her. She was about six years behind us in school."

"Lora, to be honest, that is why I'm here at this diner. I am looking into Ellen and her boyfriend Adam's disappearance. It may be connected to a case we are working right now."

"Oh, Damon, it would be so wonderful if you could uncover what happened to them. Norma has not been herself since her sister disappeared over a year ago. She figures she might be dead, but the not knowing is driving her insane. Watching her suffer is hard for me to deal with."

"I know you must be good friends and I am sure you feel bad for her. You had nothing to do with her sister's disappearance, did you?"

"Did I do anything to or with them? No, of course not. Why would I? I just feel bad that I can't relieve her mind and worries."

"I don't see that happening unless you know where they are and what happened to them. That's what we are trying to find out. While we are on the subject, Lora, do you happen to know a Tom Knight?"

"Yes, I do, but I can't tell you much about him. The times I did meet him he seemed secretive and stand offish. Norma can, though. She mentions him often. He is the brother of Adam Knight, the man who disappeared with Norma's sister. I think they're in contact with each other on a regular basis, maybe even dating."

"Lora, can I get Norma's address and phone number from you?"

"No, I don't think it's necessary for me to give it to you."

"Why not Lora, I'm sorry I don't understand why you won't give it to me?"

"Because she just came in the door and is on her way over here."

I turned to look and saw a very attractive woman, who I would have never recognized as Norma. She was approaching the table.

"I tell you that I don't think that I can meet you for lunch, and what do you do? You go out and find a handsome man to have lunch with instead!"

Norma then turned her eyes from Lora and looked at me.

"Hi, I'm Norma, a friend of Lora," she said as she acknowledged me.

"I know, Norma. I 'm Damon Carter. We went to school together."

"Damon. Huh, I thought you looked familiar. I haven't seen you for years. I guess high school was the last time. Where are you living? What are you doing now?"

"Damon lives here in town, or just outside of town a few miles, I should say. He's a Lieutenant on our police department," Lora offered.

"Thank you, Lora, but can't Damon speak for himself?"

"Norma, Lora did a better job than I would have. I would have only said I'm a cop and live here."

"What kind of cop are you?" Norma asked.

"A good one, I hope, or at least I try to be," Damon replied.

"No, I mean what type of cases do you handle?"

"Homicide, but I dabble in other major crimes as well. Right now, I am working on the grave robber case. Have you heard about it?"

"I'm not familiar with it. I don't read the paper much."

"I was just asking Lora for your address and phone number when you came in, Norma."

"Oh really, I'm very flattered, but I'm seeing somebody."

"You misunderstand. I wanted to talk to you about Tom Knight. I thought you might know how to get in touch with him."

"I'm sorry, Damon. I don't know the man," Norma replied. She then asked the server to change her order in to a to-go order.

"Norma, I just told Damon that you did know Tom Knight and that you talk about him all the time," Lora spoke up.

"You must be mistaken, Lora. I know who he is, of course, but I don't know him. I don't know where to find him, either. Now if you will excuse me, my order's ready, and I need to go."

With that, Norma paid her check, picked up her order, and left the diner without so much as a glance back or wave good-bye.

"I'm so sorry, Damon. I don't know what got into her. Normally, she's a very friendly and polite girl," Lora explained.

"That's alright, Lora. I think I might've touched on a sour spot with her. I should be the one apologizing for intruding on your lunch."

"You didn't intrude. I invited you, and I am glad I did. If anyone intruded, it was Norma. She told me she wouldn't be here today. Then she just showed up and joined us for lunch. On top of that, she outright lied to you when you asked her about Tom Knight."

"I'm sure she had her reasons, Lora. Not to change the subject, but I would like to ask you something that I should've asked you a long time ago."

"Really, what could that be?" Lora said inquisitively.

"Would you like to have dinner with me Thursday night and maybe take in a movie or something?"

"Oh, I'm afraid I can't."

"How stupid can I be? I should have known you're seeing someone."

"No, I'm not, but I have a basketball game Thursday night. I coach a girl's basketball team. If you'd like to come to the game, we could go out for an informal dinner afterward."

"Fantastic. That sounds like a great first date to me."

"Damon, are you making fun of me?"

"No, Lora, I really mean it. It really does sound great. I've wanted to ask you out since high school. To be honest, a very impromptu and informal date seems to be just the right way to start."

"Okay, then. It is a date. The game starts at seven at the James Douglas High School. You can pick me up at six-thirty. Here is my address and my phone number. Here's the address and phone number for Norma also. Just please avoid telling her you got it from me, if you can."

"Thanks, Lora, I got your lunch check, and as much as I hate to, I need to go play policeman for a while."

"Yes, I need to get back to the office also. This whole city could come to a standstill if I'm two minutes late getting back from lunch. There's just on more thing, Damon. There's something I want to give you before you leave," Lora said as we both stood to leave.

"What's that?"

"I don't believe in leaving things to chance." With that said, she put her arms around me and gave me a big hug and a kiss right there in the diner.

"Just an ice breaker, so you know where I stand with you. I've wanted you to ask me out for years," Lora said.

Icebreaker was right. That first kiss thawed me out all the way down to my toes. I was actually weak in the knees as I walked her to her car.

"I'll see you Thursday, at around six-thirty," she confirmed as she gave me another quick kiss.

I opened her door for her and replied, "Yes, absolutely, I'll be there."

I had not dated much since my divorce two years earlier. Actually, I had not really tried to. I cannot believe that I stumbled into this the way that I did. It could not have gone better if I had planned it. Now, I had a date with a woman I had admired since I was in high school.

As I drove away from the diner, I tried to concentrate on the case, but my mind kept drifting back to Lora. She really was a wonderful woman. I could not believe she was available, and I really could not believe she was so receptive to me. I needed to get my mind back on the case, though. Public opinion was important to the police department, and the public did not like the idea of their departed loved ones unearthed from their eternal sleep in the middle of the night.

My short encounter with Norma left only one thought in my mind, and that was that she was hiding something more than just her relationship with Tom Knight. She had become very nervous and uncomfortable with the mere mention of his name. I was going to need to pay Norma a visit in the next day or so, whether she liked it or not. I got the impression she knew a lot of helpful information, but I also knew it would be like pulling teeth to get it out of her.

I was only a couple of blocks from the diner when I noticed a black Chevy van with a kayak rack on top of it just a couple of cars behind me. I moved over to the left lane and made a left turn at the next corner. The black van was still behind me. I drove down a couple more blocks and made another left turn. The van followed. This was an interesting development, so I turned onto a dead end street, wanting the van to follow me. I stopped, and it passed me. I now had it trapped.

When the van reached the end of the street, it turned around and just stopped. No one got out. It just sat there with the motor running. I could not make out whom the driver was; it was certainly likely it might be Tom Knight. Why would he be following me, though? I got out of my car, walked up to the front of my car, and leaned against the fender. I just stood there watching what the person in the van might do next.

Suddenly it started toward me, picking up speed as it came. I pulled out my badge and held it up with one hand, signaling the van to stop with the other. I got in its path, but it made no effort to slow down. Soon, it was obvious that it would run me down if I did not move out of the way. I jumped out of its path just in time, but I got a good look at the driver. It was not Tom Knight, it was not even a man. It was Norma Christian.

Chapter 2

Norma had looked right at me as she almost ran me down in the van. She knew that I would have recognized her, and I am sure she was expecting me to come by. As I drove up to Norma's house, I looked up and down the street to see if the black van was around. It was not. She did not have a garage, so I was not sure if I would find her at home or not. I had checked with the Division of Motor Vehicles, and she did not have a van registered to her. The only vehicle she had registered in her name was a Ford sedan. I had not noticed what kind of car she had driven to the diner. I figured that the van was Tom Knight's, but why was Norma driving it?

I got out of my car and approached Norma's house with some caution. As I walked to the front, I noticed the storm door closed but that the main door was wide open. I looked in and saw Norma sitting on the sofa with her hands over her face. I knocked, and she looked up at me and motioned for me to come on in. She then put her face back in her hands.

"I've been expecting you, Damon. I guess I have some explaining to do."

"Yes, Norma, I think you do."

"I thought you would have been here earlier. Are you here to arrest me?"

"No, Norma! Not right now anyway. I thought I'd give you the chance to explain why you were following me and why you tried to run me down."

"Oh, Damon, I wasn't trying to run you down. I just panicked. I knew you would get out of the way before I hit you. I don't want to hurt anyone."

"I don't know, Norma. Seemed to me you were pretty intent on hitting me. I can charge you with a couple different crimes, like failing to stop for a Police Officer and Attempted Murder, even."

"Damon, I don't know what I was thinking. I don't even know why I was following you for sure. You had asked me about Tom, and I wanted to know what you were doing, I guess."

"Is that Tom's van you were driving?"

"Yes, he took my car to get it inspected today and gave me the van to drive."

"Where is Tom now?"

"I honestly don't know. When he brought my car back to the place I work, they told him I hadn't come back from lunch. He showed up over here. I told him you were asking questions about him and that I followed you. I also told him about you blocking me in on that dead end street and how I accidently almost hit you when I was trying to get away. He got in his van and drove away quickly. He didn't tell me where he was going."

"You lied to me about Tom at lunch today. How do I know you aren't lying now?"

"Damon, I'm too scared to lie right now. I know you can arrest me and put me in jail for what happened this afternoon."

"Okay, Norma, why don't you tell me what all is going on with you and Tom Knight?

What have the two of you got to hide, and why?"

"I can't tell you. I love Tom, and he would never speak to me again if I tell you anything."

"Norma, I guess we'd better go down to the police station then."

"No, Damon, I can't. What would I tell my children?"

"Norma, I'm here now more as a friend than as a police officer, but if I have to be a police officer to get the truth out of you, believe me, I will be. So, what's it going to be?"

"Oh my God, I don't know what to do. I wish I could talk to Tom.

All I wanted to do was to find out what happened to my sister. Haven't I suffered enough?"

"Norma, maybe it'll help if I tell you that we know that Tom has been digging up graves."

She started crying hysterically and jumped to her feet. She ran to the bathroom and locked the door before I could stop her. I could hear her moving things around, and it sounded like the medicine cabinet being open and closed. I could also hear the water running.

"Norma, open this door and talk to me right now, or I'm going to break it down."

"No! My life is over. My kids are going to think I'm some kind of monster who's involved in digging up dead bodies!"

"Open this door! I mean it, Norma. If you don't, I'm breaking it down."

"Go away, Damon. Please just go away and leave me alone. I'm ruined. I have to do this my way. May God forgive me!"

I backed up a few paces and hit the door hard. It moved but did not open. I tried a couple more times. It was weakened greatly but still had not opened. I backed up further and gave it one last hard hit. This time, the jam shattered and the door burst open.

There were pill bottles and pills all over the floor. Norma was sitting in the corner crying. I picked up a couple of the bottles to see what she may have taken as I ran to the phone to call 911. When I returned, I tried to make her throw up, but I was unsuccessful. I started walking her around, and by the time I heard the sound of the siren in the distance, Norma was barely conscious.

A few minutes later, the rescue squad arrived and took over for me. I don't think I have ever been happier to see anyone. They gave her ipecac syrup right away and loaded Norma up to rush her to the hospital. The medic told me not to worry and that she was going to be all right. I followed the ambulance to the hospital just to make sure.

On the way, I radioed Detective Williams. I told her to put out an all-points bulletin for Tom Knight and a description of his van. I then had dispatch patch me into a phone line so I could call Lora. I wanted to tell her about Norma. What had happened and what hospital they were taking her to.

I had more questions for Norma, but I knew it would be tomorrow at the earliest before I could try to get any answers. I cannot believe that I let her do this to herself right in front of me. I cannot believe that I could not stop her.

The hospital was only a few blocks from the Mayor's office, so I knew that there was a good chance that Lora would get there before me. Sure enough, she was following Norma's gurney through the emergency room doors as I looked for a place to park. A few minutes later, I found myself facing a rather upset Lora.

"What on earth is going on, Damon?"

I knew this was going to take a while, and I sure could use a cup of coffee.

"Lora, let's go down to the cafeteria. They aren't going to let you anywhere near Norma for a little while anyway. I'll try to explain this whole mess, but I need some coffee."

"Okay, Damon, but I just don't understand how everything got so messed up so fast."

We got our coffee and sat at a table in the cafeteria to talk. I told her why I was at the diner and that I was looking for a lead to Tom Knight because he was a suspect in the grave robber case. I explained that meeting Norma and seeing her suspicious response to the mention of Tom had gotten my curiosity up. It only increased when she followed me in Tom's van and tried to run me down. I then told her how I went to her house and how she got hysterical and took a bunch of pills.

"I can't believe Norma tried to run you down. That just doesn't sound like her."

"Well, she did, sound like her or not."

"What are you going to do with her now?"

"She as much as admitted to me that she's involved in the digging up of the graves, so I'm going to have to place her under arrest when she's well enough."

"Norma admitted to digging up the graves? Why would she do that?"

"That's what I hope to find out when I talk to her. I need to know what her connection to Tom Knight is and what part she played in digging up these graves. I also need to know what motivated her to put herself in this position."

"No wonder she tried to kill herself. This is going to ruin her."

"I don't think she actually dug the graves up. I think Tom did that. If she cooperates, I will see what I can do to help her. I could probably help her get a light sentence, maybe probation. That's where you come in Lora. I want you to talk to her first. Maybe you can convince her to cooperate with me."

"I can try."

"Great, but tell her she has to come completely clean with me about everything she knows or I won't be able to help her."

"Do you think you can keep her out of it altogether?"

"I don't, but it depends on how much and what she tells me. It also depends a great deal on what part she took in the desecration of these grave sites. This is a serious crime and the penalties can be very harsh."

"I'm sure it will be a while before they allow me to see her. If I bring it up right away or not will depend on her state of mind."

"I understand, Lora. You handle it the way you think best. I'm leaving it up to you. Just let me know once you've talked to her about it. Then I'll pay her a visit and see what she can or will tell me. Meantime, we are trying to locate Tom Knight. He's the one that I really want to talk to."

We finished our coffee, and I walked Lora back up to the emergency room waiting area. We sat and talked for about an hour before I had to leave. I was glad to know that Lora did not blame me for what Norma had done. We were still planning on going out after the game on Thursday. I would have hated it if this mess had upset our plans. I have waited a long time to date Lora. I did not want to start on the wrong foot.

When I got back to the office, Detective Williams was waiting for me with a very impatient look on her face. I walked strait to my office with her hot on my heels. I had not had time to remove my jacket before she closed my office door behind her as she entered.

"Lieutenant, why assign me a case if you're going to solve it for me? The least you could do is to keep me informed as to what you are doing."

"Kelly, believe me, I didn't plan on any of this. I simply went to lunch at a diner on a hunch, and things just started happening. The important thing is that the case is solved, which it isn't solved as of right now. I think it's going to get more involved as time goes on. Things just don't add up."

"What exactly are you referring to?"

"The first thing that I question is why Tom Knight was digging up those graves. Then there's Norma Christian. She's a classy woman, who has a good job and kids. She just doesn't seem like the type of woman who would have anything to do with this."

"There must be a reason, though. When can we talk to her?"

"Later this evening, if we're lucky, but it'll probably have to wait until tomorrow morning. I'll be asking all of the questions of Norma, but I want you and Bill to be there with me."

"Yes Sir, Lieutenant, we'll be there just in case you want us to do anything."

"Get off your high-horse, Kelly. This is still your case, but something tells me that there are going to be a great deal more developments uncovered in this case. When that begins to happen, which I think it will, it could require the attention of the entire squad. Besides, I went to school with Norma, and she's more likely to talk to me than anyone else."

"I'm sorry, Lieutenant. I'm just a little aggravated that I wasn't kept informed as to what was going on."

"I called you as soon as I could, and I told you as much as I could under the circumstances. I did have a woman full of sleeping pills dying on me when I called you. Besides, we are a team. A team who works together solves cases together."

"You're right. Please accept my apology again."

At that exact moment, Bill Austin knocked on the door, stuck his head in, and said, "Kelly, the hospital just called and said that Mrs. Christian wouldn't be awake until tomorrow morning."

"Okay. Thanks Bill. I guess we can get some rest tonight."

I then asked Kelly about Norma's kids.

"They're adults," she replied. "One is twenty-one, and the other is twenty-three. Both are married."

"Really I didn't know. I got the impression that they were much younger. It must've been the way she sounded so worried about them."

"I guess even you can make a mistake, Lieutenant," Kelly said as she left the office, smiling from ear to ear.

"Alright, Detective Williams, you made your point. I will see you and Bill in the morning. Don't go to the hospital until I get here to go with you."

I left the office around six and headed for home. I could not get Norma off my mind. I felt guilty that I had not been able to stop her from taking those pills. I just don't understand how a woman with so much to lose could have gotten involved in this whole mess.

When I arrived at the house, I could hear Ranger barking. He always knew the second I got home. I went straight to the refrigerator and got a beer. Ranger and I then went out on the deck to watch the sunset. As the sun slid down behind the mountains on the other side of the valley, the clouds took on a red glow with gold trim against the blue sky. The sunsets were usually very pretty from the deck, especially this time of year. Tonight was no exception. It was truly breathtaking. My thoughts then turned to another beautiful thing, Lora. I had been deeply concentrating on this case so much and Norma so much that I had not even thought about her much sense leaving the hospital.

I was looking forward to Thursday night with a great deal of anticipation. Even though it was to be a rather informal date, I was hoping that it might lead to a great many more. I hated the fact that this case may affect her, even indirectly, since Lora is close friends with Norma. I don't consider it a great way to start a relationship, arresting her friends.

It was getting a little chilly, so I went into the house to light a fire and settle down with a book for a short time before fixing a bite to eat. I had only read a few pages when I dozed off to sleep with Ranger on the floor by my feet.

I could not have been asleep more than twenty minutes or so when Rangers barking woke me up. The doorbell rang, and I quickly got to my feet. I did not get many visitors up here on the mountain.

When I opened the door, to my surprise and delight, it was Lora. I had no idea that she knew where I lived.

"Hi, Damon, am I interrupting anything?" She asked.

"No not at all. I was just reading my dog and drinking a book. I mean, reading a book and drinking a beer. Would you care for one?" I asked as I motioned her in.

"Care for one of what, a book, dog or beer?"

"A beer, I also have some wine if you would prefer that."

"A glass of wine would be wonderful, if it isn't too much trouble?"

"Trouble? It's no trouble. Come in and make yourself at home. I'll get your wine. Oh, this is my dog, Ranger. He'll love you. He makes quick friends with all of the women that come here."

"Oh does he really? You have a lot of women visitors, do you?"

"No, I didn't mean it like that. What I meant was what few women have ever been here, like my sister, mother and women like that."

"Maybe you had better just go get me some wine. You might want to wake up before you come back so you won't put your foot in your mouth any further," Lora said, laughingly.

"I'm thinking you might be right. I'll be back in a minute."

I went to the kitchen and splashed a little cold water on my face to wake up and to make sure I wasn't just dreaming. I opened a new bottle of wine and poured a glass for Lora. At the same time, I grabbed a fresh beer out of the refrigerator for myself.

Handing Lora her glass of wine and sitting on the sofa next to her, I almost could not control my curiosity. I was dying to know why she had shown up. Then, again, she could be here for any reason, and it wouldn't bother me. I was just glad to have her sitting on my sofa in my house.

"To what do I owe this honor? I wasn't aware that you knew where I lived. It isn't public information."

"I'm the Mayor's secretary, remember? I can find out most anything. When I looked up where you live, I knew the house right away. I sometimes take drives up this way, and I have always liked this house. It's always struck me as inviting and comfortable. I even parked across the street from it a couple of years ago and just sat to admire it for a few minutes."

"So, you just wanted to see what the house is like inside?"

"No, Damon. I wanted to see you," Lora said with hesitation.

"That is great! I wanted to see you also."

"I don't mean that I wanted to see you. I mean that I needed to see you. Oh hell, I don't know what I mean," Lora stammered.

"It isn't comfortable, is it?" I asked.

"What isn't comfortable?"

"Having your foot in your mouth as much as you do?"

"Damon, what I mean is that I did want to see you. I wanted to tell you that I had a phone call from Tom Knight. He called to see where Norma is and if she had been arrested."

"What did you tell him?"

"I told him that I wasn't sure but that she was in the hospital under police protection. I also told him about the sleeping pills. He wants to talk to you, Damon."

"I want to talk to him also. Where is he?"

"He wouldn't tell me where he was. He did say that he was where you wouldn't find him. He went on to tell me that he would call you soon, after he knew that Norma was out of danger. He also said that she has nothing to do with any of this. He told me that her only crime was being in love with him and that he wants you to please leave her alone."

"In the few minutes that I did talk to Norma, it was very obvious that she knows what Tom was doing and was probably involved in some way. The knowledge of what he was doing and not reporting it is a crime in and of itself."

"I understand, Damon. After all, she lied to you at lunch and then followed you, almost running you down with the van. If that was not enough, when you confronted her, she tried to kill herself. Those are not the acts of an innocent person."

"I'm so glad you understand and don't think I'm at fault, Lora."

She slid her hand behind me and started playing with the hair on the back of my head. She had a strange far away look in her eyes as she slowly leaned toward me. She seemed to be acting in an almost dazed manner, as if in response to an uncontrollable urge. Her lips slowly parted, her eyes closed, and her grip on my hair tightened as she moved closer to me. My hand slid around her waist, pulling her into me. As our lips met, it was like magic. It was as if they had always meant to be together in a kiss such as this. The embrace became more heated the longer it lasted, and it lasted a long time. I think it was obvious to both of us that we had a little more than a passing interest in each other. That was for sure.

"Wow, Damon, you're a very good kisser. You took my breath away."

"Lora, I haven't even gotten warmed up yet."

"Then I don't think I should hang around long enough for you to get warmed up. I don't think I could control myself."

I laughed, "I'm sure you can take a lot more than that without losing control. In any case, I'll behave myself. Although, I don't think that I'm the one that started this."

"I know. I don't know what happened. I suddenly had this uncontrollable urge to kiss you. I'm not a person that would do anything like that, or at least, I never have before. I apologize for being so forward. I honestly don't know what came over me. I guess it was the same thing that came over me at the diner this afternoon."

"Lora, don't be silly. I've had the same urge to kiss you since the tenth grade. Anytime you get that urge, don't hesitate or hold back. Just let yourself go and kiss me anytime you like."

"Are you sure? Because I think the urge is coming over me again."

This time she put both her hands behind my head and pulled me into her as both of my arms found their way around her, pulling her in tight against me. Her lips were full and soft, and her skin was smooth and tantalizing to the touch. This is the kind of passion that leads to the bedroom in short order, and if that is where it takes us, then so be it. I had no plans on lightening up.

Ranger had other plans for us, though. The mood was broken when he started barking. I think he was jealous, but it may be that he knew where this was heading and figured he better put an end to it. He wouldn't have wanted us to get out of hand and do something that we might later regret.

Neither of us had eaten, so we went to the kitchen to see what we could find. Together, we fixed a rather nice meal. We ate at the table next to the windows and looked out on the deck and the lights in the valley below.

We were able to restrain our emotions for the rest of the evening. We limited ourselves to holding hands, light cuddling, and not so passionate kissing.

Over dinner Lora said, "You know, Damon, I could have just called you and told you that Tom had called me. For that matter, it was not that important. I could have waited to tell you tomorrow."

"Why didn't you?"

"I wanted to see you. I couldn't wait until Thursday."

"I know. I'm the same way. I wanted to see you also, but I couldn't think of any excuse to use. Even with everything that has happened today, I still found time to think about you."

She reached across the table and took my hand in hers, squeezing it then just holding it as we sat looking longingly into the eyes of one another. I could not believe that I had spent so many years alone or in empty relationships. Just when it seemed like I was destined to live out my life without ever knowing true love, a chance meeting at lunch had dropped an angel in my lap, an angel that I had dreamed about for years.

"Damon, I shouldn't be telling you this, but I want you to know how I feel. I have wanted you to ask me out since high school. I would see you around town or at the police station, and I would just wish for a good excuse to talk to you."

"I don't believe this. That's exactly how I've felt, but I always thought you hardly knew I existed. You never even looked at me."

"Oh, I looked. I looked all the time, but when I would see you turning to look at me, I would look away. I'm sorry. Now I wish I hadn't."

"I wish you hadn't looked away, either. It wouldn't have taken much encouragement for me to ask you out. We've wasted too much of our lives as it is, I don't want to waste anymore time."

"I don't either, Damon, but I don't want us to rush things, either."

"Rush what?"

"You know, like making love," Lora said as her face turned a little red.

"I know, and you're right. We shouldn't rush it. I want things to be perfect when we reach that point in our relationship."

"Oh, Damon, I knew you would be just like this. You would be understanding and considerate, loving, caring, and a great kisser. Is that what you want? You want a relationship?"

"Yes, don't you?"

"Oh, yes. I want and have wanted a relationship with you for a long time."

"I wish I could be as bold as you. I can't muster the courage to tell you how I feel, not like you can" Damon confessed shyly.

"I'm sorry, Damon. I guess I'm being rather forward."

"Don't be sorry, please. One of us needs to be, or we would still be at square one. You're doing great so far. Don't stop now."

"So are you, but I need to get home."

"I know. Call me when you get there so I'll know that you're alright."

"Okay, I will."

We gave each other a long and passionate kiss goodnight, and I watched her walk to her car. It was about twenty-five minutes before Lora called. To tell me that she had gotten home. We did not talk long. I knew I needed to get up early and be at the hospital to ask Norma some questions.

Chapter 3

T he next morning, I left home a little earlier than usual. I wanted to be at the hospital and get an early start on the questioning of Norma Christian. I called the office and left word for Kelly and Bill to meet me there.

When I arrived, they were already there waiting for me with a badly needed cup of coffee.

"Coffee great, Thanks Kelly. You keep this up and you'll make captain before I do."

"Yeah right, Lieutenant. I just figured you would need some before we went in to talk to Mrs. Christian."

"That's what I mean, Kelly. You are always thinking and one-step ahead of everybody. Have you talked to the doctor yet? Is it okay for us to question Norma?"

"Yes, he said it would be fine. He thinks that she's out of danger and would be pretty much back to normal by the time we arrived."

"Okay, that's great. Let us get this show on the road. What room is she in?"

"Room 210, Lieutenant," responded Bill.

I asked Kelly and Bill to wait outside the room for a little while. I did not want to take a chance on scaring Norma. She might be more agreeable to questions if she did not think we were ganging up on her.

As I entered the room, she was lying in bed, just staring out of the window. She was in the security section of the hospital, so there were bars on all the windows. As I approached her, she turned to look at me. She did not appear overjoyed to see me but did not seem surprised that I had shown up.

"Good morning, Norma."

"I've been expecting you, Damon. I am surprised that you waited 'til this morning to come see me."

"You feel up to telling me what's going on with you and Tom Knight?"

"He's my boyfriend. We are lovers. I would've thought you would have figured that much out by now."

"Norma, you know that isn't what I'm talking about. Tell me about the graves."

"Graves, what graves are you referring too? I don't have the slightest idea what you are talking about."

"Norma, you pretty much implicated yourself with Tom Knight and digging up those graves when I talked to you yesterday."

"I could have said anything yesterday. The doctors will tell you I was not in my right mind. I won't be accountable for anything I might have said. I was temporarily insane."

"I like you, Norma. You are a friend of Lora's, and I want to help you. Before I can do that, you have to help me. Tom has already tried to contact me, and he is due to call me back soon. It would go better for you if you tell me what you know now."

"Okay, Damon. I know I am entitled to a lawyer before and during any questioning by the police. I want to talk to an attorney before I answer any questions. How is that for what I know?"

"Norma, I'm trying to help you, but if that's the way you want it, you better make sure you get a real good attorney."

"I'm sorry. I know you are trying to help me. I just cannot tell you anything until I can talk to Tom. To be honest, I really don't know much of anything. He has not confided in me that much. He said it was for my own safety, and he told me one other thing too."

"What's that, Norma?"

"Not to trust the police, to tell them nothing."

"He told you that because he didn't want them to arrest him for his crime."

"No, this was months ago that he told me not to trust the police, way before he had done anything. That is, if he has done anything illegal."

"This isn't over. I am coming back to talk to you further. If you want an attorney to be here, you better get in touch with one or tell us you cannot afford one. We'll appoint one for you."

"Damon, wait," Norma said as I was about to leave her room.

"What?"

"Tom is a good honest man. In my heart, I really believe that to be true. If he has done anything wrong, it was in an effort to find out what happened to his brother and my sister. I know Tom, Damon. I'm telling you that he is not a criminal."

"Norma, nobody is a criminal until they commit a criminal act. The jails and courts are full of good men who only made one mistake. I'm sure Tom is everything you say he is, but right now, you are both acting like criminals."

"He had a good reason for what he did!" Norma exclaimed.

"He may have, but a crime is still a crime, good reason or not."

Norma broke down into tears as I left her room. It seems like every time I see her, I upset her and make her cry. I did leave her room with a feeling that she was telling me the truth. I don't really believe she knows much, except that she feels a need to protect Tom Knight.

When I left Norma's room, Lora was waiting outside with Kelly, Bill, and the uniformed officer assigned to watch Norma's room.

"Good morning, Damon. This nice officer said I have to have your permission to see Norma."

"Morning, Lora. Of course you may see her, but before you do, I want to talk to you a moment."

"Of course what would you like to talk about?"

We walked a short distance down the hallway, away from the others. I asked Lora to try to convince Norma that it was to her advantage to talk to me.

"Lora, Tom has told her not to trust the police. See if you can get her to at least trust me."

"Can you be trusted, Damon?"

"What does that mean?"

"I'm just kidding you. I will tell her to trust you."

"It's to her benefit, Lora. I promise you that."

I told the officer outside of Norma's door that he was to tell Lora that I would be waiting for her in the coffee shop downstairs when she was finished. I was on my second cup when Lora showed up.

"I tried, Damon. I really don't think she knows anything. She said she drove Tom's van one night while he checked two graves. They were the same two graves that were not re-covered. It had taken him much longer than he had thought it would, and he didn't have time to reseal the graves before it was time for the caretaker to come in."

"So it is Tom Knight doing this?"

"Apparently so, but I don't think Norma even knew what he was doing until that night and then only after the fact."

"Did Norma happen to mention why Tom was digging up these graves?"

"No, but she seems to think that it has something to do with his brother and her sister's disappearance."

"You think it would do any good for me to try to talk to Norma again?"

"No, Darling, I don't."

"Darling, you called me darling."

"Oh, I'm sorry. It just rather slipped out. Do you mind?"

"No I don't at all. I like the sound of it."

We had not even had our first date yet, and I was already feeling like I was in a relationship. It was a good feeling after so many years of loneliness and empty relationships. With a light but meaningful kiss from Lora, we parted, and I headed to the office to see what other entanglements awaited me there. I cannot imagine that anything could seem as important as it would have a few days ago, before I learned of Lora's feelings for me. I had a warm and comfortable feeling deep within me, a feeling I had not experienced for a long time. I felt wanted and needed by a wonderful woman. For the first time, I felt that my life was in order. I felt that I had a future.

It was still a little before ten in the morning when I reached the squad room. There were only two officers at their desks when I walked in.

"Lieutenant, some guy has called for you three times this morning. He seems impatient to speak with you. Said he would call back at ten-thirty and that he really needed to talk with you as soon as possible," Detective Morris informed me.

Jack Morris was a fine officer but a little slow when it came to understanding and analyzing the evidence in a case, he was working. I guess that is why he is still a detective after twelve years with the squad. He was with the squad when I was green and straight off the street. Now I am his boss, and he is still a detective.

"Jack, did he say who he was?"

"No, he did not give his name. Said he was calling on behalf of Tom somebody. I didn't write it down."

I just shook my head in disbelief as I continued to my office thinking, *"What an attentive cop. That is exactly why he is going to retire without ever getting a promotion. Seems like Jack would wake up and smell the roses after seeing one person after another get promoted over him."*

I looked up to see Jack Morris heading toward my office carrying two cups of coffee.

"Lieutenant, I thought you might want a cup of Joe. I also wanted to speak to you about this grave robber case."

"Really, Jack? What is on your mind? Oh, and thanks for the coffee, but I have already had about six cups this morning. I think I've had enough for a while."

"Well, Lieutenant, I know it isn't my case, but I was thinking. I bet that they exhumed the bodies to steal their wedding rings. They're gold, you know?"

"Yes, I know, Jack, but a wedding band isn't really worth a great deal, and it's the only jewelry you're permitted to be buried with. Even then, the wedding bands have to be plain with no valuable jewels encrusted in them. And why would they only dig up people buried on April 30th, 1989?"

"I guess you're right, Lieutenant. I'll keep thinking about it, and I'll let you know if I come up with any other ideas."

"Okay, Jack, you do that. If you do come up with anything, you should tell it to Kelly or Bill. It's their case, and you should share any ideas or information with them first."

After hearing an idea like that, one might tend to think of Jack Morris as a complete idiot. Some may wonder how in the world he ever even became a police officer, let alone a detective. It takes all kinds to outwit the criminal element, though. Whether you believe it, or not, some of Jacks crazy ideas lead to the arrest and conviction of some of the most cunning criminals.

I remember a case that involved a young boy who had attempted to kill his family. Everyone thought that the boy had been a hero in a house fire incident, but it turned out that he had only saved his family's lives by accident. Jack had talked to the boy's grandparents, who told him that the boy had asked his mother and father for a dirt bike. His parents denied the boy's request, but his grandparents wanted to get him one anyway. Jack felt that wanting a dirt bike was motive enough for this young boy to want to kill his parents. As crazy as it sounds, he was right. When confronted, the boy confessed to setting his house on fire so that he could go live with the grandparents.

I set up a tape recorder on my phone so that I could record my conversation with Tom when he called. Even though I felt it would be a waste of time, I also contacted the phone company to request a trace.

At exactly ten-thirty, the phone rang. When I answered it, the voice said, "Is this Lieutenant Damon Carter?"

"Yes, it is," I replied.

"My name is John Payne, and I'm a ham radio operator. I have a man who says his name is Tom Knight and that it's important that he talks to you."

"Is he there?"

"No, he's on a CB radio and has asked me to patch him through to you on the telephone. I will have to key the microphone, so when you are finished talking, you have to say, 'over.' That way I'll know when to let Mr. Knight speak."

"Okay, Mr. Payne, I understand. Do you know Mr. Knight?"

"No, I'm afraid I don't. I just replied to his call for assistance. Lieutenant, are you ready to talk to Mr. Knight now?"

"Yes, Mr. Payne. Put him on."

"Lieutenant, first I want to know how Norma is." "Over"

"She's fine and out of danger, no thanks to you." "Over"

"I know. I should have never allowed her to get involved in this. I am sorry for getting her in trouble, and I am sorry for this unorthodox method of communication, Lieutenant. I just cannot afford to be bothered with this right now until I find out a few more details.. Then, I will turn myself in willingly. I am not afraid of being arrested or of you or your police department." "Over"

"It would go better for you and Norma if you turn yourself in now." "Over"

"I told you, Lieutenant, I can't, not yet anyway. Norma had nothing to do with this. All she did was drove my van for me that last night. She did not even know what I was doing until I came back to the van." "Over"

"What were you doing, Mr. Knight?" "Over"

"You know damn well what I was doing, Lieutenant. I admit to it, but I had a good reason. You think I enjoyed desecrating those graves?" "Over"

"Then why did you do it, and why only graves of people buried on April 30, 1989?"

"Over"

"Because of the treasure, also because someone led me to believe that I could find information about my brother in one of those graves." "Over"

"Are you telling me that you desecrated nine graves in seven different cemeteries looking for a treasure?" "Over"

"No, Lieutenant. I was looking for information. Some papers that might tell me where I could find it, I mean them. My brother was looking for the treasure when he and Ellen disappeared." "Over"

"Why would you think for one minute that one of those graves might hold a clue to where your brother might be?" "Over"

"I got an anonymous message to that effect, or at least that's what I thought it to mean. I know this all sounds crazy, and maybe it is. Maybe I am crazy. I don't really know anymore." "Over"

"Then you should have brought it to the police." "Over"

"I can't trust the police. I'm almost sure that this group of treasure hunters, who may have had something to do with my brother's disappearance, is connected to the police department in some way." "Over"

"What makes you think that, Tom?" "Over"

"I can't tell you right now. I need more evidence. I have to go, but I will call you again in a couple of days. Give Norma my love." "Over and out"

"Hello? Hello, Tom?"

"This is John Payne, Lieutenant. He's gone."

"Okay. Thank you, Mr. Payne for calling and helping with the transmission."

"No problem. Glad to help. Would you like me to patch him through again if he wants me too?"

"Yes, if you don't mind."

"I don't mind at all. I find this all very exciting. As long as everyone knows I have nothing to do with any criminal activity of any sort, I'm glad to help."

"We appreciate your cooperation, Mr. Payne, but the next time he calls, can you try to get a fix on him? The direction that his signal is coming from would be helpful."

"Actually, I tried this time, Lieutenant, but he was moving the whole time. All I can tell you is that he was transmitting from something that moved like a car and was somewhere south of here."

"Thank you again, Mr. Payne, for your assistance and cooperation. If you hear anything else from Mr. Knight, please let me know."

Just then, I saw Kelly and Bill come into the squad room.

"Kelly, you and Bill get in here ASAP."

"Yes, Lieutenant, right away."

"I got a call from Tom Knight. We couldn't get a trace because he used a very unusual method of calling. He patched into the phone line through a ham radio operator, using a CB radio. This isn't a stupid man. In fact, he's very intelligent. I want a complete background check on this man, and I do mean complete. From the time he was born until today, I want to know every detail."

"We'll get right on it, Lieutenant."

Just then, Jack Morris came rushing into the office.

"Lieutenant, the phone company called. They got a trace on that call. It came from the home of John Payne at 12765 Browns Mill Rd. You want me to send some units over there?"

"No, Jack. I already know where the call came from. The man told me when I answered the phone, but thanks anyway."

"No problem, Lieutenant. I want to help in anyway that I can."

"Kelly, I'm going back over to the hospital to try to talk to Norma Christian again. Maybe now that I've talked to Tom and know a few facts, she might be more cooperative about answering some of my questions."

"Mind if I tag along? Bill can handle the background investigation."

"Sure, I think you should be there."

Kelly and I arrived at the hospital during mealtime, so we sat in the cafeteria until it was over. We then went to see Norma.

"Good afternoon, Norma. You up to answering some questions now?"

"Damon, I told you that I don't know anything."

"I talked to Tom. He sends you his love."

"Is he okay? Where is he?"

"I don't know where he is. He told me that you drove the van the last night that he went out to dig up graves. Now can you tell me why he was digging them up?"

"No. I assumed he was looking for Adam and Ellen's bodies."

"I don't think so. He's too smart for that. He was looking for something else. What do you know about a treasure?"

"The Beale treasure, you mean the one that Adam was so fascinated with for so long? Ellen told me that he spent a great deal of time messing with documents and papers about that treasure."

"No, not the Beale Treasure. You must be kidding, not that old wives tale? There is no evidence that there is a treasure or ever was one."

"Adam seemed to think that the treasure was real. He also knew some other important men here in town who also thought it was real treasure."

"People have spent fortunes looking for the Beale Treasure. They've been looking for that thing for about two hundred years now. Some have even gone to jail over it. Looks like Tom might be joining them soon."

"Tom didn't seem to think he would get in trouble. I asked him about what he was doing, and he told me that he wouldn't go to jail. He told me that he had some kind of protection. I don't know what he was referring to, though."

"What does Tom do for a living?"

"I know this sounds really stupid, but I don't know. He often goes away for a week or two, but I don't know where he goes or what he does. He has told me not to ever question him about his work. He said that it's enough for me to know that he loves me and that he isn't doing anything wrong. I trust him, so I don't ask. In fact, I didn't even know anything about him before Adam and Ellen disappeared. Neither one had told me that Adam had a brother. I was surprised when I met Tom one day about a month after Adam and Ellen had disappeared, but it was comforting to know that I didn't have to go through this alone."

"What else do you know about him?"

"I know that he was in the Army, that he finished college, and that he speaks at least four languages fluently. He is very intelligent, and he is a good man. He couldn't treat me any better. I think he was in the Vietnam War, but he never talks about it. I don't know where he came from before he arrived here. I know nothing about his family or anything about him. That is, except Adam. I know that he's Tom's younger brother. I don't even know if his parents are alive or not."

"What did he do in the Army?"

"I don't know."

"What was his rank? Was he an officer?"

"I don't know that, either."

"Norma, how can you date a man and not know or want to know anything about him?"

"I love Tom and I trust him completely."

"Where does Tom stay when he's in town?"

"He stays with me at my house, of course."

"Do you have any other address for him or a phone number? Do you have anything at all?"

"No. Well, yes. He gave me a number to call in extreme emergencies only. He wouldn't let me write it down. He made me memorize it."

"What's the number?"

"I don't remember, Damon. It was a while back, and I just cannot remember it. I swear I really can't."

"Okay, Norma, tell me more about this treasure business."

"I just know what Ellen told me. She said that Adam had figured out what the key was to some code or something like that. She said that he didn't know where the treasure was but that he knew where to find another clue. She told me that the day before they disappeared."

"Did she say anything else?"

"No, I don't think so."

"Get some rest, Norma. Thanks for your help."

"Oh, Damon, wait. There is one other thing she mentioned, a date."

"What date?"

"April 30th of '89. She said it was the key to everything. That I should put my trust in the Lord and our founding father and not on but under the stone bearing that date. She wanted to make sure that I understood the difference between 'on' and 'under'. She also said that if anything happened to her or Adam, the answers could all be found under that date."

"When did she tell you this?"

"The day before they disappeared, April 28th of last year,"

"I assume you have passed this information about the date on to Tom."

"Of course I did. I tell him anything I can that might help find Adam and Ellen."

"That explains why he was digging up graves."

"How does that explain the grave thing, Damon?"

"All the graves that Tom dug up were buried on April 30, 1989."

"I guess it is kind of my fault then that he dug them up; since I am the one that told him."

"Thank you, Norma, and don't worry. I don't think you're going to be in any trouble. I'm not going to press charges involving the van incident, and I don't think that you knew what Tom was doing. We're going to dismiss the officer who's been assigned to keep watch over you during your stay here, so when the hospital releases you, you're free to go home."

"Oh, thank you so much, Damon. Now I know why Lora likes you so much."

That put a smile on my face as Kelly and I left Norma's room and headed back to the office. On the way, I told Kelly to have Norma followed when she is released from the hospital. I had a feeling that she might lead us to Tom Knight.

When I got back to my office, I called Lora at the Mayor's Office and told her that I wasn't pressing charges against Norma and that her involvement with the grave desecrations did not warrant her being charged in that matter, either. I gave her the news that Norma was free to go home after her release from the hospital.

"Damon, that's wonderful! I know that Norma is thrilled and very grateful to you. Is it alright for me to go and visit her now?"

"Yes, of course."

"Damon, are you free for dinner this evening?"

"Why yes, just so happens that I am."

"I would like very much to fix you dinner; sort of a celebration for you helping my friend and being so understanding."

"Oh, is that all? A reward for a favor and for no other reason, nothing personal?"

"Well, not exactly. I do want to see you."

"That's more like it, and yes, My Dear, I would love to have dinner with you. I do have to go check on Ranger first."

"I love your house and your dog. May I just bring everything to your house that I'm fixing for dinner? I do know my way around your kitchen now, so I could fix dinner there, no problem."

"Sounds good to me. If you get there first, look for a white stone in the flowerbed. There's a key to the front door under it. Ranger knows you, so he won't bother you. I'll get there as quickly as I can now that I have a reason to rush home."

"I need to go by the grocery store first, so it might take me a little while to get there." "Bring a bathing suit with you. We might want to get in the hot tub after dinner."

"And a hot tub requires a bathing suit?"

"Not as far as I'm concerned, but that's up to you."

"I'm just teasing you, Damon. I'll bring a bathing suit."

"Oh! Okay if you must."

"Shame on you, Damon for such thoughts. If I didn't know better, I'd think your intentions toward me are less than honorable."

"I could say the same thing about you, Ms. Lora Jean."

Lora responded laughing, "In that case, I'll have to think about the bathing suit."

"You mean, you might not want to get into the hot tub?"

"No, I do. It's the bathing suit that I haven't decided on."

"Does my vote count?"

"No, I think I know how your vote would go. I just need to think about it."

"I guess I'll find out tonight."

"I guess you will, but I have to go for now. The Mayor wants me."

"I understand. I know how he feels."

"Till tonight Darling."

"Tonight, Lora."

I was dreaming about what the evening may hold in store for me when I saw Kelly and Bill walking toward my office. Bill was carrying some papers, and they both had serious looks on their faces.

"Lieutenant, you aren't going to be very pleased with what Bill has found on Tom Knight," Kelly started out.

"Okay, Bill, what'd you come up with?"

"Thomas J. Knight graduated from his high school in Fairfax, Va. with honors. He then went to college at the Virginia Military Institute in Lexington Va., where he graduated at the top of his class. He entered the Army as a Second Lieutenant in 1962 and served six years before he got out as a Major. Then there is nothing, accept a Fairfax paper that reported his attendance at his parents' funerals. Other than that, there's nothing until he showed up here almost a year ago. He purchased a van from the Chevrolet dealership, and paid cash for it. That's the only thing that I can find titled in his name since he got out of the Army."

"What about social security, a driver's license, taxes, police records, anything?"

"We could find nothing at all on him, Lieutenant. No records."

"Okay, at least get me his military records."

"No can do, Lieutenant. They seem to have been misplaced by the Army."

"Did you check with the FBI? Do they have anything on him?"

"No one has anything. Seems as though the man hasn't existed for the last twenty some odd years."

"I sort of figured this is what you'd find."

"What did you figure, Lieutenant?" Kelly asked.

"He's a spook."

"Spook, you mean like a ghost?" Bill asked.

"No, I mean like an undercover agent for one of our government secret agencies, like the DEA, CIA, FBI, or NSA. He could even be an agent for one of those agencies that are so secret that they don't even have initials. He knows he's above prosecution for any criminal act that he commits. As far as the world is concerned, Mr. Thomas J. Knight no longer exists. The government could never allow him to be under arrest or be in court for anything. If he did get in some kind of very serious trouble, he would just disappear. No one would miss him because he doesn't exist."

"So what do we do now, Lieutenant?"

"Do now? We do nothing. We're police officers; we investigate crimes. If Knight is a spook, which I'm sure he is, no crime has been committed. Where there is no crime, there is no case. Close the files on it and bring everything to me. I'll go see the Captain about it, but I'm sure that in light of this, he'll agree with me."

Kelly and Bill started out of the office as I remembered one more thing, "Oh, Kelly, cancel that tail on Norma."

Chapter 4

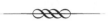

Reluctantly, I headed for Captain Mirant's office to inform him about what the investigation had uncovered. That in my opinion the case possibly should be abandon at this point. I was just hoping that he would come to the same conclusion, after he heard what the background check on Tom Knight had turned up.

When I finished bringing Captain Mirant up to date, he stood up, walked over to the window, and looked out for a moment. He then turned to me and asked, "You think Tom Knight is a spook, don't you, Damon?"

"Yes, Captain, I do."

"For what agency do you think he's a spook for?"

"That I don't know, Captain, but there's no other explanation for the fact that the man has no history for the last twenty years."

"I think you're right. Give me every bit of information you have on him and any files that you've made. Also, I need anything you may have uncovered about the treasure."

"Treasure, Captain?"

"Just bring me all the information you have," Mirant said sharply.

"Of course, Captain."

As I walked back to my office, I signaled Kelly and Bill to come with me.

"Did either of you mention the treasure to Captain Mirant?"

"No, Damon, I mean, Lieutenant. Neither Bill nor I have talked to the Captain in days."

"Have either of you mentioned anything about this treasure business to anyone?"

They both responded with a "No."

"Okay, that's fine. Just keep it that way. Don't talk to anyone about the case or the treasure. I want you to take all of the files and documents to the Captain, except the tape of me talking to Tom Knight. Also, Kelly, make me a copy of everything before you take it to him, and then forget you made the copy. Is that clear?"

"Yes, Lieutenant," Kelly responded quickly.

Bill left the office but Kelly did not. Instead, she closed the door behind Bill and turned to me.

"Okay, Lieutenant, what's up?"

"What do you mean?"

"You're asking me to withhold information from the Detective Bureau Commander, the man that has the final say so in the promotional process. Have you forgotten that I put in for sergeant? I feel I have a right to know what's going on."

"You're right, Kelly. I need to trust somebody, so it might as well be you. Tom and Norma both said that they couldn't trust the police. I don't think Tom Knight, with his apparent background, would say that without justification or knowledge. Just now, when the Captain asked for all of the files on Tom Knight, he also told to me to bring him everything that we have on the treasure. How did he know about the treasure if you or Bill didn't tell him about it? I know I didn't tell him about it, so how did he know?"

"I see where you're going with this, Lieutenant."

"I don't even know where this is going, but what I just told you need not leave this room. No one else and I mean, no one, is to know about any of this."

"I understand, Lieutenant," Kelly said as she let herself out of my office.

I needed to talk to Tom Knight again, so I needed to go see Norma. I was hopeful that when I tell her that Tom won't be charged with anything that maybe she will be willing to tell me where I can find him or how to get a message to him.

I had started out of the office when Jack Morris came running up to me.

"Lieutenant, I have another idea about the grave digger case. You told me to let you know if I had any more ideas."

"Forget it, Jack. The case is closed."

"You have arrested someone?"

"No, Jack, the case is just closed, so just don't worry about it anymore."

"No arrest, just closed? Isn't that a little odd, Lieutenant?"

"Not in this case, Jack. Don't worry about it."

I left Jack standing in the hall with a dumb look on his face, which was a normal look for Jack to have. Sometimes I wonder how he finds his way to work.

I went straight to Norma's room at the hospital, just to find it empty. I went to the nurse's station and asked about her. The nurse told me that she left with a doctor that she did not recognize. It was not out of the ordinary for a nurse not to know every doctor, and she had assumed that he was from another ward.

I would be willing to bet, that the man was no doctor but was really Tom Knight. I am sure that in his line of work, he knows a great many tricks. Posing as a doctor wouldn't be that difficult for him.

It was getting late and I had much more important things to think about. Like Lora. I needed to go by the grocery store and pick up some wine and snacks to munch on. I had no idea what Lora would be fixing for dinner, but whatever it was, I was sure it would be great. Love has a funny way of making everything spectacular.

To my surprise, Lora was already there when I reached my house. It felt good to walk in and have someone there to greet me, besides Ranger that is. Walking into a house filled with the smell of dinner cooking, to be welcomed with a kiss, and asked how my day was were all things that I had not experienced in a very long time. Suddenly, I realized how much I had missed them.

She was wearing an apron, which she must have brought with her, and a sweater that accentuated her figure as it clung to her breasts. Her blue jeans were tight but not too tight. They hugged her just tight enough to outline her perfect hip line and the shape of her legs without looking like she was pored into them. The grand finale for her lovely outfit was a pair of fuzzy pink bedroom slippers that looked like she had retrieved them from the city dump. I could tell that they used to look like two bunny rabbits; only now, one was missing an eye and an ear. The other looked like it had played the role of a dog toy for years. In any case, she was a delight to see.

I went to the bedroom to take off my suit, shower, and to put on a comfortable pair of jeans and a shirt. I did not usually shave when I got home, but with my expectations for the evening, I felt that it might be a good idea. I finished off my preparations with a few sprinkles of Polo.

Upon my return to the kitchen, Lora was standing in front of the stove slowly stirring a red sauce that smelled absolutely, heavenly. There was a large pot boiling on the back burner, and a skillet had something simmering in it. I could smell the unmistakable fragrance of baking bread coming from the oven.

I walked up behind her, put one arm around her waist, and used my other hand to move her hair away from her neck. Kissing her lightly just behind her ear.

I said, "Dinner smells good, and you smell great. Is there anything I can do to help you?"

"Yes, Darling, you can get the salad out of the refrigerator and put it in the spinner to get all of the water out of it. Then you can toss it with the Caesar dressing that you will find in the orange container in the refrigerator door. You smell good also. Polo, if I'm not mistaken?"

I got the salad and dressing out and set it on the counter next to a very small green bag.

"What's this little green bag, Honey?"

"Oh, that's just my bathing suit. Just set it aside for now."

I was a little disappointed, but it could not cover up much if it was going to fit in that little bag. I had noticed another bag in the bedroom. It resembled something closer to an overnight bag. Maybe she was planning to spend the night. That was an enlightening thought, as well as a very pleasant one.

During dinner, I discovered that Lora was a wonderful cook. She had prepared spaghetti with an Italian sausage meat sauce. While starting in on my second plate, I told her that we had closed the case that involved, Norma and Tom. There will be no charges in the case. I told her to pass the news on to Norma if she saw her since Norma had left the hospital before I could relay the information.

"That's wonderful, Damon, but I thought you were absolutely sure that it was Tom digging up those graves?"

"I was sure, and he did do it. He even admitted it."

"Then how can you not charge him?"

"I can't tell you anything about why he isn't being charged, but I can tell you that the case is closed and that Tom and Norma are in the clear now."

"Sure sounds mysterious."

"You have no idea, Lora, how mysterious this whole thing has become, especially with this treasure business and all."

"What treasure, Darling?"

"Oh, the Beale Treasure got involved in this matter somehow."

"Tell me. I know all about the Beale Treasure. I would be interested to know how it's related to your case, and I know the Mayor would be, too."

"What do you know about it?"

"Just about anything you would like to know. It is the Mayors favorite hobby. Maybe I should say passion or obsession. He's always having me look up information in old documents and books. I put what I find on a floppy disc for the computer. He has a program that he keeps in a safe. It numbers all of the words in the document, and he uses it to key in this list of numbers. He told me that he's looking to see if the numbered words say anything that makes sense."

"Well, it sounds like you know more about the treasure than I do. Would you mind telling me about it and what the Mayor does with the information that he has learned about it?"

"No, Darling, I don't mind at all, but for the last year he really hasn't spent much time messing around with it. Anyway, I'll be glad to tell you what I know but not tonight."

"No, I think it can wait 'til tomorrow."

"I didn't get off work early, go shopping, and fix you dinner to talk about some dumb old treasure and the Mayor's hobbies. In fact, it seems to me that there was some mention of a hot tub and wine. That sounds much more appealing than discussing what I do at work."

"I agree. I'll clean up while you go change."

"I think not. Let's both clear the table, do the dishes, and then we'll both get changed."

"Okay, Beautiful, you got a deal."

"I saw a couple robes in your bathroom. Do you mind if I wear one out to the hot tub?"

"Not at all, help yourself to anything your little heart desires."

"I might just take you up on that, so remember you said it," Lora laughed.

We must have set some kind of record cleaning up after dinner. Lora was heading off to the bedroom in no time to change. While I put the wine in an ice bucket and took it out to the hot tub with a couple of glasses, I couldn't help but notice that she had not taken the little bag with her that contained her bathing suit.

I poured two glasses of wine and settled into the bubbling water to await Lora's arrival. As I saw her coming through the living room in my direction, she was clenching my bathrobe tight around her. The excitement and expectation building up within me was almost more than I could stand.

She came out, closing the door behind her and looking at me with such a wonderful smile on her face. It was as if she was about to give me a gift, that I had long dreamed of but had never expected. She turned her back to me as she opened the robe. She held it wide open and away from her body as she turned to face me.

I was dumb founded by the sight that my eyes beheld. She was wearing one of those old-fashioned bathing suits my grandmother wore. It covered her from her knees to her neck. It was black with white lace on it.

I sat in the hot tub with my mouth open and a dumb look on my face while she laughed hysterically,

"I just couldn't resist doing this. I bought this silly thing for a Halloween party a couple years ago, and after our conversation earlier today, I just had to do it."

"What a surprise. You really had me going. Now would you mind doing me a favor?"

"I guess I owe you one after this. What is it?"

"Would you mind turning your back again and giving me that robe? I noticed that you did not take that little bag with you that you said your suit was in. I'm sitting here stark-ass naked. So, maybe under the circumstances, I should probably go put a bathing suit on."

"Sorry Damon. I can't do that."

"What? What do you mean you can't do that?"

"Well, of course I can. I'm just not going too. I have a better idea."

Lora turned her back to me once again and slowly began removing that ridiculous looking bathing suit. Although, I must admit that even a horrendous granny suit was no match for her natural beauty. She could make anything look good. I looked on as she revealed more of her lightly tanned body. It reflected the dim light of a candle that sat nearby, which only served to outline every curve in a soft glow. She was obviously nervous as she turned to face me, but she had no reason to be. She was beautiful; no words could express my feelings at that moment. I simply looked upon her naked body with wonder and excitement. She had far exceeded my wildest expectations. Not in anyway was I disappointed.

I stood up to give her my hand and to help her into the hot tub. I hoped that allowing her to see me would relieve some of the awkwardness that she must have been feeling. As I led her into the water by her trembling hand, she submerged her body beneath the bubbles. She seemed to relax and feel more comfortable. I wanted to hold her close to me and to feel her body against mine, but I resisted the temptation. Lora needed a little time to get used to her surroundings. I felt that when the time was right, she would let me know in some way or another.

She was sitting at the far side of the hot tub, which allowed us to stare into each other's eyes as we made small talk about how beautiful the night was. The bubbles concealed our bodies from each other's view, exposing only our shoulders and above.

I leaned forward, finally reaching out my hand to hers. She responded with both hands. As our finger tips touched, we could feel the magic of the moment. I pulled her gently toward me, and she came willingly, being careful not to reveal the wonders that waited just below the water line. We kissed as she took a seat beside me. My arm found its way around her shoulders, leaving my hand to rest upon her upper chest. I felt her hand against my leg, and beneath the bubbles, her hip rubbed against mine.

We just sat relaxing, talking, savoring the taste of our wine, and enjoying each other's company. This seemed to be enough for the both of us at the time. It was a true display of our love to be so close and naked with the presence of want and desire but with the absence of lust. There was no question that we wanted each other. It was out of love not lust.

"Oh, Damon, you just can't believe how wonderful this feels. It's so relaxing and enjoyable."

"Yes, I know. I really enjoy the hot tub."

"No, the hot tub is wonderful, but what I'm talking about is being with a man who's respectful of me. We're naked, yet you're able to treat me like a lady."

"I respect you and care for you, but I also feel great passion for you. I've always felt a strong desire to have you, but now that I know you in a more personal way, I feel somewhat restrained. It is hard to explain because I've never held back when I've wanted someone so much. Of course, I don't know that I've ever wanted anyone as badly as I want you."

"I know. I feel the same way about you," Lora added.

"Strange, isn't it? We've known each other for over twenty years, yet we've never really known each other, except from a distance."

"Damon, I know that it's crazy to feel this way about someone so quickly, but I feel like I'm falling in love with you."

My hand tightened around her shoulder, bringing her closer to me. We kissed, and then I found myself saying those words that I have so seldom said,

"I don't think I love you, Lora. I know I do."

"Damon, I have to be sure. I've only been with two other men in my life. I hope you understand. I have to be absolutely sure that this is the real thing and that I'm not just allowing my desires to override my judgment and common sense."

"Lora, I do understand because I feel the same way."

"Damon, I think you must be the most wonderful man I've ever met. You seem to understand and feel my every mood. It is almost like we're meant to be together but that circumstances have prevented it up until now."

"Yes, I've always felt closeness to you, Lora, without being close. Now that I'm close to you, I feel it's more like a bond. There's a need and desire that I can't explain with rational thinking."

"I know. It's like it's a continuation of an endless love from another lifetime," Lora said with some hesitation.

"That's a beautiful thought, but I don't believe in past lives."

"I don't either, Damon. That's what makes this all seem so strange to me. Maybe it's the wine, or maybe we've been in this hot water too long. Whatever it is, the feeling is almost overwhelming."

"I think you're right."

"You mean about past lives?"

"No, Sweetheart, about being in this hot water too long. You want to get out?"

"Maybe we should. Would you mind if I take a shower?"

I helped Lora out of the hot tub and into my robe before I wrapped a towel around myself.

"Of course not, you can do anything you like here, Lora. I want you to feel comfortable. My home is your home."

"What a wonderful way you have of saying yes to me taking a shower. Damon, you are a perfect gentleman. I wish I'd known you better earlier in my life."

"My great attraction to you goes back a long way. Do you remember when I asked you to sign my yearbook near the end of our senior year?"

"Damon, really, I signed a lot of yearbooks."

"I'm sure you did, but when you signed mine, you dropped your lipstick on the floor. I picked it up for you. Remember?"

"You know what? I think I do remember. Later, when I went to put some fresh lipstick on, I couldn't find it."

"You couldn't find it because after you finished signing my book, I didn't give it back to you. I kept it and still have the tube."

"You're joking. I can't believe you still have that tube of lipstick after all these years?"

"Yes, I do. Let me show you something in the bedroom."

"Okay, Damon, but I've already seen it and I was very impressed."

"No, I want you to see something in my yearbook from High School."

I turned to the page with Lora's picture on it. The photo had a heart drawn around it with lipstick. I then showed her the empty tube that once held the lipstick.

"Oh my God that is so sweet. You drew that heart around my picture, Damon?"

"Yes, I did. I even wanted you back then. Lora, you have always been my dream girl."

"Oh, Damon, I couldn't be happier. What happened to the lipstick that was in the tube?"

"I carried that tube of lipstick as my lucky piece in the Army. I never went anywhere without it. During one scorching hot day in Vietnam, the lipstick melted, but I kept the tube anyway."

"Did it bring you luck?"

"Oh, yes, if it hadn't, I wouldn't be here today."

Lora walked up to me, and put her arms around my neck. Lifting one foot from the floor, she leaned her body against mine and kissed me ever so sensually. She moved her hand down my back, loosening then removing my towel. She allowed the robe that she was wearing to slip to the floor. I pulled her body toward mine, picked her up, and gently laid her on the bed. We stopped kissing just long enough for Lora to utter the words,

"Damon, my Darling, I love you."

"I love you, too, Lora," I responded.

Having Lora in my bed, in my arms, and making love to her was not a conquest or a challenge. It was the fulfillment of a life long dream. She was the pot of gold at the end of the rainbow, a treasure worth having and keeping forever.

It was a wonderful feeling, waking up with a beautiful woman beside me in bed. She was resting her head on my shoulder. It sure beat waking up to Ranger licking me. It was a feeling that I had not experienced in a very long time, and I had missed it. I had forgotten how good it was to share the morning with a woman, to have coffee together as I watch her get dressed for work. I think watching a woman dress is even sexier than watching her undress. They put so much more effort into dressing than undressing. It is a slow and sensual procedure, which they always take a great deal of effort and care to perform.

Lora sat on the edge of the bed watching me shave the stubble that had shown up since the night before. Not saying a word, she just smiled each time that I looked over at her. Once, I stuck my tongue out at her just to get a different reaction. She stuck her tongue out, too, and smiled.

I don't think I have ever had so much that I wanted to say to someone before, but I was at a total loss for words. I could not bring myself to put into words what I felt in my heart. Instead, I came up with something stupid,

"If you want, Lora, you can use the other bathroom to finish up in."

"No thanks, Damon. I am content watching you. You just blow me away with everything you do."

Laughing I said, "I had better be careful what I do then, I might get in some real trouble."

"Don't worry, Darling, I'll try to restrain myself. It'll be hard, but I'll make a real effort."

Lora had to leave a little before me. She needed to go by her place to feed her cat and change clothes.

As I was driving toward town, I felt different. I felt that I was a complete man, a man with a purpose. Lora had restored a feeling in me that I had lost a very long time ago and had long since forgotten. I had dated some, but that was all that it was, a date. With Lora, it was different. This was not just a date it was a new beginning.

Chapter 5

Upon my arrival to the office, Kelly and Bill were waiting impatiently. "Lieutenant, we'd like to continue working on this case. We feel there's more to it than meets the eye."

"Kelly, the case is closed. We have too many open cases that need our attention."

"What about Adam Knight and Ellen Christian? They're still missing and may very well be dead."

"Kelly, that case is assigned to Missing Persons, and until their bodies are found, that's who will be handling the case."

"But, Lieutenant, Missing Persons and Lieutenant Gant just don't seem to be doing anything to resolve this matter."

"You want to be promoted to sergeant, Kelly?"

"Yes, of course."

"Well, you don't get promoted by questioning the acts of department heads, like Charley Gant. I hope you haven't said anything to anyone else about your feeling in regard to how he handles his cases."

"No, Lieutenant, I haven't."

"Good. Now keep it that way. I'll forget you mentioned it."

As Kelly and Bill left my office half heartedly, I began to feel bad about being so hard on them. After all, I shared the same gut feeling that they did. I just felt like this case was not over and that I had to know more about this Beale treasure and why Tom Knight refused to trust the police department or maybe just someone in it. I could not let Kelly and Bill continue working on it, but I could do some checking on my own. I wanted to know more about this Beale treasure. It seemed to be at the center of multiple cases. Even though I considered it a old wives tale, it warranted further looking into. Mainly because there were those that did not consider it to be a old wives tale.

I called Lora and asked her if she had time to discuss the Beale Treasure and the Mayor's interest in it over lunch.

"Damon, the Mayor is out of the office today, so why don't you bring lunch over here. I have all kinds of information about Beale and his treasure at my fingertips."

"Okay, Beautiful, I'll be over around noon. Do burgers and fries sound good?"

"Sound's great. I'll go ahead and pull my files on the information that you want. See you then, Darling."

Promptly at noon, I showed up at Lora's office with three double cheeseburgers, a couple orders of fries, and two vanilla milkshakes. Lora seemed delighted to see me. I was hoping that she was glad to see me, and not just the burgers that I was bringing for our lunch. After a very passionate kiss and a tender hug, we settled down to business.

"Okay, first tell me what the Mayor's interest is in all of this foolishness."

"Damon, I really don't think its foolishness. The Mayor and several of his prominent friends take it very seriously."

"I don't put much stock in hunting for treasure. Many prominent men and women have been taken-in by fables about treasures and spent their lives and fortunes trying to find them. Do you know anything about Captain Kid's treasure on Oak Island in Nova Scotia? Many fortunes have been lost, not to mention more than six lives, looking for that treasure. Then there's The Lost Dutchman Mine. Again, many fortunes and lives were lost."

"It's funny you should mention The Lost Dutchman Mine. There's speculation that the Beale Treasure originated there."

"Who are these other people that belong to this treasure club or whatever it is?"

"I don't know for sure, but I think Doctor Kline, the hospital administrator, might be one of them. Mr. Doorman, who owns that big funeral home near the city cemetery, could also be a member. I can't say for sure because the Mayor's kept their names a secret, but those two call him quite frequently. I also get the impression that the group involves a member of the police department.

"Why do they keep this group and its members a secret?"

"I have no idea, Damon. I do know that the Mayor would be very upset with me for telling you all of this, though. You have to keep this information confidential, and you can never reveal that I was your source."

"Okay, but why?".

"It would cost me my job. The Mayor's very possessive and secretive about this treasure business and about his friends who are involved in it with him."

"Is that all you can tell me about the Mayor and his friends' involvement?"

"That's all I dare tell you, Damon. I want to be honest with you. You have to understand that I can't betray the confidence that some people have placed in me. I just can't tell you more about the group at this time."

"Alright, then tell me what you know about the treasure."

"Okay, Damon, you might find more information at the library, but this is what I know about it. In 1817, Thomas Beale and a number of other men went out west, looking for a new beginning. They were not looking for gold. They made camp somewhere, possibly in the New Mexico or Arizona area, which was still part of Mexico at that time. Beale and his party were looking for buffalo when they set up camp in a ravine for the night. One of the men found something that looked like gold. Beale and his party mined the site for the next year and a half. In addition to discovering a large amount of gold, they also found a deposit of silver nearby. They decided to let one person bring the treasure back to Virginia via a stop in St. Louis to trade some of the silver for jewels. The exchange would allow the person to reduce the amount of weight that he had to carry, and that person was Thomas Beale. When Beale arrived in Lynchburg in 1820, he was alone and spent several months in the area. During that time, he found a suitable location to hide the treasure and buried it. Also during his stay in Lynchburg, Beale met a man by the name of Robert Morris. Morris owned the Washington Hotel in Lynchburg. While Beale was hiding the treasure and meeting new people in the area, the other men were still working in the mine."

"How is all of this known?"

"Because of a letter he left with Robert Morris."

"Okay what else?"

"Beale returned to join his companions at the mine site, and when he came back to Virginia about two years later, he added even more treasure to what he had buried earlier. Because Beale and his associates were in a rather dangerous area at the time, they felt that they should leave a way for their relatives to find and distribute the treasure among themselves should something bad happen to the group. Beale's instructions were to find a person who was trustworthy and to leave that person with information regarding the treasure. Mr. Morris was his choice."

"Not being sure that he could trust anyone with such a great treasure, Beale made a code, or ciphers, that would have to be decrypted to obtain the information that would reveal the location of the treasure. Each cipher was a page full of numbers, and each page required a key document that would allow someone to decipher the message it contained. In 1822, Beale left a metal box containing the ciphers and a note written in plain English with Mr. Morris. Beale left Lynchburg to never return, and wasn't heard from again. After twenty-three years, Morris, thinking that Beale would never return to retrieve it, opened the box. Inside, he found the note and three sheets full of numbers. The note told the story about the discovery, journey, and burial of the treasure. It also explained the plan to leave the information with a trusted friend.

"More importantly, the note explained how the numbers worked. Each number represented a word in a key document. The problem was that there were no documents listed. Each cipher gave different information. One told exactly how to find the treasure. Another told what the treasure was comprised of, and the last told the names and next of kin of Beale and all of his associates.

"After twenty years of failing to break even one of the codes and knowing that he was near death, Morris made public in 1862, everything that he knew about Beale and the treasure, including the three pages of ciphers.

"After Morris's death, one of the ciphers was decoded using the Declaration of Independence as the key. It read,

> *"I have deposited in the county of Bedford, about four miles from Buford's; in an excavation or vault, six feet below the surface of the ground, the following articles. The deposit consists of two thousand nine hundred and twenty-one pounds of gold and five thousand one hundred pounds of silver; also jewels, obtained in St. Louis in exchange for silver to save transportation. The above is securely packed in iron pots, with iron covers. The vault is roughly lined with stone, and the vessels rest on solid stone, and are covered with others"*

"Do you have any idea what all that would be worth today, Lora?"

"From what the Mayor's said, I understand it to be worth somewhere between thirty and fifty million dollars. A lot depends on the value and quantity of the jewels, which is unknown at this time."

"Wow. That is a lot. People have been killed for a great deal less."

"That's for sure, Damon. Would you like a copy of the ciphers? Here is the one that's of such great interest to everyone. It's the one that tells the exact location of the treasure."

"You have copies of the ciphers?"

"Of course I do, silly. You can find them in any library. They're not a secret or anything. Anyone who wants them can have them. Without the key to unlock the code, they're useless, though. A great many people have spent their lives trying to decode them. Many have spent their entire fortunes trying to locate this treasure, and some have given up their lives and freedom for it."

"What do you mean, 'their freedom'?"

"I understand a number of people have gone to jail for trespassing and damaging private and public property. Also, several have gone to jail for digging up peoples' graves."

"Yes, if you don't mind, I'd like a copy."

"Okay, but don't you get crazy on me and start trying to figure it out. Here it is."

As I stared at the piece of paper that Lora handed me, a multitude of numbers stared back:

"71, 194, 38, 1701, 89, 76, 11, 83, 1629, 48, 94, 63, 132, 16, 111, 95, 84, 341, 975, 14, 40, 64, 27, 81, 139, 213, 63, 90, 1120, 8, 15, 3, 126, 2018, 40, 74, 758, 485, 604, 230, 436, 664, 582, 150, 251, 284, 308, 231, 124, 211, 486, 225, 401, 370, 11, 101, 305, 139, 189, 17, 33, 88, 208, 193, 145, 1, 94, 73, 416, 918, 263, 28, 500, 538, 356, 117, 136, 219, 27, 176, 130, 10, 460, 25, 485, 18, 436, 65, 84, 200, 283, 118, 320, 138, 36, 416, 280, 15, 71, 224, 961, 44, 16, 401, 39, 88, 61, 304, 12, 21, 24, 283, 134, 92, 63, 246, 486, 682, 7, 219, 184, 360, 780, 18, 64, 463, 474, 131, 160, 79, 73, 440, 95, 18, 64, 581, 34, 69, 128, 367, 460, 17, 81, 12, 103, 820, 62, 116, 97, 103, 862, 70, 60, 1317, 471, 540, 208, 121, 890, 346, 36, 150, 59, 568, 614, 13, 120, 63, 219, 812, 2160, 1780, 99, 35, 18, 21, 136, 872, 15, 28, 170, 88, 4, 30, 44, 112, 18, 147, 436, 195, 320, 37, 122, 113, 6, 140, 8, 120, 305, 42, 58, 461, 44, 106, 301, 13, 408, 680, 93, 86, 116, 530, 82, 568, 9, 102, 38, 416, 89, 71, 216, 728, 965, 818, 2, 38, 121, 195, 14, 326, 148, 234, 18, 55, 131, 234, 361, 824, 5, 81, 623, 48, 961, 19, 26, 33, 10, 1101, 365, 92, 88, 181, 275, 346, 201, 206, 86, 36, 219, 324, 829, 840, 64, 326, 19, 48, 122, 85, 216, 284, 919, 861, 326, 985, 233, 64, 68, 232, 431, 960, 50, 29, 81, 216, 321, 603, 14, 612, 81, 360, 36, 51, 62, 194, 78, 60, 200, 314, 676, 112, 4, 28, 18, 61, 136, 247, 819, 921, 1060, 464, 895, 10, 6, 66, 119, 38, 41, 49, 602, 423, 962, 302, 294, 875, 78, 14, 23, 111, 109, 62, 31, 501, 823, 216, 280, 34, 24, 150, 1000, 162, 286, 19, 21, 17, 340, 19, 242, 31, 86, 234, 140, 607, 115, 33, 191, 67, 104, 86, 52, 88, 16, 80, 121, 67, 95, 122, 216, 548, 96, 11, 201, 77, 364, 218, 65, 667, 890, 236, 154, 211, 10, 98, 34, 119, 56, 216, 119, 71, 218, 1164, 1496, 1817, 51, 39, 210, 36, 3, 19, 540, 232, 22, 141, 617, 84, 290, 80, 46, 207, 411, 150, 29, 38, 46, 172, 85, 194, 39, 261, 543, 897, 624, 18, 212, 416, 127, 931, 19, 4, 63, 96,

12, 101, 418, 16, 140, 230, 460, 538, 19, 27, 88, 612, 1431, 90, 716,
275, 74, 83, 11, 426, 89, 72, 84, 1300, 1706, 814, 221, 132, 40, 102,
34, 868, 975, 1101, 84, 16, 79, 23, 16, 81, 122, 324, 403, 912, 227,
936, 447, 55, 86, 34, 43, 212, 107, 96, 314, 264, 1065, 323, 428, 601,
203, 124, 95, 216, 814, 2906, 654, 820, 2, 301, 112, 176, 213, 71,
87, 96, 202, 35, 10, 2, 41, 17, 84, 221, 736, 820, 214, 11, 60, 760"

"This is really something. Why would anyone go to so much trouble to commit a hoax?"

"Exactly, that's what the Mayor and his friends think also."

"So, let me understand this correctly. Each number represents a word in some historical document?"

"That's correct, but it doesn't have to be a historical document. It can be anything like a song, a book, a poem, anything out of millions of things. Just because the Declaration of Independence was the key to the one cipher does not mean that a historical document is the key to the others. I have put all kinds of things on computer discs for the Mayor. He uses it all to compare with his program that he has in the safe."

"What is Buford's, Lora?"

"It's an old inn or tavern near Montvale."

"Thanks so much, Beautiful, for all your help. I remember hearing people mention the Beale Treasure before, but I just figured it was bull. This is really interesting, I think I'll visit the library and pick up a book or two about it."

"You better not become so engrossed that you forget about our first date tonight. I expect to see you at the basketball game. Oh, and like we discussed, I'm still expecting dinner afterward."

"How could I ever forget our date, Lora? I haven't been able to get you off my mind for years. You really think I would forget?"

"I'm just warning you. You better not forget."

"Does six-thirty still work for you? You might want to bring the clothes you plan to wear to work tomorrow."

"Hey that sounds to me like you have more than just dinner planned for us, and yes, six-thirty still sounds good."

"What do you mean? Remember, this is our first date. You think I would put a move on you on our first date?"

"Yes, I do, but that's alright with me. If you're not going to make a move on me, I'll just plan on making some moves of my own."

I left Lora's office with a laugh and a big smile on my face. Apparently, what I did last night had been satisfactory. She seemed eager to try it again tonight, and that was just fine with me. I was glad that we ended our meeting the way that we did. To know that I had performed up to her standards secured my sexual confidence in a needed way.

There was nothing pressing at the office that I knew of, so I decided to stop by the newspaper office that Adam Knight used to work for as a reporter. I wanted to see what information I could dig up on him that might shed some light on what may have happened to him and Ellen.

As I walked into the building, I looked across the street. There on the corner was the old Virginian Hotel. It had not been a hotel for years. It was now a dilapidated office building that had a few cheap one-room apartments on the top floors. The people that rented rooms there were guests in our jail when they were not residing there. I vaguely remember someone telling me that it was once the Washington Hotel. They destroyed the hotel after the Civil War. Then years later in the late eighteen hundreds, they built a new hotel named The Virginian.

I found the people at the news office to be very cooperative about answering questions regarding Adam. It seemed that Adam was well liked and highly regarded by his fellow workers. They were glad to answer all of my questions, knowing that anything might be helpful in finding Adam. I learned that he had a very high IQ and was a genius. They also told me about his treasure hunting activities. It seemed that everybody knew more about the Beale Treasure than me.

When I left the newspaper office, I headed for the library, which was just down the street. I found several books about the Beale Treasure, and it seemed like Lora was right. The Beale Treasure was no secret, and I had a good selection of books from which to choose. I checked out a couple of books to look over in my spare time. I also felt that it would be a good idea to find out who else may have checked these books out in the last couple of years. The librarian was very helpful and gave me a list of people who had checked out the two books that I had chosen plus a list of those who had checked out any books concerning the Beale Treasure.

I scanned over the lists quickly, taking only enough time to notice that Adam Knight had checked out every book and that the Mayor had checked out none. I gave Lora a call to ask if she knew if the Mayor owned any of the books on the list. She told me that he had all of them in addition to some that were not on the list.

I decided that it was time to get back to the office and make sure that everything was running smoothly. I was just nearing the police station when a man who appeared to be in a hurry bumped into me. He mumbled that he was sorry and kept going. I did not think anything of it until I got in my office and found a balled up piece of paper in my jacket pocket. I straightened it out only to discover that the man who bumped into me must have slipped it into my pocket and that the man must have been Tom Knight. It read:

> *Lieutenant Carter*
> *You are on the right track to finding what happened to my brother and Ellen. I think I can trust you and will be in touch with you soon.*
> *Tom Knight*

Well, for a case that was no longer a case, this was certainly becoming more involved. It was also becoming more interesting. It had been a while since I had worked on something that kept my attention so strongly; well, except Lora. I was looking forward to Tom contacting me.

Before going to my desk, I stopped by Charley Gant's office to find out what he had learned about the disappearances of Adam Knight and Ellen Christian.

"Good afternoon, Charley. You got a few minutes?"

"Sure, Damon, what can I do for you?"

"Well, I was wondering if you've made any headway on the Knight and Christian Missing Persons case."

"No, we haven't. I figure they're dead or have skipped the country.

We haven't come up with anything to indicate that they're alive, so we're assuming that they're dead. When their bodies turn up, you can have the case. Until then, we've put it on the back burner. More or less, it's closed."

"Did anything come up about the Beale Treasure in your investigation, Charley?"

"Why, No. Why would that have come up in a Missing Persons case? The Beale Treasure sounds more like a lost and found case, or should I have classified that as a never found and never existed case." Charley laughed.

"Yeah, you're right. I don't know what I was thinking. Sounds like you know about the treasure, though."

"I know what I've heard about it. Everyone who has ever lived here knows about that treasure. I've just never developed much of an interest in it. If you ask me, I think it could be a hoax, that some prankster came up with to make fools out of people. It never existed, Damon."

Well, that conversation did not turn up much to help me. I went back to my office to look back over the lists of names that the librarian had given me. Tom Knight's name had not popped out at me earlier, but I just wanted to double check to make sure that it was not on any of them. As I read over the lists, I did not find it, but I did find another interesting name. Charles Gant had checked out a few of the books over the past two years. For someone who thought that the treasure was a hoax, he sure did do a lot of research about it. I wondered why he tried to mislead me. Was he the member of the police department who belonged to the Mayor's treasure hunting group?

I had legitimate cases that I should have been working on, but this was all too intriguing to me. The more that I thought about it, the more Charley's "misleading" became lying. I think saying that he was being misleading was giving him too much credit. I called Lora to ask if Lieutenant Gant was a regular visitor of the Mayor's.

"He's never come by himself, but he has shown up a couple of times with other officers. In fact, I remember him coming here with you once."

"Oh yes. I remember that. What about phone calls, does he ever call the Mayor?"

"Damon, I can't discuss the Mayor's calls."

"Okay, I'll see you tonight at six thirty. Thanks for your help, Honey."

Over the next couple of hours, I reviewed the cases assigned to the squad over the last year. I then left a little early to get ready for my first formal yet informal date with Lora.

When I arrived at her house, she was almost ready to go. She sent me back out to the car with a large suitcase that felt heavy enough for a weeks worth of clothing. It was only a few minutes later that Lora came bouncing out to the car wearing sweat pants, a tee shirt, and sneakers. She had pulled her hair back on her head into a ponytail, and she was carrying another bag that looked like more of an overnight bag.

She jumped in the car and kissed me before I even had a chance to speak.

"Let's go, Damon. I don't want to be late."

"Yes Ma'am. Believe me you won't be late. If I have to, I'll turn on the lights and siren to get you there on time."

"Wow, that's right; this is a police car. Are you supposed to be using it while going out on a date?"

"Yes, Darling, I'm a Lieutenant. I'm on-call twenty-four hours a day, so I need my car with me at all times."

"Do you own a car?"

"Yes, of course. It's in the garage at the house. I keep it covered up."

"What kind of car is it?"

"Corvette convertible"

"What color?"

"It's black with a matching top. What difference does it make? I never get to use it."

"Just being curious Darling."

When Lora and I arrived at the school, I dropped her off at the gymnasium's back door. She wanted to go in through the locker room to give her girls a pep talk before the game, so I drove around front, parked, and went in to find a seat. The game was close, and at half time, Lora's team was trailing by four points. They made a good recovery, though, and came back to win the game by ten.

While Lora celebrated with her team, I went outside to pull the car around back. When she came out, she was all smiles.

"Oh, Damon, didn't the girls play a great game tonight? I'm so proud of them."

"Yeah, I don't know what you said to them at half time, but they really turned it around."

"I know that we had plans for dinner, but would it be too much to ask if we could go to the burger joint instead?"

"No, I don't mind. I know that it must be important for your girls to see how proud you are of them."

"Thank you for understanding, and I promise that I'll make it up to you later tonight."

"If I'm giving up a steak and baked potato for a fast food cheeseburger and greasy French fries, I'm going to hold you to that promise."

When we got to the burger stand, it was clear to me that; I had been had. The whole team was there and waiting for us to arrive. It seemed that Lora had promised to buy them all burgers, fries, and shakes before she had even asked me if it was okay to change our plans.

"Honey, what if I had wanted to go to the restaurant instead of coming here?"

"I knew you wouldn't do that."

"Oh really, you know me that well already?"

"Yes, I do, and I also know that you love me too much not to grant me this small favor."

"Well, in the future, I'll try not to be so predictable."

"Darling, you can't help it," Lora said as she laughed and managed to insult me all in the same sentence.

"Oh, really"

That night, Lora kept her promise far beyond my wildest expectations. She aroused feelings in my body that I did not even know existed. We moved together in perfect harmony, seeming to know each other's thoughts, desires, and needs. I could not imagine a more perfect union as we consummated the love and desire that we shared for one another.

As she lay at my side with her head on my shoulder, her fingers danced among the hairs on my chest. Nothing needed to be spoken aloud the communication was there all the same.

Each look and every touch that we shared screamed aloud that this union was destine to be and was long overdue. As we drifted off to sleep in each other's arms, I felt that peaceful serenity and comfort that had escaped me before learning of Lora's feelings.

In the morning, we awoke with the same passion that we had experienced the night before. A surge of energy that I did not even know I was capable exploded into a continuation of our lovemaking. Afterwards, we laid there as I thought about how morning sex was the perfect way to begin a new day. I then heard the coffee maker cut on, and I thought to myself, *there is the second perfect way to begin the day.*

As I poured two cups of coffee, I noticed that Lora seemed to have something on her mind. Just as I was about to ask her what she was thinking, she asked,

"Damon, what would you think about me spending the weekend here with you?"

"Sweetheart, I think that's a great idea."

"There's one little problem, though."

"What's that?"

"Smokey."

"What is a Smokey, Lora?"

"My cat, his name is Smokey. I'll need to bring her here with me, or I'll have to go home a couple times a day to take care of her."

"I don't mind if you bring your cat over. I don't know what Ranger will think, but he'll just have to adapt to it. I want you to spend a lot of time here, and if that means that your cat has to come too, then so be it. I'm sure that we'll all get along fine."

"Okay, I'll go by my place after work and get Smokey. I'll be waiting here with dinner ready when you get home."

"Well, you might want to wait on fixing dinner until I can call you and tell you that I'm heading home. Remember, I am a cop, and cops can't rely on a schedule like most people. It's Friday night, and anything could happen to delay me."

"I know, Darling. I understand, but I hope nothing happens. I'm looking forward to spending the weekend with you. It'll be almost like we're married."

"Yes, Sweetheart, it will be," I said after groping for words.

Wow, we have only been dating for a week, and the M-word has already been used a couple times. That gave me something to think about but not concerned about. I did love Lora and could not think of a better-matched couple than the two us, but the fact remained that we did not really know each other that well yet.

We got ready and left for work early. As I drove Lora to her house to get her car, she must have noticed that I was saying very little,

"I scared you when I mentioned marriage, didn't I, Damon?"

"No, you didn't scare me. I just hadn't really considered anything that serious yet."

"I wasn't insinuating that I was expecting you to marry me or anything. I was just saying that it would be as if we are married. I guess that it was a poor choice of words."

"No, it wasn't that. I just think we need to get to know each other a little better before we get swept up in our emotions and start talking about marriage."

"I'm sorry, Damon. Maybe I shouldn't spend the weekend at your house."

"Don't be ridiculous. I want you to. I can't think of a better way to get to know each other than by spending as much time as possible together."

"Are you sure? I don't want to push myself on you or be too forward."

"You aren't. I love you, Lora. I have always loved you. I am just having a little difficulty coming to the realization that after all these years you love me too. It's just hard to believe that I could have everything that I've always wanted."

"Then I'll see you at the house tonight," Lora said with a farewell kiss.

"Yes Darling."

As I drove toward my office, I played our conversation back over in my head. After several reviews, I admitted to myself that I had probably hurt Lora's feelings. I stopped at a nearby florist and ordered a dozen roses. I had them delivered to her office with a note that told her that I could not wait to spend the weekend with her. The last thing that I wanted was for her to feel anything less than confident that I desired her deeply.

Chapter 6

As I arrived at my office, the last thing that I was thinking about was police work. My mind was preoccupied, with memories from the night before and the romantic weekend still to come. Lora was a wonderful woman, and I could not get her off my mind. The passion that she so willingly ravished me with each time we were intimate was unbelievable. If someone had told me back in high school that some day the most beautiful girl in the class would be sharing my bed, I surely would have thought that they were crazy. Suddenly, the phone rang, and my mind switched to work mode as I answered,

"Lieutenant Carter, Homicide."

"Damon, it is Lora."

"Hi Beautiful I was just thinking about you."

"Damon, Norma's at home, and she called me. Tom Knight wants to meet with you."

"I would like to talk to him also. When and where does he want to meet?"

"He will be at Norma's house in an hour. He wants you to come alone."

"Sure, that's no problem. I wasn't planning on bringing anyone with me."

"I don't know what's going on with this whole thing. I thought the case was closed?"

"The grave business is closed, but there's still that looming matter of his brother and Norma's sister's disappearance."

"Isn't that a Missing Persons matter? I thought that you only worked homicides."

"Yes, but it could be homicide. It depends on what happened to them."

"Be careful, Damon. I don't know if I trust Norma anymore."

"Don't worry, Honey. I'm not going to let anything interfere with my weekend with you."

"You better not. I have some things planned for you that I think you'll like, starting with dinner tonight."

"I'm really looking forward to it. Did Norma say anything else?"

"No only that you should call her back if you couldn't come."

"I'll be there."

"Okay, I'll call Norma back and tell her. I'll see you tonight, Darling."

Before leaving, I tried to make a few notes regarding questions that I wanted to ask Tom. Soon, it became apparent that I had more questions for him than I had originally thought. Each one made me think of two or three more. I did not want to take a chance on being late and Tom leaving, so I started on the fifteen-minute drive to Norma's house. On the way, I was still coming up with more questions. This whole thing was so bizarre, and so many things remained unanswered.

When I arrived, the black van was not there, and I immediately became disappointed at the possibility of not meeting him. When I walked up to the door, I was pleasantly surprised.

"Tom Knight, I'm glad to finally meet you in person," I said to the man who motioned me in the door.

"I'm glad to meet you too, Damon. I've heard a lot about you. Norma told me that I could trust you. Is that true?"

"I think you can. Before you get too carried away with trusting me, I have a few questions that I would appreciate the answers too. Remember, I'm still a cop."

"Okay, what are your questions? I'll answer them if I can and if they aren't too personal. I should also let you know that I won't answer any questions that may go against any oath that I may have taken."

"Judging from the background check we did on you and the total lack of information that we were able to obtain, I have to assume that you're a spook for the government. What agency do you work for and what do you do with or for them, if you can tell me?"

"Well, first off, we don't like to be referred to as spooks, but I am what you would call a spook. As far as what agency I work for or what I do, I can't tell you that. My work is classified at the highest level, and my agency will protect me from any prosecution that is associated with my work related activities."

"Tom, we figured that out already. That is why we didn't pursue any charges for the desecration of those graves, which brings me to my next question. What did you hope to find in those graves?"

"I hoped to find out something in reference to the disappearances of Adam and Ellen, but I wasn't really sure what I was looking for. I was on my way out to my van one day when it started sprinkling. As I jogged closer to it, I noticed a note under one of the windshield wiper blades. The rain had smudged some of the ink, but I could make out most of what it said,

The proof ---t your broth-- and Ellen -- --ding for their own ----y can be found -- - grave dug on April 3-, --89 on the L---- ---m in ----- -- -e-- -------- I am tel--ng you th-- to s--- --- from sea------ fo- then an to --- y-- ---- they are ----.

"I took it to mean that information as to what happened to them was buried in one of the graves."

"I didn't find anything, though, and I can tell you that, it had to have been one of the most distasteful things that I've ever done. The night that I dug up two graves was the hardest. I struggled through it so much that I didn't have time to cover them back up."

"Well, if you weren't able to make out the entire note, how did you come up with what you did? What did you hope to find in the coffins?"

"There are only thirty days in April, so I knew that 'April 30' made sense. Norma had also told me what Ellen had told her about the date and the rest of it. Adam disappeared in 1989, so I just filled in the blanks with that. After that, I'm not sure. As to what I hoped to find. I really didn't know what, if anything they could have hidden in one of the coffins. Could be a note giving a clue to their location or possibly a letter from Adam. It would be easy to slip something into a coffin at a viewing or anytime prior to burial. It is hard to imagine a safer place to hide something. At this point in my search, I was grasping at straws. Someone was trying to tell me something for some reason. I didn't know what they were trying to tell me or why. I just knew I needed to take my best shot at what they may be trying to tell me."

"What do you mean?"

"I didn't know what letters were missing or how many. I can only go by the blanks and the size of the writing. Then guess at how many letters were in each word. As for the 'L----,' I could only think of Lord or Lords since the letter is a capital. Also because of what Ellen told Norma the day before she disappeared. Either way, none of it really fits together."

"So, you're telling me that one little note prompted you to dig up nine graves?"

"I've devoted the last year to finding out what happened to my brother. That note found me at a desperate time. The police weren't sharing any information with me, and I'm not even sure that they were really making an effort. What I do know is that Lieutenant Gant is of no help. He won't answer any of my questions."

"You mentioned to me over the phone, something about the Beale Treasure. How does that enter into this whole thing?"

"I think it has a big part to play. My brother was a genius; he had an ability to figure out codes and ciphers that seemed very unbelievable sometimes. My agency with the government even used him several times over the years to decipher codes that the computers could not even figure out. He truly had a gift for it."

"He told me about a year ago that a group of prominent men here in town had asked him to look over the Beale Treasure ciphers for them. He told me these men where obsessed with finding this treasure and offered to cut him in if he helped them. About a month before he and Ellen disappeared, he called me and told me he thought he had figured out the key to decoding the cipher that told the location of the treasure. That he thought the author, Thomas Beale had put it on a curve, something like a teacher in school would grade on a curve, if test scores all seemed low. I didn't understand what he meant by that at all."

"Then about two weeks later he called and told me that he had told these men about his findings, but he didn't trust them. That he had told them enough, that it wouldn't take them long to figure out the cipher and when they did they wouldn't need him any longer. He felt his life may even be in danger that these men in their positions could easily do away with him with no problem or questions asked. He also was afraid to tell me too much over the phone, because he said that they had the means of taping it and could be listening to his phone conversations."

"Tom, did he ever mention any names in regard to who was in this group?"

"No, he didn't. He was afraid to tell me, but he did tell me he could not go to the police for protection. Because he did not feel they could be trusted."

"Do you have any idea who any of them might be?"

"I'm not sure, but I think the Mayor might be one of them. I also suspect that Captain Gant might be involved in someway, I'm not sure how."

"What about any Doctors or any business owners?"

"I think maybe at least one doctor, but I'm not sure of that either. There is a doctor that has shown a great deal of interest in the treasure. He has dug for it at least two times, about ten years ago. He had a partner back then, a respected attorney, which is now your city Mayor. That Doctors name is Kline and he lives just down the street from the Mayor."

"So that is why Norma became friends with Lora, to get information from her about the Mayor and also who he may be connected with?" I asked.

"Yes, but she also liked Lora a lot, they had been friends in school. We both trust her completely that is why we think we can trust you."

"Thanks Tom, I like to feel I am trustworthy. What is your best guess as to who, you think left the note on your windshield and why?"

"I have no idea who, but I think the reason why is so I will find Adam for them. They know I have resources to find people, but so far I haven't come up with anything on Adam or Ellen."

"You don't think their dead, do you?"

"No, I think Adam cracked the last cipher, then he left here and he and Ellen are laying low somewhere. Waiting to come back and get the treasure."

"How do you know they don't already have the treasure?"

"Because if they had found it, they wouldn't still be looking for it, would they? For some reason I don't think the last cipher told the exact location of the treasure, but was just another clue."

"How would Adam and Ellen be living, there hasn't been any activity on the bank accounts or any of their credit cards?"

"I don't know Damon, I just have the feeling they are still alive and are hiding out until it is safe before they come back or let anyone know where they are."

"Tom in your position, you could be a big help to Adam. Why wouldn't he get in touch with you, if he were still alive? It would seem only natural that he would contact you, which I am sure he could do in total secrecy."

"How should I know, maybe fear or the overwhelming desire to find the treasure have warped his way of thinking?"

"Tom, do you really believe this treasure is real?"

"I don't know, it is possible I suppose. I know if it does exist, it is worth over thirty million dollars and there have been many people killed for a great deal less. It does not matter if it exists or is a hoax; if there are people out here that believe it is real they will kill for it."

"Norma, you haven't said a word, what is your opinion of this whole matter?"

"I don't honestly know Damon; I just want my sister and Adam back. I don't care about some silly treasure. I believe in Tom, I think he will find them. I just hope they are alive and okay."

"I would like to help the two of you if I can. Not as a police officer of course but as a friend."

"That would be great Damon; I was hoping you would offer. Lora is already helping us and has been for a couple months."

"What? You mean she has known about everything going on all the time?"

"No, Not everything, but most of it I think. She is the one that told us that you were interested in finding what happened to Adam and Ellen. She also told us that you where asking about the Beale Treasure. It was Lora that convinced us to trust you."

"She has done it to me again. I guess I'll be eating a lot of greasy hamburgers and french-fries in this relationship."

"What Damon? What in the world are you talking about?"

"Oh nothing it is just how Lora gets me involved or to do things without me knowing what is going on."

Norma smiled and said, "Damon if it is any conciliation, I happen to know you aren't going to be eating hamburgers and French fries tonight. Lora has a very special dinner for you and a dessert that will knock your pants off. I mean that in a literal since."

"I hope so; I have had enough hamburgers for today."

There was one thing that seemed wrong or out of place about everything, that Tom had just told me.

"Tom, you just told me that Adam and you have spoken at least a couple times just prior to his disappearance. For some reason I was under the impression you had not spoken to each other for years."

"Damon, in my line of work, we must keep family as much a secret as what we do, for their own safety. I can see where you may have gotten that impression. But I assure you we spoke frequently."

I left Norma and Tom. Then headed back to the police department to hopefully find an answer or two to some of my questions. I was really beginning to wonder what role Charley Gant played in this whole affair. I know he had something to do with it, because he lied to me. In addition, there was his total lack of cooperation with Tom. Charley knew something, but what did he know and how could I get it out of him?

Then my thoughts turned to what Norma had told me about Lora tonight. Every time Lora entered my mind, I know I would get a smile on my face. I could not help but smile with such a pleasant thought in my head. I could not wait to see her tonight, she would be waiting for me when

I got home, and that was a wonderful feeling. I hoped it would be a quiet weekend and there would be no calls for any police business. I wanted to spend as much time as possible with Lora.

Funny, driving home seemed longer today than usual. It seemed like it took me forever to be pulling into my driveway. When I opened the front door, Ranger was not there to meet me as usual. There was a delightful smile coming from the direction of the kitchen along with the sound of music. Nothing was as it normally was when I got home and it felt great.

I walked quietly into the kitchen and Lora was just closing the oven door and did not hear me come in.

"Hi beautiful" I said rather loudly.

"Oh my God, you scared me." Lora exclaimed as she turned quickly.

"I'm sorry I didn't mean to scare you. Where is Ranger he wasn't at the door to meet me."

"Oh Damon, you aren't going to believe this. Come here I have something to show you."

I followed Lora to the bedroom, and there on the bed was Ranger and Lora's cat Smoky. They were both asleep, but woke up and looked at us as we came into the room.

"Can you believe how well they are getting along? Just a few minutes after Smoky and I got here they became instant friends; Once the initial shock had passed of seeing each other for the first time."

"I didn't think Ranger would mind much, but I didn't expect any thing like this."

"Dinner won't be ready for almost two hours. Is there anything you would like to do while we are waiting for dinner to finish cooking? I got the most beautiful bunch of roses today. All the girls at the office were envious of me all day long."

"Yes, I want to talk a little."

"Talk about what, Damon?"

"How you have been constantly in touch with Tom Knight and Norma. How you know a great deal more about this whole situation than you have let on. That you have been working with them for the better part of a year."

"I was hoping they wouldn't tell you. I wanted to tell you myself, before you found out from another source. I wanted to tell you that day you came to the office to ask questions about the Beale Treasure. Tom did not know if you could be trusted at that time, so he made me promise not to tell you. Tom is sure that at least one high-ranking person in the police department is involved in his brother and Ellen's disappearances. Not knowing who it is for sure, he did not trust anyone connected with the police. Even if a high-ranking police officer is involved, I don't feel that it is in a bad way. In fact, this person may be working to protect Adam and Ellen. If the officer involved is one of the Mayors group. I know the Mayor wouldn't harm or allow anyone to harm Adam and Ellen. I know one thing I will never give a pledge of secrecy to anyone again. It is far too hard to keep, when I see people I care about being mislead and hurt by it."

"It is okay Darling; I have thrown in with Tom and Norma also. So I guess it will be the four of us now."

"That is great. I knew you would, there wasn't a question in my mind that you wouldn't be willing to help."

"Yes Darling. That brings me to another subject I wish to discuss, which is how you seem to assume I will go along with things."

"What can I say my love, you are a predictable man I'm not assuming, I know you are a good man and caring person. Being a good man, you will naturally do what is right."

"That isn't exactly what I wanted to hear, but not bad for openers. Did you predict this?"

As I laid her on the bed gently while in a passionate kiss. We sent Ranger and Smoky running out of the bedroom.

"Yes Darling I did, that is why I waited for you to come in the front door before putting dinner in the oven."

"You heard me come in?"

"Of course, I saw you pull into the driveway."

"So I didn't scare you when I came in the kitchen."

"No Darling, I'm afraid I was acting. But you seemed so intent on scaring me; I didn't want to disappoint you."

"You are a she Devil. a beautiful one though."

After we made love, Lora got up and went to the kitchen to check on dinner. I just laid there thinking how fantastic she was. If this was an example of how our weekend was going to go, I was a dead man. She was going to kill me with passion, love and plan spoiling me.

She came back into the room and stood in front of the dresser mirror brushing her long blonde hair. She was wearing a sweatshirt and thongs. She was a vision of loveliness to me, her shapely, tanned legs topped off with the smooth perfect cheeks of her buttocks. Just watching her got me all excited again. She turned to me to say something, but stopped when she saw that I was in the mood again, even though the encounter we had just had moments before was very exhausting. She walked over removing her sweatshirt and thongs on her way. Then she mounted me like a horse and leaned into me for a kiss. I was definitely a dead man; there was no way I was going to survive this weekend.

We had no sooner finished making love than the buzzer on the stove went off, to alert us that dinner was ready. Lora jumped up put a robe on and ran to the kitchen, while I decided to grab a quick shower.

As soon as we finished the fantastic dinner of some kind of Lobster casserole along with salad and fresh baked bread. We decided a little time in the hot tub was in order. We had not been in the hot tub more than ten minutes when my pager went off. I got out and called the station to see what was going on. The sergeant on duty told me that a Doctor Kline and his wife were involved in an automobile incident and they are both presumed dead.

"Sergeant, I don't handle automobile wrecks, I'm homicide not traffic."

"Lieutenant, it was Chief Lewis that told me to call you and I understand it was Mayor Caldwell that told him. Seems the Mayor does not think this is an accident.

"Okay Sergeant, give me a quick explanation of what happened."

"According to the officer on the scene and witnesses, the Doctor and his wife where going to a party. They had pulled out of the driveway and had driven about a block, where they where to make a right turn, toward the highway. There was an explosion in the car and it became totally engulfed in flames instantly. They never had a chance to escape."

"All right, Sergeant what is the address, I will head over there as soon as I get dressed."

I went back out to the hot tub to explain to Lora what was going on and to tell her I had to leave. When I mentioned the Doctors name, Lora said.

"Damon, don't you remember? Doctor Kline is the Hospital Administrator, that I told you may be involved with the Mayor in the Beale Treasure thing."

"Really, I had forgotten but that makes sense, because the sergeant said the Chief told him to call me and he was pretty sure the order came from the Mayor."

"Can I go with you Damon?"

"I don't think you should, these two people were burned to death. That doesn't make for a very pleasant sight."

"Oh Damon, Please I won't get in the way, I can just wait in the car."

"Okay, but if you see things that you wish you hadn't seen, it isn't my fault, I tried to talk you out of coming."

"Good, I'll hurry and get dressed; we can do the dishes when we get home."

In a very few minutes, Lora and I were on our way to the location where the explosion had taken place. It was in one of the higher-class sections of town and on the same street that the Mayor lived on.

When we arrived, the Kline's charred bodies were still in what little was left of their car. They had extinguished the fire; with that exception, nothing had been touched. The officers at the scenes instructions were not to remove or handle anything until I had arrived.

You never get use to the smell of burnt human flesh; I don't care how many times you smell it. An unforgettable smell I had gotten very familiar with, in Vietnam. I got a flashlight out of the trunk of my car and started examining the Doctors car. It was obvious that the gas tank had exploded, but gas tanks don't just explode without help. The filler line going into the gas tank seemed to be the source of the initial explosion. The force of the blast had blown it into little pieces. Then I found the remains of a wire that had no business where I found it. I followed it and found it connected to the right turn signal.

In a gas tank with the cap on the fumes alone would be the equivalent of several sticks of dynamite. Combined with the gas in the tank you had a very lethal bomb. Someone had obviously put a wired detonator on the filler line going into the gas tank. Then run a wire to the signal light. When the Doctor turned on his right signal to make the turn, the detonator exploded in the gas tank causing it to explode.

I had the officers there search the area very closely, for anything that might be a detonator or used as one. A sparkplug wired to any source of power, placed in the filler line to the gas tank. In this case the source of power appeared to be the right turn signal. Anything that would make a spark, in that tank full of fumes would have detonated it.

I informed the Traffic Sergeant that Homicide was taking over. Then I went back to my car to radio the station, to get my people over here right a way. Then I told the Sergeant to close off the area as a crime scene and to tell the coroner that they could go ahead and remove the bodies.

Then I turned to Lora. "Honey I'm going to be a while. If you want me to, I will have one of the officers, drive you back to the house?"

"It isn't an accident is it, Damon?"

"No, it isn't."

"If you don't mind, I would like to stay here with you. Is that all right?"

"If that is what you want to do, but if you change your mind, just let me know."

"Okay Darling, don't worry about me, I will be fine. I find this all very interesting."

I was looking around when I noticed a familiar face in the crowd. It was Tom Knight. I walked over to ask him what he was doing here.

"What are you doing here Tom?"

"I heard it over my police scanner, when I heard the name Doctor Kline, I decided to come over."

"Well I'm glad you did, maybe you can help."

"Fine with me, Damon, I would love to help. I think this connects to all the other things we have been talking about recently. But you know I have to keep a low profile."

"Sure Tom, I understand. This is what I have found so far.

I told him about the wire to the gas tank and the turn signal. He had already suspected Doctor Kline was in the treasure group of the Mayors.

Jack Morris was the first of my squad to arrive. He started looking around as soon as he got there. I went up and asked him if he had any idea of what he was looking for.

"I just figured I would look and see if I saw anything out of place or out of the ordinary, Lieutenant." Jack told me.

"We are looking for anything that could be used as an electronic detonator Jack. A tube a sparkplug, wire, anything that would cause a spark or explosion when twelve volts, was put to it."

"Don't forget a twelve volt light bulb, Damon. With the glass gone it is perfect." Tom spoke up.

"Yes, I hadn't thought about a light bulb, but that is a good idea."

"Who is that Lieutenant?" Jack asked.

"He is an explosive expert I borrowed from the government."

"How did you get him here so quickly Lieutenant?"

"He is a friend of mine, Jack, he was already here visiting, I asked him to give me hand on this investigation."

"Good thinking Lieutenant, very good thinking considering, you didn't even know it was our investigation fifteen minutes ago."

"Jack, go do something, anything."

I took Tom and showed him the filler pipe to the gas tank.

"Damon, you can stop looking for anything unusual that could have been used as a detonator. They used a real detonator, possibly home made, combined with a small explosive charge. I would say C-4 maybe. Not much about a quarter pound or less."

"How do you know Tom?"

"If something like a sparkplug or light bulb had been used, it wouldn't have blown this pipe in to pieces like it did. Neither would a commercial or military detonator by itself, so it had to have a charge with it."

"Tom, it doesn't make any sense, why would anyone want the doctor dead?"

"It makes a lot of sense to me Damon. Thirty Million plus is a lot of money."

"Yes it is, but why would they start killing off their own members of the group."

"Maybe they aren't."

"What do you mean, Tom?"

"There might be a fly in the ointment we don't know about. Whoever it is, knows explosives and the affective way of using them. I would say they were ex-military and with demolition training."

"How do I know you didn't have anything to do with this, Tom?"

"You don't Damon. I will give you my word that I did not. That is if my word carries any weight with you. You can consider it given."

"Well Tom, you are here. You are ex-military, I am sure you have had demolition training, and I am sure you wouldn't have any problem acquiring any explosives you want."

"You're right on all counts. So why aren't you arresting me then?"

"Because I don't think you did it. In addition, from what little I have found out about you, it wouldn't do any good to arrest you. You would be out with one phone call."

"Right again Damon, I guess you have never run into this type of situation before, aggravating isn't it, my friend?"

"If I thought you did this, it would be. I don't think you did this because you are missing one primary thing to commit a crime like this. You don't have a motive to kill the Doctor, not that I know of anyway. You are not interested in finding the treasure; your only interest is finding your brother, Adam. Killing off the people that might give you a clue as to what happened to him doesn't make any real sense at all."

"Damon, don't waste your time and brain power thinking about why I did not do it. Lets concentrate on who did, get me an evidence bag, let us get some residue off this gas filler line. Maybe your lab can tell us what kind of explosive they used. That should narrow down the field a little, because if it was C-4, not just anyone can get their hands on it. In fact get me two bags, I'll send a sample to my lab also, I know they will have some answers for us on it."

Either Tom was telling me the truth or he was a very good actor. At this point I was not sure which, but I would give him as much rope as I could. He would either help me tie up this case with the rope I give him or maybe hang himself with it. Which one remained to be determined, for right now, I would allow him to think I trusted him.

Chapter 7

I started walking back to my car, where Lora was waiting patiently. I was thinking she was not going to be too happy with me, when I told her I was going to talk to Mayor Caldwell about this completely unpleasant affair.

"Lieutenant, Lieutenant." I turn to see Jack Morris coming toward me. Speaking of acting, I just got the feeling some times that Jack was not as dumb as he sometimes seemed. But then again why would he want to appear stupider than he is?

"Lieutenant, Do you know who that man is that you told me was your friend, the explosive expert?"

"No, Jack, just because he is a friend, doesn't mean I really know him."

"That is Tom Knight, Lieutenant."

"Jack, Of course I know who he is."

"Tom Knight, the person we suspected to be the grave robber?"

"No, Jack. Do me a big favor and don't arrest him.

"I know Lieutenant; he is a big shot special agent for the government?"

"Jack, that is one reason, the other is that he can be a big help in solving this case."

"You think he is smarter than the detectives on your squad?"

"What is your point Jack, What are you getting at. Stop beating around the bush and just say what is bothering you."

"Oh nothing, it is just that you think you are so smart at times. When in reality you are not so smart. You just think you know it all. You don't know jack shit. You really don't know jack.

"Jack, I will just pretend you didn't even say that."

"Fine Lieutenant, We will see who has the last laugh."

"Jack you are assisting in this case and it is very involved. Much too involved to go into it with you right now, Jack. Why not ask Kelly or Bill when you see them? Which should be in a few minutes, they should be on their way here?"

"Oh, that reminds me, dispatch gave me a message for you. They haven't been able to locate your two little friends, Kelly or Bill. But everyone else in the squad should be here very soon."

"Really, that is odd that neither of them answered their pager. That is very odd."

I finally got that idiot Jack, out of my hair and continued to the car. Lora was watching me closely as I approached her. I could tell she was just full of questions.

"Damon, what is going on and why is Tom here?"

"Well there is no question that Doctor Kline and his wife were murdered. The car was set to explode when he turned on his right turn signal. Tom heard the dispatcher on his police scanner, so he came over. With his knowledge and resources he can be a big help, so I ask him to do just that."

Just then I saw Tom heading in our direction, looked like he may have found something else.

"What do you have there, Tom?"

"I found the remains of a detonation device, enough to know we will never be able to trace it."

"Why, what is it?"

"It is home made, a simple device. A coiled wire made like a light bulb filament, placed next to a flash device, probably matchstick heads, and then placed in a plastic tube with black powder or gunpowder. Then the ends of tube were probably sealed. They may have used a substance like hot glue only leaving the two wires sticking out of it. A crude and but very effective detonator. When the turn signal was turned on, the wire got red hot, ignited the matches which set off the gun powder that exploded the C-4."

"Wow, how did you come up with all that?"

"I found this."

He opened his hand to show me a very thin peace of wire coiled like a spring, and a small peace of plastic tubing, with a little what looked like hot glue on it.

"Still Tom, I don't see how you figured that out from this."

"Damon, in my line of work, sometimes we don't have everything we need, so we have to improvise with things that are readily available to us. It is one of the ways they showed us how to improvise an electronic detonator, in demo school. I am assuming, whoever did this, when they got the C-4, they could not get their hands on detonators also. Don't you have C-4 in the police arsenal at the station?"

"Yes we do."

"Where do you keep the detonators, with the C-4?"

"Of course not, that would be far too dangerous. We keep them in a safe that only a couple people have the combination to open it."

"Yes, a situation like that is what I am talking about, Damon."

"I see where you are going with this Tom; I think I will have them inventory the explosive's stock pile at the police department first thing Monday morning."

"That would be a good idea, Damon. You know that I think at least one person in your department is involved in this."

"You need a requisition signed by an officer to check out explosives."

"Charley Gant is an officer."

"Tom, I know Charley may have his flaws, but I can't believe he would be involved in anything like this. I went to the academy with Charley."

"Well, It still won't hurt to check."

"No, it won't and I will take care of looking into it first thing Monday morning. Mean time Tom, we both have a beautiful lady awaiting our attention."

"Your right, I told Norma I wouldn't be long. I should get back to her. Here is all the stuff I found, except for the sample I'm going to send to my office."

"Okay Tom, I'll be talking to you later. I am going to take Lora back home and let my squad finish here. The main thing left to do was to clean up the mess."

"You aren't leaving that older guy in charge are you? The one you call Jack, he doesn't strike me as being on top of things."

"No, Sergeant Dorsey, will be here in a minute, he will handle things when I leave."

Driving home, Lora was full of questions. Some I could answer but most I had to tell her, we don't know yet. It was a good time to inform her that I was going to have to talk to the Mayor. I need to question him about his knowledge of the whole matter. Anything he might know about the Beale Treasure and the disappearance of Adam Knight and Ellen Christian.

To my surprise Lora did not seem the least bit upset that I was going to talk to the Mayor. She understood that it was my job. Now that there were two people dead and two missing, my solving the case had priority over her job as far as she was concerned. I told her I did not see any reason why it should affect her job. I did not intend to let the Mayor know how I found out about his evolvement in this case.

I did have to clear this with Chief Lewis, after all Mayor Caldwell was our boss. However, he was not above the law, neither was the Chief for that matter.

By the time Lora and I got to the house, it was very late and we were both very tired. Tired or not, we had both been looking forward to making love all day and night. If it was on the news that there were creatures from space invading the town and they had landed a space ship in my front yard, It wouldn't have made any difference. We were making love regardless.

I kept in touch with the office by phone the rest of the weekend. This was Lora's and my weekend and I did not want it to be spoiled. Besides there really was not anything going on that the other detectives in my squad could not handle.

Kelly and Bill finally called in Saturday morning about five minutes apart. Seemed a little strange to me, that maybe there was more going on between them than just being partners. I could easily see that they could get romantically involved with one another. Kelly was a pretty girl and had a great personality. Bill was just a few years older than Kelly and a nice looking man that took good care of himself and they were both single. It did not really matter to me as long as it did not affect their work. I could not deprive them of the same thing I had found with Lora.

The weekend was way to short and Monday morning came much too quickly. But short or not it had been a fantastic weekend with Lora.

I remembered what I had told Tom, Friday night and I went straight to the Sergeant in charge of all the weapons and explosives. I told him to take an inventory and have those results to me as soon as possible. He assured me he would take care of it right away, he did not even inquire as to why I wanted it.

The autopsy on the Doctor and his wife showed that they died because of the explosion and fire. There were no drugs or alcohol in their blood or stomach. I did not think the autopsy would turn up anything new, I was sure the explosion had killed them both.

Kelly and Bill had gone to the Doctors home and with the permission of the family, conducted a search. They found a lot of information in the doctors office about the Beale Treasure, and a great many historical documents that had the words all numbered. They also discovered many old books and a couple old versions of the Bible. His computer loaded down with things that pertained to the treasure. Seems he was a very active member of the group.

They found nothing to help us identify the other members of the group or anything that might help locate Adam and Ellen.

I called the Chief to see if he had any problem with me questioning the Mayor and he did not.

I called Lora at the Mayors office and asked her when he would be available. She put me on hold while she went and asked him. When she came back to the telephone, she told me,

"Damon, he would like to see you right away."

That was a surprise. As secretive as this whole thing had been, I would have thought he would try to put me off.

"Okay beautiful, I'll be right over." I told Lora.

When I reached the Mayors office, Lora told me to go right in, that he wanted to see me right away.

"Mayor Caldwell, I want to thank you for seeing me so quickly."

"Thank you for coming, Lieutenant, would you like a cup of coffee. I want to wait until someone else arrives before we start our discussion."

"Who, are we waiting for your attorney or Chief Lewis?"

"Neither of them will be coming. Excuse me while I get my secretary to bring some coffee in."

In a few minutes, Lora came in with two cups of coffee, she of course knew how the Mayor liked his coffee and how I liked mine. She only brought the coffee no cream, sugar or sweetener. A pack of sweetener and a little cream had already been added to my coffee.

"You like your coffee black, Lieutenant."

"No Mayor, I drink it with a pack of sweetener and a little cream."

With a big smile on his face, the Mayor looked at me and said.

"It's funny that my secretary would just happen to know how you like your coffee Lieutenant. Please don't be embarrassed there is very little that goes on in the town that I don't know about sooner, or later. When it comes to the city hall and especially my secretary, I usually know about it sooner more often than later."

The intercom went off, and the Mayor picked up the phone instead of using the speaker. He then told Lora to "Send him right in."

As the door opened slowly, I turned to see whom the person was that was going to be sitting in on our meeting. I could not hide my surprise from the Mayor when Tom Knight came through the door.

"Mr. Knight, won't you join us, I believe you already know Lieutenant Carter and I know the Lieutenant already knows you. Now Gentlemen if you wouldn't mind taking a seat, I will get Lora to get us all a cup of coffee and one for herself. Then I am going to ask her to join us, if you don't mind. Seems she also had a deep interest in this case, so I asked her to join us as well. In fact I would have liked Ms. Christian here also, but I'm sure you will convey what I have to say to her, Mr. Knight."

"The reason I want to see you all, is because recent developments, leads me to believe that all of our lives are in danger. The sudden demise of my friend and associate Dr. Kline and his wife has convinced me that my fears are justified. Doctor Kline and I have both received death threats in the last few weeks. I am correct in assuming that the death of Doctor Kline, was not an accident was it Lieutenant?"

"No Mayor, it was not, it was murder."

"This is why I have you people here instead of the members of my treasure group. I don't know whom to trust any longer. I don't know if the killer is a member of my group or not, but whoever it is knows we are very close to locating the Beale Treasure."

"Tom, Your brother Adam was hired by our group to decipher the Beale code. He came to us just prior to his disappearance and told us he was very sure that the key to the code was the Inaugural Address of President George Washington. He gave the address on April 30, 1789. I believe it to be just a coincidence that happens to be the same month and date your brother Adam took it upon himself to disappear. However, I could be wrong about that. Your brother told us that he believed that Beale used an alternative method of using the key to decipher the code a curve or twist to the norm is how he described it. He also told us that he was days away from the complete decoding of the message. A couple days prior to April 28, he let us know that he had deciphered the code. That it would lead him to two hundred pounds of gold and another cipher. That Ellen and him were going to the location and see if the gold was there. If in fact they did locate the gold, it would be solid proof of the treasures existence. The cipher located with the gold would be the last and that once decoded it would lead to the treasure.

His plan was to locate the gold, melt down a portion of it into small pieces and sell them to live on while he worked on the new cipher. That he would keep the gold with him and go into hiding until he had broken the final code. He would select one person either in or out of the group to keep in touch with every two months. That person would remain anonymous for their safety and wouldn't know Ellen and his location. That person would keep us informed as to his progress on deciphering the code. The person he selected as a contact would keep the group informed by anonymous letters in the mail, which they have. Every two months we each receive a letter. The last letter was received over three months ago. That was the last we ever heard from Adam or Ellen directly."

"Then you have no idea what happened to Adam and Ellen?" Tom asked the Mayor.

"Adam was concerned that he and Ellen were being followed and watched. If it leaked out that any portion of the treasure had been found. It would start a firestorm of people looking for it. That there were people that would stop at nothing to get their greedy little hands on such a vast treasure. Adam had lead us to believe that their disappearance wouldn't concern anyone accept Norma which was Ellen's only living close relative. Adam said he only had you Tom and that he had not heard from you in over a year. Since you worked with the government as a spy, he could not contact anyone to find out if you were alive. You always had to contact him. Sense he had not heard from you he presumed you to be dead. That is why everyone was so shocked when you showed up and started looking for information about Adam."

"Are you telling me that my brother and Ellen are alive and well?" Ask Tom.

"Yes, as far as I know they are. We haven't heard from him recently. The last we heard was that he was very close to the final answer and would be returning soon to share it with the rest of us. That was the last we heard from him, unless the contact person has just not relayed the message."

"Why would you keep the knowledge that my brother and Norma's sister are alive from us? You think we would do or say anything that would jeopardize their safety. They are our blood, my brother and her sister. We would both die before we would allow anything to happen to them. You have made us suffer, while all the time you had the knowledge that would relieve our anguish."

"I know Tom and I felt so bad about that. I wanted to tell Norma, but at the same time, I found comfort in the fact that I believed she might already know and was putting on a act. I believed her to be Adam and Ellen's contact person. Then you showed up, that made me think she was not. I left the note on your car. I presumed that if you went to the Lords farm, that you would realize that they had gone into hiding and why."

"Instead of being up front and honest with us, you leave some stupid riddle in a note on my windshield. No name or way to contact you, just left use to figure out what it all meant on our own. I would expect a little more honesty and courage from a man in your position, Mayor."

"Tom, I owe you an apology. Apparently, the note I left on your windshield was not clear. It led you to digging up graves, which was not my intention. What made you think the answer was in one of those graves you dug up?"

"The note had gotten wet, and part of it was missing, I interpreted, it wrong I guess. So you are the person that left me that note, Mayor."

"The note I left you read like this." The Mayor said as he handed Tom a peace of paper."

The proof that your brother and Ellen are in hiding for their own safety can be found in a grave dug on April 30, 1789 on the Lords farm in Bedford near Montvale I am telling you this to stop you from searching for then an to let you know they are safe.

"This is what the last page of Beale's ciphers says. When you use the curve on George Washington's Address, it is sort of a poem."

Follow this trail and you will find,
What belongs to me and friends of mine,

Go three mile south to the farm of Lord
Find in with family a stone baring a sword.

The date on the marker is the same
The date on the key that bares his name.

Follow a hundred the direction of aim
Go a bit further about the same.

You will find a rock resembling a seat
In the direction of the back go eight feet.

Then turn sharp left and go eight feet more
There if you dig half a foot times four.

Here lies two hundred pounds of pure gold
Also the direction to the treasure will be told

Now hold the secret of exactly were
You must find our kin and give them their share

Each number is a word but the words are not clear
Perhaps to read it you must begin at the rear

Each word in the key you cannot count
You only need half of the total amount

"We checked the records for the period and found that a farm located three miles south of Buford's Inn, was owned by the Lords family. The current owner is a Mr. Calvin Brown. On the property, we found a family cemetery. There was a head stone with a sword carved on it, which marks the grave of a boy that had died at age three on April 30, 1789. His name was George Washington Lords. We went two hundred feet in the direction that the sword was pointing. Where we found a rock shaped like a chair. We measured off eight feet in the direction that the back of the chair pointed, turned ninety degrees and measured off another eight feet. The digging was easy. Obviously, the area had recently been disturbed. Someone had been there before us. We dug down two feet and found a empty stone vault area. Well it wasn't completely empty there was a 1989 quarter in it."

"Someone had gotten there before us, removed the gold and the letter or cipher that told the location of the rest of the treasure. Later we found that it had been remove by Adam and Ellen. He had left the quarter in case we came behind him. That we would know that he had recovered the gold. Gold last year was valued between $358.50 at its low, to $417.15 at its highest in 1989. That would mean that two-hundred pounds of pure gold was worth about, one million two hundred and some odd dollars."

"Tom, your brother Adam, found that gold and the final clue to the remainder of the Beale Treasure. Knowing his life might be in danger and needing time to figure out the last cipher to the treasure. Adam and his girlfriend went into hiding until they could come back and find the rest of the treasure. You can do a lot of hiding with over a million dollars."

"My brother wouldn't double cross you and your friends, Mayor. I know he wouldn't, it just isn't in his make-up or upbringing."

"I don't think he would either, Mr. Knight. I think he will come back and share with the rest of us when he knows the exact location of the treasure."

"Doctor Kline and I went to the Lords farm alone to check out if we felt the location was valid, and then we would inform the rest of the group. Doctor Kline paid Mr. Brown two hundred dollars to dig on his land and gave Mr. Brown his name and phone number. The day after we had been there, Mr. Brown called Doctor Kline. He was upset that we had not covered over the hole we dug, as we had told him we would. The thing was that we had covered the hole, we put it back just the way we had found it. Someone had gone to the location and dug it up again after we left. We found out a few months later that two of our other associates were there the next day. The Browns were not home, so they went to the site and dug it up. I don't know why it took them months to inform the rest of us about it. That in its self made question their motive and intentions. Dr. Kline and I had informed everyone in the group that we had been there and what we found."

"Mayor, who else has a copy of the decoded cipher leading to the two hundred pounds of gold?"

"Everyone in our group has a copy."

"Mayor, you know I have to ask you. What are the names of the other members, of this treasure group? Also who the two were that were there the next morning."

"I can't tell you Lieutenant, not without their permission to do so."

"If their lives are in danger also, it would be to their benefit for me to know all their names."

"I'm sorry Lieutenant; we took an oath not to tell anyone who was in the group. I will contact each of them over the next couple days and ask them if I can give you their names."

"Okay Mayor, I guess that will have to do. Remember that the sooner we know who they are, the sooner we can take measures to protect them."

"I'm sorry Lieutenant, but that is the way it has to be. I am sticking my neck out telling you people everything I have told you. I honestly cannot believe that anyone in our group could have had anything to do with the murders of Doctor Kline and his wife. I have known all these men for years."

"Lora, I had you sit in on this because I have been aware for sometime now that you were working with Norma and Tom. Then when you started seeing the Lieutenant here, I did not think it would take you very long to get him involved. Now with the murder of my dear friend, the Lieutenant is very much involved now."

As Lora looked up at him, like she felt she had betrayed his trust. The Mayor continued.

"You should know by now Lora, that there is nothing goes on here at City Hall that I don't know about sooner or later."

"I'm sorry Mayor, I feel like I betrayed your trust." Lora said almost in tears.

"Not at all my Dear, You didn't tell the Lieutenant anything that he couldn't have found out at the library. All you did was give him a history lesson about the Beale Treasure. For future reference, I will tell you that all conversation that takes place in my office, are recorded. But only if my office door is open, and of course if I haven't turned off the recorder, like I have for this meeting."

"Well Mayor, I for one don't care about any of this treasure business. My only interest in this matter is to find my brother and Ellen. But if the treasure will lead me to the answers, then I will be looking for it."

"Mr. Knight I don't feel that any person in this room, other than myself, are interested in the treasure. That is why I feel I can trust you with the information that I have given you today. I also am relatively sure that none of you had anything to do with the death of Doctor Kline and his wife. Due to your relationships and why you are interested in this case."

"I saw you and the Lieutenant talking Friday night, and it appeared from my vantage point that you were assisting the Lieutenant in his investigation."

"It is my hope now that we can all work together, to find out whom the murderer is and be reunited with Adam and Ellen." The Mayor said as he concluded our meeting.

Tom and I left the Mayor's office and went up to my office to talk. Lora of course remained with the Mayor. I am sure they had a few things to discuss between themselves. When Tom and I reached my office, it caused quiet a commotion. I was sure there was going to be a lot of questions asked of me by my detectives and fellow officers. Why I was being so chummy with Tom Knight, but I was not going to let it bother me, and I was not planning to answer the majority of their questions either. Every set of eyes in the squad room followed the two of us as we went into my office and closed the door behind us.

"Tom, what do you think about everything the Mayor told us?"

"I believe he was leveling with us, Damon. But I want to go out to that farm and talk to the owner."

"You mean Mr. Brown, at the old Lords farm."

"Yes, don't you want to talk to him, Damon?"

"You are dam right I do, Tom, and the sooner the better. About everything, the Mayor told us. I think it was a half truth, he knows something he isn't telling us."

"You mean about my brother or the treasure?"

"Both of them just call it a gut feeling. But I could tell he was lying to us about several things that he told us."

"Be more specific Damon, I'll tell you more on the way and over lunch. I hear there is a great little restaurant out that way to have lunch at."

"What are we waiting for Tom, let's go to lunch?"

I placed a quick call to the Bedford County Sheriff's office and got directions to Calvin Brown's farm. Of course, we really were not interested in eating lunch, so we headed straight to the farm.

When we arrived, there was a man plowing a field with a tractor. We got out of the car and waited for him to come in our direction. He had seen us pull into the drive, so it did not take him long to make his way to our location.

He pulled up in front of us and turned off the tractor, but made no effort to get down off it.

"What can I do for you fellows?"

I showed him my badge and identification. "Mr. Brown, we would like to ask you some questions about a couple people that may have asked you if they could dig on your property."

"Sure Boys, I'll be glad to tell you anything I know. Come on up to the house, we can sit on the porch, out of the heat and I'll get my woman to bring us some cold drinks."

We followed him up onto the porch, where he stuck his head in the door and called to his wife to bring us three ice teas. Then he sat in a rocker, pulled an old pipe out of his pocket and packed it carefully with tobacco from a pouch. Once he had lit his pipe and had taken a few puffs, he turned and said.

"Okay boys, what did you want to ask me about?"

"About this time a year ago, did a man and woman, come here and ask permission to dig on your property?

"Sure did, don't have any trouble remembering them, that is for sure." He took a quick look to make sure his wife was not coming. "That woman was a real looker and those shorts she was wearing gave me a lot of happy thoughts for a long time. I hope she aint no kin to either of you and I am not talking out of turn. But she was a looker that is for sure, that is for dang sure."

"No Mr. Brown, she isn't related to either of us. What did they ask you?"

"Well they told me they wanted to dig over at the Lords family cemetery. Of course, I told them I could not allow them to dig at the cemetery. They said they wouldn't be digging near the cemetery but would be digging a couple hundred feet away from it. I didn't see any harm in that, so I told them it would cost them, five hundred dollars and they had to fill in all the holes they dug before they left."

"So they gave you the money?"

"Yep, they sure did. They told me they were not going to be digging big holes just one little one, so I only charged them five hundred. I make more money off these fools looking for that treasure than I do off some of my crops. I had one man paid me twenty thousand, to dig up on the ridge over there for a week."

"So do you know if they found anything?"

"I don't know for sure, but they may have. They did act a little strange when they came back down here to the house."

"Anything else you can tell us Mr. Brown." By this time, Mrs. Brown had brought us all a nice cold glass of ice tea.

"Well there was these other two older gentlemen, that came asking question, one said he was a doctor. They came a few days later, and wanted to dig in the same exact spot. I only charged them two hundred, because I knew there wasn't anything there. But I should have charged them more, because they didn't put the dirt back in the hole, I had to send my boy up and fill the hole in the next day."

"Was his name Doctor Kline?"

"Yep, I think that was the name he gave me."

"Has anyone else been around here that seemed interested about the couple or that area where they had dug?"

"That is what I don't understand; why you fellows are here asking the same dang questions I have already answered. Don't you people keep records; I told all this to those other two police officers from your department just a week or so ago. Might a been two weeks ago, I don't rightly remember."

"Two other police officers were here? Why were they here and what was their names?"

"I did not catch their names; don't think they threw them out. They where asking about the pretty woman and her friend also. I told them the same thing I am a telling you. Then they wanted to see where they had dug a hole so I showed them and they dug a hole at the same spot."

"What did they look like?"

"I don't rightly remember that either, but that one fellow looked kind of like your friend here."

"You mean this gentleman."

"Yes, looked a lot like him if I remember right, but maybe a little older, you really can't tell when they have a beard and he also was wearing a hat and sun glasses."

"He had a beard? Not a big beard; like Santa Claus, not that kind of beard. He just had not shaved for a couple of week or so. Didn't you think it was odd that a police officer had a beard?"

"No, on TV lots of them are wearing beards when they work undercover. Besides, up in West Virginia, the Sheriff had a beard."

"Tom, have you ever been here?"

"No, of course not Damon, he must be mistaken. I just learned about this today the same as you."

"Is there a chance you are mistaken, Mr. Brown?"

"Of course, my memory ain't what it used to be. I didn't say it was this here fellow, I said he resembled one of the fellows. The fellow he looked kind of like didn't talk much and was kind of stand offish and shy acting. He also weren't wearing no suit like the other feller, so I figured he was just sort of a helper."

"What did they find?"

"I don't rightly know, they made me come back to the house while they dug."

"Did they also pay you to dig on your property?"

"No, Hell no, I can't ask the cops for money."

"Did they show you their badges and ID, Mr. Brown?"

"No, and I didn't ask for it neither. Who in the world would lie about being a cop? Besides I could hear the radio in the car and it sounded like police chatter to me. You know all the ten this and ten-four that, like on TV."

"Would you mind if we took a look at the cemetery and the area where they dug the hole."

"You fellow's, going to be digging or anything?"

"No Mr. Brown. Not now we just want to see the location."

"Okay, as soon as we finish our drinks I'll take you boys over there on the tractor; it's a far walk from here."

Tom and I chatted between our selves. While Mr. Brown just puffed, his pipe and sipped his tea, while he stared out across the field. He seemed to be thinking about something.

We stood on the back of the tractor while Mr. Brown drove us over to the cemetery. We found the grave with the sword on it that belonged to George Washington Lords he had died on April 30, 1789. Then we walked down the hill and Mr. Brown showed us the location that everyone else had been digging up. Everything was just as the Mayor had told us.

We got back onto the tractor and he drove us back to the house and our car. We thanked him and headed for the car for the drive back to town.

"Officer, There is one more thing, that I didn't tell any of the others. It has been a weighing on my mind a right smart recently. Especially since those other two policemen, was here."

"What is that Mr. Brown?"

"You boys come with me down to the barn. I got something down there I want to show you."

This must have been what he was thinking so hard about, as to if he should show us whatever it was in the barn. Tom and I gladly followed him to the barn. He opened the door wide and grabbed a pitchfork off the wall. Then he started moving some hay piled in one stale. In a few minutes he had uncovered enough of it for us to tell it was a car cover with a tarp. Tom went over and lifted the tarp up enough to see the car.

"Damon, this is Adam's car. A 1988 black Mustang convertible. With his personalize license plates still on it."

"Mr. Brown, you have some explaining to do."

"Oh Lord, I knew this was going to get me in trouble, that is why I hadn't told anybody about it before. That fellow and that pretty girl gave me this new car for my old 1972 Chevy Pickup. It was just to good a trade for me to pass on. I did not mean to do anything illegal. They gave me the title and everything, and I gave them the title to the truck."

"Can we see the title, Mr. Brown?"

"Sure thing officer. I haven't moved that car. Not one mile have I moved it. The day after I made the trade, with them folks. I got to thinking about it. I figured there was something that ain't right about this. I pulled the car down here to the barn. Covered it with that tarp then covered it with hay and that is where it has been since the day they left it here."

"What happened after they traded you the car for the truck?"

"They drove the truck back over to where they had been. Said they had to cover the hole up, and then they would be leaving. They were only there a few minutes, and then drove off. They did not stop by the house or anything. They just left."

Mr. Brown showed Tom the signed title. It was dated April 30, 1989.

"This is Adam's signature, Damon. No question about it."

"Officer, Am I in any trouble over this thing? It has been bothering me for might near a year now that I might have done the wrong thing."

"No, Mr. Brown, You aren't in any trouble, the car is yours all legal and proper. I would like to send a couple officers out to go over it real good before you do anything with it though."

"Sure thing officer, anything I can do to help. Be plum glad to do it."

"Thank you Mr. Brown, you have already been a great help. Thank your wife for that ice tea also. Don't you worry, you made a good trade."

After we got back in the car and started driving in the direction of town. Some of the things I was thinking wouldn't make Tom happy.

"Tom, looks like the Mayor was right about everything. Adam and Ellen must have found the two hundred pounds of gold and went into hiding."

"Yes, Damon. It is starting to look like that might be what happened. But I can't believe Adam wouldn't even get in touch with me in all this time."

"Money can make people change, Tom. It can make people do things they wouldn't normally do, even commit murder.

"What are you insinuating Damon? That Adam might have killed the Doctor."

"Tom, you have to admit, That Adam seems to be doing things you wouldn't have thought he would do. So yes it is possible he may have killed the Doctor and his wife."

"That is crazy. If you knew Adam, you would know how crazy that is. Just get that thought out of your mind."

"Tom, If Adam is alive. His connection with this whole treasure mess makes him a suspect. I'm not saying he did anything, I'm just saying he is in a position of suspicion at this point."

"Go to Hell, Damon. Next thing you know you will be telling me I'm a suspect."

"Actually Tom, You are. I don't think you did it, but you are a suspect. Just because of the closeness of your relationship with the case. You have also all the technical skill, knowledge and opportunity, to have done it. You combine that with the grave robbing episode. If you had a motive, you would be our prime suspect in the case. Actually millions of dollars in treasure is a good motive for anyone, you included."

"Okay, Damon, you have made your point."

By the time we reached my office again, the discussion was beginning to become a little heated, between Tom and I. Tom had put me on the spot so I was glad to hear the phone ring, gave me the chance to change the subject before I got him upset.

The phone call was the sergeant that had been doing the inventory on the explosives. He reported to me, that there was a pound of C-4 missing. In addition to that, there had not been any signed out for use by anyone in the department sense the last inventory.

We kept the explosives in the evident locker area. So actually, a great many people in the police department had access to it. C-4 was no more dangerous than modeling clay, without a detonator so the security on it was a little lax. Only an officer or sergeant could check it out, but most anyone could have stolen a pound of it. A pound of C-4 is not very big, about two inches square and a about six inches long. An item that size can be concealed long enough to remove it from the evidence room. Then be carried out of the evidence room, by almost anyone on the force. Maybe I need to mention to the chief that we need to keep it locked up, like all the other weapons and explosives from now on.

Chapter 8

I felt there was a need to let the rest of my team, know what was going on. I told everyone to be in the squad room at three that same afternoon. There where eight people in my squad, Sergeant Mike Dorsey, Kelly Williams, Bill Austin, Sara Johnson, Carl Leftwich, Bob Leonard, Alan Custer and of course Jack Morris.

They all arrived and by three o'clock were all seated, everyone seemed eager to get into this case with both feet. I told them almost everything I knew, I left out a few things, like finding Adam Knights car. I even told them about the Mayor's treasure hunting group and informed them that I was hoping to know the names of all the members in a day or so. The Mayor had decided to offer his cooperation, with the death of his old friend Doctor Kline and his wife. I also told them about the Beale Treasure and that the final cipher seems to have been decoded, it apparently just led to a small amount of the treasure and another cipher. That we assume the final cipher was in position of Adam Knight and he was working to decode it. At present we had know idea where Adam may be. Then I ask if anyone had any questions.

"Lieutenant, What about Tom Knight, what role is he playing in this case?"

"Kelly, Tom is aware of everything I just told you. He was at the Mayor's office by invitation of the Mayor. The Mayor told us all that he knew about everything connected to the case. Tom is willing to help us on this case, because it involves his missing brother. He works for one of the secret agencies of the government and has resources and contacts that we cannot even imagine. Not to mention his skill as an investigator is very impressive. He came up with evidence Friday night that we may have overlooked."

"Maybe he came up with that evidence so fast because he knew what to look for, because he is the one that blew up the car."

"Good point Kelly, but I don't think Tom Knight wanted to see the Doctor dead. Tom's primary interest in this case is to find out what happened to his brother. He is not interested in the treasure. Whoever killed the Doctor is interested in the treasure and is eliminating the competition or reducing the number of people they would have to share with."

"Lieutenant"

"Yes Sergeant Dorsey."

"Why do I get the feeling you haven't told us everything you know, that you are holding back on us?"

"That is very perceptive of you Sergeant. Your right I haven't told you everything. I have a good reason for keeping certain facts from you."

"What reason, Lieutenant? How are we supposed to work on this case and attempt to solve it when we don't know all the facts? Yet I am assuming Tom Knight and outsider. Does know all the facts, you trust him more than us?"

"No, Sergeant, I trust everyone in this room. Leaks have happened in the past and I can't take that chance. I will let you know everything in the near future.

"I don't know about everyone else but I'm not happy working with a handicap."

"I understand that, but I have reason to believe that a police officer in this police department may be mixed up in this. I have come into knowledge that I wouldn't want to get to him or her."

"Does this have to do with the missing pound of C-4 from the department, Lieutenant?"

"How may I ask, do you know about the C-4, Detective Leonard?

"Things get around; there is a rumor that there is a pound of C-4 missing, Lieutenant."

"Thank you, Detective Leonard. You just proved my point. You got any more objections to me holding back information, Sergeant Dorsey?"

"No, Lieutenant. I apologize for questioning your wisdom in the matter."

"I have another question Lieutenant."

"Yes Leonard, what is your question?"

"Did Tom Knight dig up those graves and if so why isn't he in jail for it? Instead he is walking in and out of this station like he owns it and being invited to the Mayors office, for secret meetings."

"I told you and everyone else, that case is closed, we know who did it, why they did it, and that is why the Captain and I decided to close the case. If you have any question, see Kelly or Bill after this briefing."

Jack Morris spoke up. "I already ask them, they wouldn't tell me anything."

"Jack, it wasn't your case and the fact that no one wants to tell you about it, should give you a hint to let it go."

"Did the digging up of the graves have anything to do with the treasure you were telling us about?"

"No, Jack. Now I have asked you, now I am telling you let it go. The case is closed and I don't want it mentioned again. Is that clear or would you like me to make note of it in your personnel file?"

Jack mumbled something to himself.

"What was that Jack, did you have something to add?"

"No, Damon, I don't."

"It is Lieutenant, Jack."

Jack mumbled again as he left the room in a bit of a huff. Maybe I should not have been so hard on him, but sometimes he just really gets under my skin. He isn't a stupid man, in fact he has his Master's in criminology, but he does a real good job of hiding it sometimes."

"Lieutenant Carter?"

"Yes Kelly."

"What did the decoded cipher say?"

"That is one of the things I am holding back. I will tell you that I have been to the location and there is nothing there now."

"You mean, there was something there and now it is gone? The Beale Treasure has been found?"

"No, Kelly, the treasure if it even exists has not been found to my knowledge. According to the message there was a small amount of gold there and another cipher or key to the actual location of the treasure. But there is nothing there now and there was nothing there when I got there."

"I find this all so exciting, I have heard about the Beale Treasure all my life. My father even spent hours trying to decipher the codes. Do you think it is close to being found?"

"Kelly, I'm not convinced that this whole Beale Treasure thing is not a big hoax. But if it does exist, yes I think it is very close to being found or proven not to exist."

"That is exciting; I can't wait to tell my Dad. He will be beside, himself with envy."

"Oh, by the way Kelly, what was going on that neither you nor Bill answered your pagers Friday night?"

"I guess we didn't hear it."

"Were you together?"

"Ah, yes sort of."

"What were you doing that neither of you heard your pager ring? No, don't answer that, I don't think I want to know."

"What are you trying to say, Lieutenant? Are you insinuating something?"

"Kelly, if there is something going on between you and Bill, I think that is wonderful. Just don't allow it to affect the job you are doing."

"Okay Lieutenant, the next time at least one of us will keep our pager on." Kelly said with a big grin on her face.

"I think that will be satisfactory to just have one on because I'm assuming you will be together."

"Lieutenant: you are embarrassing me!"

"I'm sorry Kelly, I'm not trying to. I am really happy for you two kids."

"I'm happy for you and Lora, also. I think you are a perfect couple."

"Thanks Kelly, I think so."

Speaking of Lora, I really needed to talk to her tonight about that meeting we all had with the Mayor this morning. If she was not coming out to the house, I needed to go by her place. I gave her a call.

"Mayor Caldwell's office, may I help you."

"Hi! Beautiful."

"Oh! Damon. Why did you take so long to call me? I've been waiting all day, for your call."

"I'm sorry, Honey. I have been rather busy since this morning. Are you coming out to the house, after work?"

"Do you want me too?"

"Of course I do."

"Okay, then I'll be there waiting for you when you get home. We can talk then."

"Great Honey, I'm going to stop and get you a key made, so you don't have to go rutting around the flower garden each time you get there before me."

"Damon, that is so sweet of you."

"You are my lady. At least I hope you are, so you should have a key to our house."

"I like the sound of that."

"Which part?"

"I like both parts. That I'm your lady and calling your house ours."

"I know this might be a little premature of me to be thinking along these lines. But I honestly hope it really will be our house soon."

"Really Damon, You really think you want that, you are really thinking like that in regard to me?"

"Of course, I have been in love with you since high school."

"Oh! Damon. That makes me so happy, that you think like that. I'm relieved that I'm not the only one thinking along those lines."

"I guess we have a lot to talk about tonight, besides this morning's meeting with the Mayor."

"I'll be seeing you in a little while, I love you my sweet wonderful, man."

"I love you also, Darling. See you shortly."

Wow! Lora and I have only been dating a week and we are already talking marriage or at least living together. Our relationship has been an express ride and manifested into a full-blown love affair in just a week. It seemed to me that I had loved Lora all my life. I would marry Lora tomorrow if she would have me. She was the exact woman, I had always dreamed of having as a wife.

On the way home I stopped at the hardware store and had a door key made for Lora. Just two doors down from the hardware store, was a jewelry store. I was very tempted to go in there and buy Lora a ring. They say, "It is the early bird that catches the worm." I did not want this worm to get away. After only a week, it would be rather premature, but beside the jewelry store was a florist, so I forced myself to walk past the jewelry store and went to the florist instead. I got her another dozen red roses arranged very nicely in a vase. For now, the flowers were just going to have to do, besides if I jump the gun on a ring. I might just scare her away and I wouldn't want to do that.

When I got home, Lora had not gotten there yet. I took the flowers in and put them on the kitchen counter, with the key tied to the vase with a ribbon and of course a note. I then went back to the bedroom to take a quick shower and change cloths. I was in the shower when I heard a noise, so I looked out over the shower door in the direction of the bedroom. At first I did not see anything so I said aloud, "Lora is that you?" Then I saw a shapely feminine leg slowly appear in the doorway. Moving upward provocatively and slowly then straightening out. It was exciting, but it became even more exciting when Lora showed her head, then said.

"Love the flowers and my new key. Honey, can I join you?"

"I can't think of anything I would rather have in the shower with me than you, Darling."

Lora joined me, and then soon we found ourselves back in the bedroom, frantically doing one of our favorite pastimes, making love. It seemed like nothing could touch us, nothing could happen to disrupt our evening of lust and love. We had not even had dinner, neither of us wanted to do or mention anything that might disrupt the magic of the moment.

Lora was without question, the most tantalizing, sexiest, woman I had ever known. Her every look and movement, gave me cold chills of excitement over my entire body. After we made love, I went to the bathroom to get a warm wet washcloth for her. I also grabbed her hairbrush so I could brush her long blonde hair. That I had messed up and tangled as our passion reached its peak. I love brushing her hair, it gave her pleasure and that made me happy, so we both benefitted from it.

As I brushed her hair, I could not help but admire her unblemished, smooth, tanned back. Her back was almost as desirable and exciting as her front view. She made almost purring sounds as the brush passed through her long hair.

"Darling can we get in the hot tub." Lora said suddenly with out warning, also with an air of excitement

"That is fine with me if that is what you want to do."

"You go get the hot tub ready and I'll go to the kitchen and fix some snacks and open a bottle of wine I brought from my house."

I slipped into a robe and headed out to open up the hot tub and get it ready. Lora also put on a robe and went to the kitchen to get busy with the preparation of snacks and finger food. It turned out to be nothing short of a feast. She had salami, summer sausage, Swiss and sharp cheddar cheese, cream cheese, olives, pickles, cauliflower, several kinds of crackers, fresh strawberries and pineapple slices.

Then Lora came to join me in the relaxing bubbling waters of the hot tub. This was the first opportunity we had taken to talk since we had gotten home.

Lora started it off by saying, "Damon, I feel the Mayor is really afraid and concerned that someone my try to kill him."

"I know, I got that impression from him this morning also."

"Do you think he is in any real danger?"

"Yes Lora, I do, along with everyone else personally connected to this case, you included. That is why I want you to be extra cautious and don't take any chances. If you have the slightest concern about anything, I want you to call me right away."

"Oh Darling, I don't think anyone would try to hurt or kill me."

"Neither did the Doctor and his wife. I don't care I want you to be extra careful from now on. I have waited too many years to get you into my life to let anything happen to you now."

"I am too happy with living to allow anything to happen to me now, Damon. I am happier now, than I have ever been."

"There is one other thing about the meeting this morning that I think you should know about. I don't think the Mayor was being totally honest with us. In fact I think he told us a few out and out lies."

"You don't really believe that do you Damon?"

"Yes, I do. I also don't think he is the only person lying to me."

"Damon, there is something that has been bothering me. I need to tell you about."

"If it is something bad about you and in the past, I don't even want to know about it."

We had just embraced in a passionate kiss when I heard my pager ringing. I had to get out of the tub to retrieve it from the table. It was headquarters of course. I excused myself and went in the house to phone the desk sergeant. As I walked toward the phone, I hoped it wouldn't be anything that would take me away from Lora for any longer than it took me to call.

No such luck, when the sergeant told me why he paged me, I knew it meant I was going to have to leave. Even though at this point it was not my case, I had a bad feeling it would be very soon.

Right now, I had to figure out how the best way to break the news to Lora would be. This was really going to upset her, so I had to handle it with tact. I sat for a few moments after hanging up the phone, out of sight of Lora in the hot tub. I knew there was no easy way to tell her or any way that would make it any easier, on her. Reluctantly I headed back out to the tub, to give Lora the devastating news with as much tact as possible.

"Lora, I'm going to have to go back to town."

"Oh! No! Not tonight?"

"I'm sorry, but this is very important."

"It had better really be important, I had a new teddy I was going to wear for you tonight, It was going to be a surprise."

She noticed the fact that I was just barely listening to what she was saying when my response, when she told me about the teddy was, "Oh, that's nice".

"Damon, are you listening to me at all? Did you hear anything I said to you?"

"I'm sorry, Lora. What was it you were saying?" My mind was occupied with the phone call and how to tell Lora about it.

"Damon, what is wrong with you, your mind is a thousand miles away?"

"No Honey, only about ten miles away. Remember what we were just talking about a few minutes ago?"

"I'm not sure, we were talking about several things, which are you referring too?"

"I am referring to our concerns with the Mayor."

"Oh my God, don't tell me something has happened to Mayor Caldwell."

"Yes Lora, about an hour ago his wife found him in their hot tub dead. It appears that he had a stroke while he was in the tub, then drown."

"Oh! No. His poor wife and Mayor Caldwell, I just cannot believe it."

"His wife is on the way to the hospital now, seems the shock of finding her husband was too much for her to deal with. She apparently had a heart attack, because when the rescue squad arrived there they found Mrs. Caldwell passed out on the floor. She still had the phone in her hand from calling 911. She is in critical condition."

Lora started getting out of the hot tub, she grabbed the tray with what was left of the snacks she had fixed and put it on the kitchen counter as she headed toward the bedroom. I quickly closed up the hot tub and followed her to the bedroom, to get dressed and go to town. By the time I got to the bedroom, Lora was already dressed and was putting her shoes on.

"Hurry up, Damon, and get dressed, I'll wait for you in the kitchen."

"Wait a second honey, who said you were going with me?"

"I did, you think for one minute you aren't taking me with you? You have another thing coming, mister!"

I just held my hands out to my side, as if I don't know what I could have been thinking of when I thought I was going alone. I knew it was a waste of time to tell her she could not go. I could also tell that the reality of this had not hit her as of yet, otherwise she would be crying her eyes out. I got dressed quickly and joined Lora in the kitchen. We rushed out the front door and headed toward the car. Lora, collapsed in tears, her legs just gave out from under her. She was sitting in the middle of the driveway crying hysterically. I tried to comfort her, but she was so upset that nothing could have helped at that moment.

I picked her up, to carry her back into the house, but she screamed at me saying that she was going with me. I turned back toward the car and put her in the passenger seat, but she fell over into the driver side still crying. I went around the car opened the driver side door and pulled her up so I could get in. She kept her head on my shoulder crying all the way to town.

With Lora crying as she was, and repeating over, and over, "I can't believe Mayor Caldwell is dead" I could not use the radio to talk to anyone. So I headed straight to the hospital, I knew the Mayors wife would be there and suspected that the Mayors body would also be there by now.

Arriving at the hospital, I got Lora settled in the waiting room outside of intensive care, where I assumed Mrs. Caldwell had been taken. I told the nurses to keep an eye on her for me and to not, let her wonder off anywhere. I headed to the basement and the morgue area, where they would take the Mayor when they brought him in.

When I entered the autopsy portion of the morgue, the Mayors body was already there. Lying covered with a sheet on one of the stainless steel tables, with the holes in it. A handheld sprayer hanging over it and the instruments, they used to do the autopsy on a covered table beside it.

I don't care how many times I see this room; it still sends cold chills down my back each time. It is so cold and impersonal. It is even worse when it is someone you know that is laying on one of those tables.

There was no one in the room, I walked on in and went over to the table with Mayor Caldwell on it. I lifted the sheet covering the body to check for any obvious signs of injury.

"Excuse me, this area is off limits. What do you think you are doing?" A voice said behind me startling the hell out of me.

I turned in the direction the voice came from. There was a Doctor in a white coat coming toward me very quickly. He was jerking the sheet covering the Mayor from my hand, telling me to leave.

I showed him my badge and ID, but his hostility toward me continued.

"Just because you are a police officer, that doesn't give you the right to just roam around this hospital at your leisure. This is not a case for the police this man obviously had a stroke that caused paralysis which caused him to drown."

"Do you know who this man is Doctor?"

He picked up the clipboard beside him. "Yes, this is a Mr. Caldwell."

"He is the city Mayor, Doctor."

"Mayor Caldwell, well I didn't recognize him. Why yes now that you mentioned it. It is Mayor Caldwell."

"Doctor, I have reason to believe this is not an accidental death, I want you to check the Mayor over very closely. Check for any drugs, injuries or marks that you can find or test for."

"I can already tell you officer. This man, drown in his hot tub after having a stroke. That is the cause of death."

"He may have Doctor, now I want you to help me find out why a perfectly healthy man with no history of heart problems, suddenly drown in two feet of water on his back porch."

"All right officer, I will check him over more carefully, but I think it is a waste of my time and yours."

"You don't mind if I stay and watch you work, do you?"

"Not at all, you can stay if you wish. I don't get many spectators in here, so if you can handle it, feel free to stay. In fact when it comes time to turn him over you can give me a hand."

I stood back out of the way of the doctor, as he went about his gory business. He was very methodical and intensely careful as he examined every inch of the Mayors body. He took blood samples and samples from the stomach, content. He was not very personable but he did seem to know what he was doing and did it well.

He looked at me every couple of minutes, I assume either to check that

I approved of what he was doing or to see if I was getting woozy or turning green. Then he asked me to give him a hand turning the body over. We had no sooner turned the Mayor body over, exposing his back when the Doctor said something under his breath, like thinking aloud, but quietly.

"Did you say something, Doctor?"

"Officer, come look at this. See these to identical marks, just below the hairline on the back of his neck. What do you suppose would cause that?"

I moved closer to examine the marks the doctor was referring too. I had seen marks like that before.

"Doctor, those are the marks made by a stun-gun. Which would have caused the Mayor paralysis making him helpless and unable to prevent himself from sliding beneath the water and downing? Doctor this is now a homicide case and you are not to release this body without my authority. I also want a complete autopsy performed on the body and a complete report of your findings."

"You mean the Mayor was murdered?"

"Exactly Doc, and for right now, I want you to keep this knowledge private. Don't tell anyone, do you understand."

"Yes, of course. Can I tell my wife?"

"Doc, I said no one. Where is a phone I can use to call out on?"

"In my office, go through that door over there."

"Thanks, Doc, and by the way, you did a good job."

I went to the Doctor's office and called headquarters, Jack answered the phone.

"Jack, are Kelly and Bill there by any chance."

"No Lieutenant, Just Bob Leonard and I are here right now."

"Okay Jack, I want you to call Kelly and Bill, and then I want all four of you to go to Mayor Caldwell's house and treat it like a crime scene. Pay special attention to the area around the hot tub, look around in the yard adjoining the area where the hot tub is located. Jack, I don't want you and Bob to do anything until Kelly and Bill get there. Two uniform officers are there already."

After I hung up the phone with Jack, I tried to call Kelly at home. She answered the phone finally after about ten rings. Bill was there with her, I told her what had happened and that I wanted her and Bill to get to Mayor Caldwell's house as quickly as possible. I did not want that bungler Jack to mess up the crime scene. I told Kelly to take over the investigation, but that I would be there as soon as I could.

Then I went looking for Lora, of course she was not where I had left her. I ask the nurse that I had asked to keep an eye on her. If she just happened to notice which direction, Lora was heading when she left the waiting room. The nurse told me that she went with Mrs. Caldwell's daughter and son-in-law. They were waiting outside Mrs. Caldwell's room to talk to the Doctor after he examined her.

I went to join them.

"Have you heard anything yet?"

"No, Damon, the doctors and nurses are still in there with her."

Lora was looking and seemed to be feeling much better. The Mayors daughter was in need of all the support she could get. I am sure that was a big factor for Lora's quick recovery. I decided that it was not necessary for Lora to know all the details right at that moment. She was being too much of a comfort to the Mayors daughter to take her off to the side to tell her. Just then, the doctor attending Mrs. Caldwell came out of the room.

"Are you the daughter?" He asked.

"Yes, I'm Carol, her daughter, and this is my husband. How is my mother doing, Doctor?"

"Not good I'm afraid, she is not helping us. She has to have a will to live or we are limited as to what we can do."

"My mother was much attached and in love with my Dad. I'm afraid she just doesn't want to live without him."

"Well, you had better change her mind, or she isn't going to live."

"Okay Doctor, I will try. Can I see my mother now?"

"Yes, but don't stay long and only you can go in to see her. I'm sorry but everyone else is going to have to wait until she is in much better condition."

When Carol went in to see her mother, I ask Lora if I could talk to her. We walked far enough down the hall so know one else would over hear what I told her.

"Lora, I am pretty sure that Mayor Caldwell was murdered."

"Oh no Damon, What makes you think that?"

"There are two small marks on the back of his neck that look like they were made with a stun gun. While he was in the hot tub, the noise of the pump on the hot tub would have covered up the sound of anyone coming up behind him. Then they zapped him with fifty thousand volts, which rendered him helpless, causing him to drown. They may have even held his head underwater to make sure. I'm having a complete autopsy performed on him that may give us more answers."

The conversation ended abruptly, when we heard a loud scream from down the hall. We turned to see Carol assisted out of her mother's room by a nurse. Carol was crying hysterically, and then we heard over the PA, "Code Blue, Code Blue room 205". That was Mrs. Caldwell's room number; she had gone into cardiac arrest. Lora ran to be with Carol, I just tried to stay out of everyone's way. The nurses rushed the resuscitator to Mrs. Caldwell's room.

After about thirty minutes, a doctor emerged from Mrs. Caldwell's room. We expected to hear the worst. It was not good, but at least she was alive. The doctor explained she had suffered another severe heart attack and her heart had stopped. They were able to resuscitate her after about seven minutes. The attack had severely damaged her heart and there was a good chance of brain damage. The lack of oxygen to the brain for several minutes can easily cause brain damage. She had partially paralysis on her left side. She had little to no muscle control on that side of her body. He gave her chances for recovery as minimal and with almost no chance of total recovery.

Poor Carol, it seemed that more than likely, she would be burring both her parents at the same time. Carol was an only child and was not what you would call a socialite. She had few friends and none that she could really turn to in this time of grief. Her husband seemed to be of little help or comfort to her; In fact, he seemed to have a disconnected attitude about this whole thing. I was glad Lora was with her, even though Lora was just her fathers' secretary. She showed a great deal more interest, understanding and sympathy than Carols, unemotional husband that did not even offer to hold her in her time of need and despair.

I needed to go to the Caldwell house and join my team there. I suggested to Lora that she remain there with Carol. That I would return as soon as I could, to pick her up. In the mean time if she needed me for anything to call the desk sergeant at the station. Lora agreed that she should remain with Carol at the hospital.

I headed out to my car, stopping at the refreshment stand to get a cup of coffee, to wake my brain up. Then I noticed, Carols husband leaving out the front door of the hospital and get into a taxi. He was a defense attorney, but I could not believe even a defense attorney could be such a bastard to his own wife at a time like this. The woman had just lost her father and could lose her mother at any moment and that selfish bastard leaves her here with relative strangers.

I got in my car and headed over to the Mayors house where I found Kelly on the back patio next to the hot tub.

"Come up with anything yet, Kelly."

"Very little Lieutenant, Jack and Bob walked all over the back yard and around the hot tub before Bill and I got here. If there, was any other evidence there to be found, they have compromised it or destroyed it. I did find a couple, small fragments of blue cloth stuck to the wooden railing next to the hot tub behind where the Mayor had been sitting. I will have them compared to see if they match any garments that are owned by the Mayor or his wife."

"I told that idiot to just preserve the crime scene until you and Bill got here. I swear Kelly, I would transfer Jack out of the squad, if I could find any other department that would take him. I can't believe that a man that can be so intelligent at times can be so stupid at other times."

"Amazing isn't it, Lieutenant"

"Do you or Bill, happen to have your stun-guns with you, I need to borrow one to take to the hospital for comparison to the marks on the Mayors neck?"

"Yes, I have it here in my pocketbook. It is the one the department issued me, is that all right, or were you looking for some other type?"

"That will be fine; I'll get it back to you tomorrow. I left Lora at the hospital with Carol the Mayors daughter so I need to get back over there. I also want to get this stun-gun to the doctor."

"You go ahead, Lieutenant, we have things under control here."

I was comfortable leaving things in Kelly's capable hands. She was a good detective. Unlike that bungling Jack Morris and he has the nerve to question, why she was up for promotion to sergeant. When she had only been with homicide for two years and he had been with homicide for fifteen years.

When I arrived back at the hospital, I found Lora still with Carol just outside Mrs. Caldwell's room just as I had left them. With the exception, that Carol's husband was no longer with them of course. When we find out who killed Carol's father, the Mayor. It wouldn't surprise me if that jerk did not offer to defend the killer. He was a good attorney I had seen him in the courtroom many times getting obviously guilty criminals, either off or with very light sentences.

I called Lora aside to ask her if she felt Carol was up to answering any questions. Her response was, she did not know but she would ask Carol if it would be all right.

In a few moments, Lora returned. "She said she would talk to you, but didn't understand how she could be of any help. You know Damon; she still thinks her father's death was an accident as a result of a heart attack."

"Yes, I know Lora."

I walked over and took a seat beside Carol, while Lora took a seat on the other side of her.

"Carol, I know this is not the best time to be asking you questions. If it wasn't very important, I wouldn't be doing it."

"That's okay Lieutenant, I don't know how I can help you but I will try."

"I need to know the names of your father's associates in this Beale Treasure thing he was involved in."

"Beale Treasure, what do you want to know about that? My father wasted his entire life casing after that stupid treasure. Why do you want to talk about that now?"

"Because, we may save someone else's life, if we know the names."

"Honestly Lieutenant, I really don't wish to discuss that silly treasure right now. My father is dead and my mother may be dying. I don't feel it is appropriate for you to be asking me about the Beale Treasure under these circumstances."

"Carol, we feel that Doctor Kline his wife and your father, were all killed because of their interest and pursuit of the Beale Treasure."

"What are you saying that my father's death was not an accident? That he was murdered!"

"Yes Carol, I'm afraid so."

"No, no Lieutenant! You must be mistaken; my father had a heart attack. He wasn't murdered, he couldn't have been."

"Yes, he was murdered and we believe it to be directly connected to the research of the Beale Treasure."

"I don't really know much about it. I know Doctor Kline and my father where involved in the treasure hunting group. I think Ed Doorman; he owns that big funeral home downtown may have been associated with it also. I also remember my father mentioning someone in the police department and a lawyer. That is pretty much, all I can tell you. I always thought it was a foolish endeavor and total waist of time, for Dad to be involved in. I couldn't believe that intelligent and prominent men like my father and Dr. Kline would waste their time with anything as unimportant as a myth about a treasure."

"We have some pretty strong evidence that it may not be so much of a myth Carol. In fact, we feel your father and his friend were getting very close to the finding of it. Now someone is killing off the members of the group."

"Why? What purpose would that serve?"

"We think someone feels that the members of the group either have the key to the location of the treasure or they know the whereabouts of Adam Knight. That may have the key to the final location of the treasure."

"Yes, I heard my father mention Adam Knight; he said he was some kind of genius when it came to figuring out codes. But didn't he disappear a year or so ago?"

"That is correct, Adam and his girlfriend Ellen Christian both vanished a little over a year ago. A recent discovery leads us to believe that he cracked the third cipher, but it only lead him to a small portion of the treasure and another cipher that would lead to the rest of the treasure. He and his girlfriend went into hiding to try to solve the code on the new cipher they found."

"Then you believe that Mr. Knight and his girlfriend are still alive. I got the impression from Dad, that they both might be dead."

"Your father thought they were dead? That is not the impression he gave me in his office yesterday morning when he told me everything."

"My father talked to you yesterday about this?"

"Yes, he talked to me, Lora and Tom Knight, Adams brother."

"Then why didn't my father give you the names of his associates?"

"He said he had to get their permission first, but he would do that and tell me in a couple days what all the names were."

"My father's attorney is Tom Kent; you may want to talk to him. I know my father talked to him on the phone yesterday. Because when I called him, he said that he was talking to Mr. Kent on the other line, and would call me back. But he didn't call me back."

"Thanks Carol, you have been a big help. If you remember anything else about who might have been in the group especially anyone connected to the police department, please call me and let me know."

"I will Lieutenant; would you do me a favor also?"

"Sure, if I can?"

"Catch the person that killed my father and see that they hang for it."

"I will do my very best to find them, but the hanging part is up to the courts."

"Okay, just catch them, and then I'll trust the system to hang them."

Chapter 9

By this stage of the investigation, things were beginning to come together. I was almost certain that a ranking member of my own police department was a member of the Mayors treasure group. I suspected one if not both of two men. Captain Mirant because he had told me to bring him all the information I had on Tom Knight and the treasure, when he told me to drop the grave digging case. At that point, he should not have known about the treasure. The other suspected member of the group, was Lieutenant Charley Gant head of missing persons. He denied knowing anything about the Beale Treasure, yet I found where he had checked almost every book about it out of the library over the last two years.

I needed to go to see Captain Mirant about the Mayors murder. With a little tact, I will lead into questioning him about the treasure.

"Damon, Great I was about to send for you. I cannot believe that Mayor Caldwell is dead. The fact that you think, he was murdered, I find even harder to believe. Tell me what you have on the case, like evidence and suspects. Then fill me in on any theories you my have as to motive."

I spent the next fifteen minutes briefing the Captain on how we believe the Mayor was murdered. I told him about the meeting in the Mayors office. I explained the connection between the Mayor's murder and that of Dr. Kline and his wife. He was interested, but seemed not surprised at anything I told him.

"Captain, now I have a question for you."

"Yes Damon, what question is that?"

"You told me to drop the case and charges against Tom Knight. You told me to bring you all the information we had on Tom and the treasure. At that point, to my knowledge, no one had told you about or discussed the treasure with you. How did you know about it and its involvement in this case?"

The Captain seemed reluctant to answer. He offered me coffee, looked out the window, walked around the room. Obviously in an effort to stall and delay giving me an answer.

"Okay Damon, I guess with Mayor Caldwell now dead, there is no harm in telling you about this. A few days ago, Mayor Caldwell asked me to come to his office. At that time he told me about the treasure and that, he and a group of friends and associates had been actively looking for it for years. He also told me that he felt they were very close to discovering where it was hidden."

"He told me all about Adam Knight and that he felt that Adam would be returning soon with the answers they needed to locate and recover the Beale Treasure. He also told me about Tom Knight and that he had left a note on Tom's car. That Tom had apparently misunderstood the note and was responsible for the digging up of the nine graves in the local cemeteries."

"It was the Mayor that told me to get you to drop the charges and the case against Tom Knight. That he felt responsible for Tom doing what he was doing. It was not his intention to get Tom to break the law in anyway. What he was doing was trying to lead Tom to the location of where Adam had found some gold and the last cipher. By doing so, he felt Tom would come to the same conclusion that his brother was alive and in hiding. That Adam had disappeared of his own free will and was trying to decipher the last code."

"The Mayor hoped that would put Tom's mind at ease enough to stop him from poking around for information about his brother and the treasure. The Mayor and Dr. Kline were afraid that if Tom continued his investigating that he would cause problems. Do to numerous threats that the Mayor and Dr. Kline had received. They felt there was a joker in the deck that is why Adam and his girlfriend went into hiding. It also explains why he and his friends feared for their lives. They felt that this person or persons would stop at nothing to be the finders of the Beale Treasure."

"The Mayor believed that Adam would return as soon as he had figured out the last cipher. He felt Adam to be an honest and honorable man that would include the Mayor and the other member's of the group and share the final reward of finding the Beale Treasure."

"Why did you not you tell me all this before Captain?"

"I had given Mayor Caldwell my word; I wouldn't reveal anything he told me to anyone."

"You could have saved us a lot of time and maybe the Mayors life if you had given me this information before."

"I realize that now, Damon. I had given my word to the Mayor and I just could not betray his trust in me. He told me that there was a joker in the deck, which is why Adam and his girlfriend went into hiding. That is also why he and his friends feared for their lives."

"Who was he referring too?"

"I don't know he didn't tell me. I am not sure he even knew who it might be. The Mayor felt that it could even be a member of his own associates. He just was not sure of anyone any longer. He did tell me that I was the only person on the police department he felt comfortable enough with to trust."

"Okay, Captain. At least tell me the names of the other members of the group so we can investigate and protect them."

"I don't know Damon, the Mayor never told me about anyone other than Dr. Kline."

"You are telling me that the Mayor told you about this just a couple days ago. Then how did you know to go to the Brown farm a month ago?"

"I don't know what you are talking about. What and where is the Brown farm?"

"You didn't go to the old Lords farm that now belongs to Calvin Brown, sometime in last couple months?"

"No, Damon, I have no idea about what you are even talking about."

"Mayor Caldwell didn't show you the decoded message of the third cipher."

"No, he didn't. He didn't even tell me what the note said that he had put on Tom Knights, car windshield."

"Is there anything else Captain, if not I have some things I need to be taking care of?"

"No Damon, except I'm sorry I withheld this information from you, I should have known I could trust you with it. I want you to put everything you have at your disposal into this case, don't spare any expense. When the news gets out that the Mayor was murdered the public is going to demand answers and they will be expecting us to provide them."

My response was, "We are on top of it Captain"

Then I headed back to my office, with a feeling of confidence that Captain Mirant was being honest with me. I had known him since I joined the department and other than a disagreement a few years earlier over a case concerning a close friend of mine. We had always worked together well and had a mutual trust in each other's judgment. He was not above pulling a few strings or kissing a butt or two to get ahead. I felt he was a good cop and his reputation and retirement was far more important to him than any myth about a treasure. He had designs on replacing Chief Lewis before he retired. A Chief of Police pension was a lot sweeter than that of a Captain.

As I entered my area, I saw Jack Morris fumbling frantically with a Rubric's Cube. It is a puzzle which you most get all the squares of the same color on each of its six sides. Challenging but a real waste of time, but at least it served in keeping him busy and out of trouble.

"Lieutenant, you have someone waiting to see you in your office."

"Thank you Jack, First I need to get another cup of coffee. Who is waiting to see me?"

"You're old friend and buddy, Tom Knight."

"It really bothers you doesn't, Jack?"

"What Lieutenant?"

"The fact that I am friendly with Tom, it seems to give you a lot of displeasure."

"Not in the least Lieutenant. It does not bother me one bit. In fact I am glad you have at least one friend."

"Jack, you know. Oh never mind, it isn't worth going in to."

I am glad I stopped myself from saying what I wanted to say to Jack. It could have gotten me in trouble, and frankly, Jack is not worth the effort. I went to the coffee room and grabbed a couple mugs of coffee. Then went to my office to see what Tom had on his mind. As I entered the office, I handed him one of the cups of coffee.

"How are you today, Tom, what is on your mind?"

"Damon, what on earth is going on? First Dr. Kline and his wife are killed, now Mayor Caldwell."

"I don't know, Tom. This whole treasure business seems to be driving people crazy. Other than my time in the army, I have lived in this area all my life. I had barely even heard of the Beale Treasure. Now I am finding out there are many people that have spent their entire lives looking for it. Many have spent their fortunes in trying to find it and others have gone to prison over it. Now people are disappearing and being murdered over it."

"I know exactly what you are saying, Damon. It all seems so crazy for something that might not even exist. It might be a total hoax dreamed up by a man almost two hundred years ago. It also may have been, discovered and removed a long time ago. Yet it is having a devastating effect on people today."

"Tom, do you have any ideas?"

"Do I have any ideas about what? Who killed the Doc and the Mayor? No, Damon, I have no idea who would be insane enough to be carrying this whole thing to this degree. How about you, do you have any idea who it may be?"

"No, but I think I know who a couple more members of the Mayors treasure group might be."

"Who are they?"

"I really can't tell you right now. I need to talk to them first."

"Damon, you are also worried that I might be the person doing the killing and you don't want to put these people in jeopardy."

"Well Tom, that is a consideration also, you are still on my suspect list."

"Damon, you really think I am interested in the treasure?"

"No, but fifty million dollars can be a big temptation for anyone, even you Tom. It seems that your brother became very interested in it also."

"You don't know my brother. He is more interested in solving the riddle and ciphers than the money. He loves the challenge of the hunt, not the reward at the end of it."

"Sense we are talking about your brother? Where do you think he might be?"

"I honestly don't know, Damon. If I know him, he has some way to keep tabs, on what is going on here, if he is still alive that is. If he is than he will know about the Doctor and the Mayor that might just bring him out of hiding."

"How would he be keeping track on what is going on here?"

"I don't know, maybe a friend, maybe he is getting the newspaper."

"The newspaper of course, he worked for the paper; he might be getting it sent to him. I am sure he wouldn't have subscribed to the paper using his own name. Tom, we need to check the list of out of town subscribers to the newspaper. I will need your help; he might be using a name that you might recognize like a relative or some other name from his past. We need to find your brother he is the key to this whole crazy thing."

"Damon, I think you might be on to something. Let's go to the news office and see what we can come up with."

At the news office I was amazed at the number of local papers that were sent to people that did not live in the area. Tom did not recognize any names on the list, but it was a shot worth looking into. It turned out to be like looking for a needle in a haystack.

"Well that didn't produce anything, Damon. So it is evident to me someone here is in touch with Adam. I would really like to know who that person might be. If you should find out whom that is. You would tell me wouldn't you, Damon?"

"I don't know Tom. I probably wouldn't, but then again I might.

Why would you need to know who that person was? As long as I got the information from them and passed it along to you."

"I may have some question for them of my own, you know about my brother and all."

I headed back to the office and Tom said he was going to look into a couple more leads he had ideas about, but they where long shots. He did not want to bother me with them until he found something a little more concrete, before letting me in on it.

I sent Kelly and Bill over to the hospital to get the autopsy report and her stun gun from the doctor. The report said that the stun gun matched up perfectly with the marks on the Mayors neck. The tissue damage in the area of the marks, were consistent with damage that would result by being shocked with a stun gun. This made the Mayors death officially a homicide, so I needed to pay a visit to Tom Kent, the Mayors attorney.

I gave his office a call to see when it would be convenient for me to come by to see him. The woman that answered, the phone, placed me on hold while she checked with Mr. Kent. Then she came back to the phone, to my surprise. She said that Mr. Kent would very much like to see me right away if possible. I told her I would be there in about ten minutes, since it was just a few blocks up the street.

When I arrived at Tom Kent's office, it was obvious that he was one of the Mayors treasure friends. On his book selves, besides many law books, was about every book ever written about the Beale Treasure. He also had books marked, "Newspaper Articles about Beale Treasure" and "Magazine Articles about Beale Treasure" he even had tapes made off TV on documentaries about the treasure. I had met Mr. Kent before; he was the typical lawyer looking man, average height and build, with a little gut. He had gray hair and wore glasses that usually sat on the end of his nose so he could look over them when he was not reading something. He was wearing a shirt and tie and the pants of a very nice suit, the jacket was hanging over the back of his chair.

He stood up behind his desk as I entered his office, holding out his hand to shake mine.

"Thank you very much for making the time to see me Mr. Kent."

"Lieutenant, I'm the one that should be thanking you, if you hadn't called me I was going to call you."

"Really what did you want to see me about?"

"Was Mayor Caldwell murdered, Lieutenant?"

"Yes sir, I'm afraid he was."

"That is what I thought. First my good friend Doctor Kline and his wife, now the Mayor."

"Mr. Kent, I take it from all the books and other items I see here in your office that you are a member of the Beale Treasure group that the Mayor and Doctor Kline were also members of?."

"Yes Lieutenant, I am and I am afraid I am going to be killed also."

"Why Mr. Kent, what has anyone got to gain by killing off the members of this group? That is what I don't understand; it doesn't seem to serve any real purpose."

"One reason is to reduce the competition looking for the treasure. The other is to either obtain information from us or to prevent us from using information we already have."

"What information Mr. Kent?"

"I cannot tell you."

"Why not, why can't you tell me? It just might save your life."

"I cannot tell you because I'm not the one that has that information."

"Who does have it and what is it about?"

"One of the other members of the group maybe, Who ever Adams contact might have been. It could have been the Mayor or Doctor Kline, I don't know, Lieutenant."

"I'm sorry, Mr. Kent, this just doesn't make sense to me."

"All right, Lieutenant, I have already spoken to the members of the group and gotten their permission to reveal this story to you and you alone. The only member I cannot get hold of is Adam Knight. One member really didn't want you to know he was a member but after the Mayor was killed he changed his mind."

"Adam Knight, then he is still alive to the best of your knowledge?"

"Yes, to the best of my knowledge he is and he is in possession of the last cipher that he found along with the two hundred pounds of gold at the old Lords farm. He is working day and night to try to decode the cipher. Then he will return and join the rest of us to go and locate the Beale Treasure."

"How do you know this Mr. Kent?"

"I know because. Adam has remained in touch with us regularly over the last year. Keeping us informed of his progress with the cipher."

"Where is Adam?"

"Only one member of the group is in touch with him. He sends all his correspondence and information through that one member. That same member, also keeps Adam informed as to what is going on here, in town."

"Who is the member?"

"I don't know. Adam chose one member, but because he feared for his life. He told us all that no one was to know who the person he chose was, except Adam and that person he chose. Because of the delicate nature of the information, we are in position of and the great value of the treasure. We have had to keep so many things secret, even from each other."

"Okay, at least tell me who the other members of this group are."

"Well you already know about Mayor Caldwell, Doctor Kline, Adam Knight and my self, of course. There are seven members in all; Adam only joined us about two years ago, at our request. Because of the talent, he had in decoding difficult codes. He proved to be a important addition to the group, he was able to figure out the third cipher in a year. It was something that many people had failed to do over the last hundred and fifty years, the boy is a genius."

Just then Mr. Kent's secretary opened the office door.

"I'm sorry to bother you Mr. Kent but there is a man on the phone that said it was very important that he speak to you right away. I told him you where in a meeting, but he said it was an emergency concerning your wife, daughter and two grandchildren. He is on line one, what do you want me to tell him?"

"I'll take the call, excuse me Lieutenant."

Whatever the person on the phone was saying to Mr. Kent was obviously very disturbing to him. He became much more nervous and began perspiring. I could only hear what Mr. Kent was saying, which was very little. The person on the phone was doing most of the talking. He only said, "I will need to make a couple calls to verify what you are telling me, then I will do exactly what you ask."

Then he hung the phone up and looked up at me.

"Lieutenant, The man on the phone said he had my wife, daughter and two grandchildren that he would kill them if I didn't do exactly what he asked. I need to call my home and my daughter's home to see if they are there. I cannot say anything else to you until I find out if what he said could be true. Would you excuse me for a few minutes?"

I went out to the secretary's office, to use the phone to call headquarters, and get some people moving, on this right away. As I was telling my people to get out to Mr. Kent's house, and was getting his daughters address from his secretary. I saw the light on line one, light up. It stayed lit for a minute of so, then it went out then lit up again.

Moments later, Kent's office door shut and you could hear him lock it. I did not like the looks of this so I headed back toward his office and tried to open the door. Then there was the unmistakable sound of a gunshot. I tried to force the door open, but was unable to. The secretary came running with her key to his door. We opened the door as quickly as possible, to find Mr. Kent sitting behind his desk. He had shot himself in the head. The gun was on the floor beside him and he was dead. I told his secretary to call 911.

There was nothing more I could do for Tom Kent, except to try to locate his wife, daughter and grandchildren as quickly as possible. Apparently whoever it was on the phone, told Mr. Kent that if he did not kill himself, they would kill his family.

I was still at Kent's office waiting for the coroner to arrive. When a older woman, a woman in her twenties and two small children arrived. They seemed very upset and the secretary went rushing to them, hugging them as soon as they came in the door.

"Oh, Mrs. Kent, I am so glad you are okay, you and your daughter and grandchildren, I was so worried."

"Where is Tom, what is going on? We had a call from the hospital, a

Doctor told us that Tom had a heart attack and for all of us to get over there right away."

"Mrs. Kent, I'm Lieutenant Damon Carter. You are telling me you haven't been being held by anyone?"

"No! Of course, not Lieutenant, why would you think such a thing? Now where is Tom, he was not at the hospital. Is he all right, where is he?"

"I'm sorry to tell you this, but you husband is dead."

I knew I needed to get Mrs. Kent and her family out of there before the coroner arrived. I got some of the office staff that did not seem quit as emotionally destroyed to drive them back to their house. I did not make it, the coroner was coming in the door with his dolly when they where going out. Mrs. Kent asked to see her husband, but I knew that wouldn't be a good idea. She was still under the impression he had died of heart failure. It was going to be hard enough to tell her the truth without her seeing the bloody mess in the next room.

I was very shaken up also and was in no condition to deal with talking to anyone. I am usually on the scene after the fact, not while it is happening. It is bad enough to arrive at a thing like this long after it happened. To be engaged in conversation with the victim, just moments before, then to hear the fatal shot.

I was glad to see Kelly and Bill. I needed to get out of there. I told them briefly, what had happened, and then I went outside and got in my car. I was far too shaken up to drive anywhere so I just sat there for a while. I watched the coroner bring Kent's body out and put it in the van.

Whoever made that call to Kent, knew I was there talking to him. Kent told me that he could not tell me anything else. Apparently, that was part of the killers' instructions to him.

I had not told anyone where I was going but someone could have heard me on the phone, talking to Mr. Kent's secretary. Someone could have also found my note that I left on my desk, with his name and number on it. The only other way anyone would have known was that someone was watching and then followed me.

Mr. Kent's murder and it was murder under any sense of the word, as the others had all the earmarks of careful planning. It was timed perfectly and every detail taken into consideration. Who ever this person or people are, they are no idiots. In fact, they seem more like professionals trying to look like amateurs. Tom Knight had not been gone from my office long, when I left to go to Kent's office. I was thinking about going to see Kent while Tom was in my office. I don't think I mentioned it to Tom, but I was not sure.

Tom Knight is smart, had the knowledge contacts and access to the equipment, so he could be the killer. I need to be very careful about what I tell him from now on or let him know about in the case.

There was one thing in Tom Knight's favor, which I don't think he would have known. Whoever, the caller was had to know Tom Kent well enough to know that he wouldn't hesitate to kill himself, if he thought he was protecting his family by doing so. To my knowledge, Tom Knight did not know Kent at all, let alone his feelings concerning his wife and family.

Chapter 10

———— ⨳ ————

When I finally got my composure back and drove to the office. I
called Lora. Even though the Mayor was dead, she still went to
the office. I told her about Tom Kent and that I would have to go talk to
his wife and family this evening. I would be late getting home, so if she
needed to do anything else tonight I would understand.

Lora sensed that I was in need of her, so she said she would go on out
to the house and fix dinner. That she would keep it warm for me, and then
we could talk when I got home. I don't know how she can be so perceptive.
How could she have known I was probably going to need to talk with her?
I guess it was just because she was such a wonderful woman and seemed
to understand my needs so well.

I was still on the phone with Lora, when I looked up and saw Charley
Gant leaning against the doorframe of the coffee room. He was sipping a
cup of coffee, but he was also looking right at me. He seemed almost in a
trance like state as he stared in my direction. Suddenly he seemed to realize
I was looking at him as well. He turned his head away and headed in the
direction of his office down the hall.

By watching me so intently, Charley had opened a door to go talk with
him. I went to his office, where I found him sitting behind his desk with
his head in his hands. You could tell he was in very deep thought about
something.

"Charley, I couldn't help but notice you looking at me. Is there anything you would like to talk about, seemed like you had something on your mind?"

I had startled him when I spoke, "Oh, Damon, No, not really. Well, yes I wanted to ask about Tom Kent. I heard what happened to him and that you were there. What happened, Damon, he was not the type of man to take his own life?"

"Did you know Tom Kent well, Charley?"

"Yes I did, I knew him very well. He was a great family man and a good person."

"Is there anything you want to talk to me about Charley?"

"No, Damon. You are the one that was there, I just wondered what happened."

"I am writing up a report on what happened, I will bring you a copy when it is finished."

"Why were you at his office anyway, Damon?"

"Mr. Kent wanted to talk to me about the Mayors murder and Doctor Kline's murder and some other things."

"What things?" Charley asked nervously, as his trembling caused him to spilling his coffee.

"Charley, what is on your mind? You seem a little upset and nervous."

"Why do you feel the need to interrogate me?" What I am thinking is none of your affair."

"I'm not interrogating you Charley, I just got the impression you wanted to talk. I guess I was wrong."

"Damon, if I wanted to talk, I would have come to your office. But since you came to mine, I thought I would ask you about Tom Kent."

"Okay Lieutenant Gant, like I said I guess I was mistaken about you wanting to talk to me."

"No Damon, I'm sorry you are right I did want to talk to you. I don't mean to come across like a bad ass, I'm just a little upset and scared."

"What about Charley, the men that are involved in this group that seem to be obsessed with the Beale Treasure, that keep coming up dead."

"Yes Damon, I don't know what is going on and I don't know who to trust."

"You don't trust me, Charley?"

"I don't know who to trust anymore, the only men I'm sure I can trust are all dead, that is how I know I can trust them."

"You are a member of the group aren't you Charley?"

"Yes, didn't Kent tell you that?"

"No, he didn't have the chance, he only told me about Caldwell, Kline, Adam Knight and himself. Then he got a phone call and the caller convinced him that if he said anything and did not kill himself. That his family would all be killed, if he didn't."

"Someone convinced him to kill himself over the phone?"

"Yes, bizarre isn't it."

"Did Tom Kent, tell you that Adam is alive?"

"Yes, he did. He also told me that one member of the group was in constant touch with him."

"Yes, that is true. Now you know why I haven't put a lot of effort in looking for Adam and Ellen as missing persons. Because I have known all along that they are in hiding and not missing."

"Are you Adams contact, Charley?"

"Even if I was, I couldn't tell you. We feel the reason this person or people are killing the members of the group is because they know one of us is keeping in touch with Adam. I think they feel that if they kill that contact, Adam will come out of hiding to find out what is going on. Adam is very close to solving the last cipher the last we heard, although that was over a month ago. We are talking maybe days away from finding it, as soon as Adam shows up. The killer wants Adam and that last cipher."

"We have known for a long time that there was someone, either in the group or not in it, which was intent and insane enough to kill to find the treasure. That is why Adam went into hiding; he knew that whoever this was would stop at nothing to get hold of that last cipher. He was afraid for his and Ellen's life, so after he found the last cipher and the two hundred pounds of gold at the Lords farm."

"We had told him to take the gold, cipher and Ellen and go into hiding. With the gold, he had plenty of money to go anywhere he wanted to go. Once he settled in to a location, he was to contact only one of us, or someone he felt he could trust. That no one, not even the members of the group were to know who that one person was. That person would keep him informed of anything happening here and he would keep the group informed as to his progress decoding the cipher through that one person. In return for keeping, the secret of what he was doing and where he was. Adam had to promise not to contact anyone. He was to keep in touch with that one person and under no circumstances was he to contact anyone else, in the group or outside the group."

"How does this person let the rest of you know what Adam is communicating, without the others knowing who he is?"

"The person is only able to contact Adam on a certain day at a certain time, once every two months. Then this person types out any message to the group from Adam and mails it to each of us in a plain envelope, with no return address. The postmarked on the letters was from the main post office here in town. The person even mails himself one apparently to reduce suspicion and avoid detection. Because we all get a letter the only person that we know for sure is not the contact is ourselves."

"So the killer feels that when Adam can no longer make contact, he will come back to find out why and what happened to his contact."

"That is what I think also. Either the killer is a member of the group or has found out how we keep in touch with Adam."

"Charley, I have to tell you. I find this all hard to believe, how did you got involved in this thing anyway. You have never struck me as a greedy man that would be interested in treasure hunting."

"My uncle got me involved."

"Who is your uncle?"

"My uncle was Tom Kent, he married my mother's sister, and Mrs. Kent is my aunt. The group felt it would be to their advantage to have someone inside the police department. The members voted me in without my knowledge. Then Tom came to me with an offer of a full share if I wanted to join the group. At first I told him, I was not interested, but then I started reading about the treasure and the more I learned about it the more interested I became. It was not the money; It was the mystery of it that intrigued me. I guess the cop in me is what got me to join the group.

In fact I didn't think they ever had a chance in hell of really finding the treasure until Adam Knight was brought into the group."

"Who are the other members that I don't know about?"

"Ed Doorman that owns the funeral home and Nick Stevens that owns the drug stores."

"They are some of our leading citizens, all men of position and prosperity in the community. Other than you and Adam, they are all also wealthy. It would appear that they all had a great deal more to lose than to gain except for you and Adam."

"You are talking about fifty million dollars. There is also money to make from documentaries, TV appearances, and book rights. The notoriety of being the men that located one of the largest, most hunted for treasures in the world today. Adam and I are probably the two least interested in the money. Adam liked the challenge of the codes and I liked the mystery of the whole thing. I have no need for money, my family left me a bit and I am comfortable and have everything I need or want."

"Are you all crazy or something, Charley? Why risk your lives and your reputations for a treasure that might not even exist. You all are little nuts, if you ask me."

"Damon, actually it was great fun, it was sort of like a game before Adam figured out the key to the code was Washington's Inaugural Address, then it became more serious. That was also the time the joker appeared in the deck. The person that has undoubtedly became the killer. It was not until Adam solved the third cipher, which lead him to the gold and the fourth cipher. That it changed from a game to serious business and the fun ended. When somehow someone found out we were getting close to finding the treasure."

"What about the note that Mayor Caldwell left for Tom Knight to find?"

"Caldwell did that without the rest of us knowing about it. He was trying to get Tom to stop looking for his brother. He was afraid that if Tom kept probing he would eventually expose every thing we have been keeping secret, including where his brother was. That would have been putting his brother in real danger of being captured, tortured and even murdered to obtain the information."

"Yes Charley I understand the Mayors motive, just question his judgment."

"We knew from the first contact with this person, he was insane and would stop at nothing to be the one that located and recovered the treasure."

"Do you have any clue to who it might be?"

"None Damon, whoever he or she is they are as clever as they are insane."

"What about Tom Knight?"

"No, I don't think so, Tom Knight didn't even show up until a few weeks after Adam was reported missing. Whoever this is has been here and on the trail of the Beale Treasure for a very long time."

"Then Charley, if you knew what Adam was doing and that he had found the gold, why did you go to the old Lord's farm the day after the Mayor and Doctor Kline?"

"I didn't, not then anyway. I went a month of so later, just because I wanted to see where Adam had found it."

"Did you talk to or have contact with Mr. Brown, the present owner of the farm?"

"No, I went to the house but there was no one home the day I was there. I just found the family cemetery and the grave by myself. Then I found where they had dug a hole about two hundred feet away from the head stone, but I didn't dig it up again."

"You did not have anyone with you?"

"No, no one was with me."

"Wow, this is even more bizarre than I thought it was. You have been a big help in clearing up some things for me.

"Sorry I couldn't be more open with you before, Damon. I had given my word to the others, and to be quit frank, I didn't know if I could trust you."

"Charley, you could do me a big favor, if you would?"

"Sure if I can, what is the favor?"

"Are you going to Tom Kent's to see your aunt, Mrs. Kent?"

"Yes, I am going out there as soon as I leave here."

"That is the favor. I will tell you everything that happened at your uncle's office. I want you to tell your aunt, I think it would be better coming from someone she knows and with it coming from a close relative it may be easier on her. Plus you can decide what she should and shouldn't know about this treasure thing."

"Sure I'll be glad to do that for you."

"Good, but there is one thing you should know. She thinks he died of a heart attack, or at least she did earlier, unless someone has already told her that he shot himself."

I told Charley everything that we talked about at Kent's office. Then I told him to be sure she understood that he took his own life because he had been lead to believe he had no choice. He did not do it because he was depressed or unhappy, that he did it because he thought he was saving the lives of his family by doing so.

I knew I would still have to go visit her soon, but I was glad it was not going to be tonight.

Leaving Charley's office, I returned to my own, where there, was a report waiting for me concerning the explosives that they used on Doctor Kline's car? The explosive was C-4, made by the same manufacture that provided the police department with their explosives.

Then I called Lora back. To tell her I did not think I would be late after all. I had a lot that I wanted to talk to her about tonight.

I still had a few concerns about Tom being more involved in this whole mess than he appeared to be. In short, I still did not trust him completely. Even though Charley felt he could not be the murderer, I was not so sure. I had nobody else as a suspect to replace him with yet, he remained as my prime suspect. If he did have anything to do with these murders, he was one hell of a good actor.

Thinking about it, I was not even sure I could trust Lora with all the information. She had canceled that she was working with Tom and Norma. She was in constant contact with them the whole time. She cancel there location even though she knew he was wanted by my department concerning the grave desecrations. That was when Lora and I had first started seeing each other though, I am almost sure I can trust her now.

I am beginning to be like Charley Gant about this whole thing. I am no longer sure who I can trust and who I cannot.

That was another thing about Tom; he did dig up all those graves, which was a sick thing to do. I know I could not have done anything like that, not as he did, in the middle of the night and alone. He probably does a great many things in his line of work that I wouldn't do.

I wonder exactly what he does do for the government; he might be an assassin and kill people for them. That is how it is done in the movies anyway you just don't hear about it in real life.

This case was beginning to make me a little nutty. My mind was whirling with ideas, suspicions, to many questions and not enough answers. I think that being there when Tom Kent killed himself. It had a profound effect on me and numbed my senses. My mind was jumping from on thing to another with no pause in between.

Did Charley say that the contact person had to me a member of this group? I don't see why they would have to be as long as Adam totally trusted them. Charley talked like it had to be a member, like there was not a choice in the matter. I need to check with Charley about that, it could be important.

What I really needed was to get my mind off this crazy case for a while and I knew exactly what would do that very thing. Lora would be at the house by now, so I headed in that direction. If anything could clear my mind of the happenings of the day, it was Lora.

Maybe we could make plans to go to the lake next weekend. I could rent a houseboat for the weekend and we could just spend a relaxing weekend in some quiet cove. Maybe do a little fishing, although we had never talked about fishing and I was not sure how Lora felt about it. It did not really make a lot difference about the fishing anyway. If we did not get to go fishing, there are many activities that we could enjoy just as much as fishing. Cooking, swimming and of course making love, just to name a few. The main thing is that we would be together in a quiet setting away from the troubles and the horrors of this case.

When I arrived home, Lora was waiting when I came in the front door, with a kiss and a cold beer. She suggested we go out on the back deck and relax a while before having dinner. That sounded like just the ticket to get my mind off things. Relaxing with a cold beer, with the woman I loved, watching the sunset and smell the aroma of the flowers and the fine dinner Lora had prepared.

I could tell Lora wanted to ask me about my day, but out of consideration for me did not. I knew we would end up talking about it before the night was over. Right now I just wanted to enjoy her company and not talk about anything except us.

"Honey, what are your thoughts concerning fish?"

"I like fish, but I fixed meatloaf for dinner, but if you like I can fix fish tomorrow night."

"No Honey, I didn't mean eating them, I mean catching them."

"I enjoy fishing a great deal. I use to go fishing with my Dad all the time."

"What would you think about me renting a houseboat up at the lake next weekend?"

"Damon that sounds wonderful. We could take Ranger and Smoky with us and just have a great relaxing weekend. We could go up after work Friday and come back Sunday evening after dinner."

"Sounds wonderful, let's make plans to do it next weekend. I will call the marina tomorrow and make arrangements to rent the houseboat for those days."

"Damon, are you going to be able to get away? What I mean is, with everything that is going on won't you have to be where they can get in touch with you?"

"I can take that new cell phone with me and if they really need me they can reach me on it or by CB radio. But that is the main reason I want us to go, I need to get away from this case for a little bit, it is starting to really drive me a little nutty."

"Oh Darling I know, I heard what happened today, it must have been horrible. I can't imagine what could have made poor Mr. Kent do such a thing, as that?"

"Please Lora; I really would rather not talk about it, right now."

"Oh Damon, I'm so sorry. It was insensitive of me to bring it up."

"No Honey, that is all right, no harm done. I do plan on telling you all about it later, but just for now I would like us to just enjoy being together and not worry about any thing."

"I understand Darling, when you are ready to talk about it, I'll be glad to listen. Mean time, are you ready for dinner. I'll go put it on the table, you just sit here and relax and finish your beer."

"Can't I help?"

"No Dear, it will just take a couple minutes. I can handle it; I want you just to relax. I will come get you when it is ready."

Lora has made such a difference in my life. I don't know how I survived without her as long as I did. She has given me purpose and reason to work and live. She has filled my life with love, understanding and joy, far greater than anything I had ever experienced before.

When I think back, and remember all the unhappiness that my first wife subjected me too. My wife had been unloving, uncaring, unsupportive, and unpredictable and a drunk. There was also her infidelity, constant nagging and bitching. I don't know what I ever saw in the woman, I must have married her out of frustration and loneliness.

Lora was nothing like her. Lora had given me more love, contentment and happiness, in the two short weeks that we have been dating, than my ex-wife did in all those years I spent with her.

After the wonderful dinner that Lora had prepared, I cleaned up and washed the dishes. While Lora got a shower and did what it is she does to make herself irresistibly beautiful. Then we settled down on the sofa with our coffee to talk.

I told her what happened at Tom Kent's office in detail, but when we got to the part where I was talking to Charley Gant. I left out some things about the conversation that I did not think I should let her know about. Like the fact that I knew all the names of the members of the Mayors treasure group now. So really I did not tell her very much of the conversation at all.

Evidence gathered and information received was a crucial part of any case. Keeping certain aspects of that information confidential could also be a very important factor in the case. Some information if revealed could also be very detrimental.

I hated the fact that I was with holding things from Lora, but it really was not due to my personal feelings. It was police procedure, certain segments of any case have to be confidential and strictly within the police department. I just hoped Lora would understand that, when this whole affair unfolded and everything was revealed.

When the phone rang, I answered quickly but it was for Lora.

"Lora, you have a phone call."

"Oh, it must be the hospital; I gave them this number to reach me in the event there was any change in Mrs. Caldwell's condition."

I handed Lora the phone then walked out on the deck, to look at the stars and think. In moments, Lora joined me. She stood by my side placing her arm around my waist just quietly looking at the stars with me.

Then she said, "Damon, Mrs. Caldwell passed away about forty-five minutes ago. That was the nurse at the ICU that just called."

"Oh Lora, I'm so sorry."

"Damon, I should give Carol a call. Do you mind?"

"No Honey, of course not. That poor girl has lost both parents within a day of each other. You seemed to be a great comfort to her at the hospital. I'm sure she would want you to call her now and if we need to go be with her that is fine also."

"Oh Damon, that is so considerate of you. I will go call her right away."

In a few minutes Lora returned and rejoined me on the deck, she was noticeably upset.

"What is wrong, Honey? Is Carol okay?"

"I don't know, I didn't get to talk with her. Her husband answered the phone and told me that he felt it was best that Carol was not disturbed by anyone right now."

"Did he ask Carol if she would like to speak to you?"

"No, I ask him to, but he said he felt he was the best judge of what was good and not good for his wife."

"Do you know where Carol lives?"

"Yes I do. She lives over on Summers Street."

"Get your jacket, we are going over there."

"Oh Damon, do you think we should?"

"Yes, I know about jerks like Carol's husband he will back off when we arrive at his front door. He is a typical defense lawyer, all mouth, no guts. I am sure when we show up at the door and I am with you. He will sing a different tune. So get your jacket and let's go."

When we arrived at Carol's house, it went down about as I had antis pated. When her husband opened the door, he did not say anything he just motioned us in. Lora went right in looking for Carol; I just stood there looking at her husband."

"I guess you might as well come in also. You are going to have to excuse me. I have a court case in the morning that I need to prepare for. I don't mind telling you that all these interruptions are very annoying to me."

"Yes, it was very inconsiderate for Carol's mother to die, when you have a case in the morning. What is your first name, Michael isn't it"

"Yes my name is Michael and it was rather inconvenient timing, I have work to do."

Carol was very glad to see Lora; she was getting no comfort from her husband at all. I could not believe what a cold, unemotional, unfeeling, callus bastard he was. I called Lora off to the side and suggested we take Carol back to our house or somewhere else where she would get a little bit of comforting and understanding for her great loss.

When Lora mentioned it to Carol, she was grateful for the offer, excepting it quickly. She really did not want to be alone at a time like this. Lora helped Carol put a few things in a bag, while I went into her husband's study to tell him what we were doing and to give him my number, just in case someone needed to reach Carol.

"Excuse me, Michael."

He looked up from his papers with a disgusted look on his face of total and complete annoyance.

"Yes, Lieutenant, what is it now."

"I just wanted to let you know, that we are taking Carol to my house. Here is my number."

"Good, maybe I can get some work done now."

"Oh yes, Michael. There is one more thing.

"Yes, Lieutenant, what is it?" He asked with a tone of disgust and impatience with me.

"I just wanted you to know, what a total asshole I think you are. You have the emotions, concern and feeling toward your wife, of an oyster and a dead one at that."

"You have no right to talk to me like that. Unlike you I am an important man."

"Important to who Michael, you mean the criminal element and bottom dwellers of the city?"

"You cops think you are so smart. You are just jealous of me, because I expose you for the incompetent idiots you are in court. You are all just a bunch of law hopefuls that could not make the grade to be attorneys like me. If you can't find evidence you fabricate it."

"I can't believe a man with your education can be so stupid."

With that said, Lora and I helped Carol to my car and we drove her back to the house.

Chapter 11

———

Carol had calmed down considerably by the time we got her in the car. She had stopped crying and had really calmed down before we got her to the house. Lora loaned Carol a pair of old shorts and a top, so she could go into the hot tub. I opened a bottle of wine while Lora fixed a few snacks and we joined her in the tub.

Once we got Carol to talking it was like a dam bursting. She, of course, talked about her parents with a great deal of admiration and respect. Then she started talking about her husband, with anything but admiration and respect. It was more about his control, abuse, usury and infidelity.

She began by telling us how he did not like her having friends of her own. They would go out with his friends only and she was to play the loving wife and keep her mouth shut. That he treated her as if she did not have a brain in her head, when in fact she had a Masters-Degree from UVA. He also poked fun at her to his friends and entertained them with intimate details of their love life; not caring if it embarrassed her or not. She was not allowed to go out alone often and when she could get away it was only to visit her family for a limited time. She didn't share much about her marriage and they had no idea of the conditions she was living under; she didn't want to worry them.

It was obvious to Lora and I, that Carol had no life except what her husband allowed her to have. It was no wonder she was talking our ears off, she had not talked to anyone since she was married, three years ago. She made us want to adopt her, so she wouldn't have to go back to her house and be under the control of that tyrant again.

Her parents were both in their forties when Carol was born and she was an only child. She had met her husband in college and they got married after they both graduated. She was only twenty-eight now. We explained to Carol that she was probably going to get a sizable inheritance and she should use it to break free of her husband and get a divorce. The environment she was living in was not a healthy one and if her parents had known how she was being treated, they would want her to do that.

Carol agreed that she should divorce her husband, but she was still afraid. He was an attorney and she knew she would also need a very good attorney. She did not know any that were not friends with her husband. We told that when it came to winning a case and money. Lawyers had no friends and no morels. That we would find her one if that is what she wanted. That Lora and I would help her in any way we could and for her to consider us her friends.

The next morning, Lora took Carol home, but not to her home. Instead, she took her to her parent's house. At least there, she would have the housekeeper and cook to keep her company and she could begin getting her parents affairs in order. Lora was also able to stay with her a while and told her, she would be back to visit and to call her if she needed any thing at all.

My first order of business for the day was to go see Charley Gant again and ask him a few more questions to clarify a few things for me.

When I got to headquarters, Charley was in the coffee room getting his morning coffee. I got a cup also, and then asked Charley if he would join me in my office.

"Charley, yesterday you were telling me about this contact person. Did it have to be a member of the group or could it be anyone?"

"We all assumed it would be a member of the group, but no, it was not stipulated that it had to be."

"So Adam could have picked anyone to be the contact person?"

"Damon, I don't think Adam would go outside the group. The person he selected would not only have to be someone he trusted but also have a pretty good knowledge of what we where doing and about the treasure."

"Okay Charley, lets just assume that it might be someone outside the group. Is there anyone you can think of that it may have been, who would a logical choice be?"

"I can't think of anyone. You might be right; he may have gone outside the group, because as I told you we were suspicious of each other. We didn't know who we could trust and who we couldn't."

"What about Ellen's Sister Norma?"

"I don't think so Damon, unless she is one very good actress. She has been constantly on my ass about finding her sister and Adam."

"All right then. Maybe we should consider a different angle. When is the next contact date?"

"I don't know, but it should have been about a month ago, the last contact was almost three months ago. Only the contact person knows how and when contact is to be made with Adam."

"How about getting a message to Adam?"

"What message?"

"That he needs to return, that three members are dead and more will probably die if he doesn't come back right away."

"I don't know Damon, first of all the contact may already be dead. Secondly Adam was told not to respond to any plead messages, because they could be false. That was put into action, in case anyone found out whom the contact person was and got them to disclose the procedure some way."

"You know Charley, you and your brainy friends have this all figured out so everything could remain secret. Well I got news for you; the killer is using your vale of secrecy against you. The only thing that all this is doing is keeping me from catching the killer before he kills again."

"I know Damon, it does seem that way."

"I need to talk to Nick Stevens, Ed Doorman and you, all together at one time. Do you think that you can arrange that Charley?"

"Yes of course, will this afternoon be all right, I will give them a call. I know they both want to talk to you also."

"That will be fine Charley, the sooner the better; around two o'clock would be great. Have them come here to my office."

Charley Gant had not been gone from my office more than twenty minutes, when I saw him coming back in a hurry.

"Damon, Tom Knight and Norma, have been in an accident down on Federal Street. They ran their van through a red light and a delivery truck hit them. The driver of the truck said it appeared like they didn't have any brakes."

"Come on Charley, I want you to go with me."

"You got it; I'll meet you at your car in a couple minutes."

We met at the car, while I got us moving in the direction of Federal Street, I told Charley to get on the radio and find out the location and condition of Tom and Norma.

"215 this is 401 and 501, over.

"Go ahead 401, over."

"What are the locations and conditions of each of the victims?"

"401, the occupants of the van are being transported by ambulance to General Hospital. The driver of the truck is being treated on the scene by a medic."

"What are the injuries to the two victims in the van?"

"The woman has a broken right arm and possible internal injuries. The man has a severe head wound and was unconscious when we arrived. He had not regained consciousness by the time they put him into the ambulance to go to the hospital."

We arrived at the scene of the accident in minutes. I got Charley to question the Traffic officers and the driver of the truck. While I went up the street to take a look at the van that was on its side. It looked to be a total wreck. It was located about fifty feet from the point where the two vehicles actually hit each other. It only took a minute to find out where someone had cut the brake line in half. There was no question in my mind about it. It was evident that the line cutting was intentional, I would say from the looks of it, with a pair of side cutters. Both ends of the line were crimped shut.

We finished up there quickly so we could go to the hospital and talk to Tom and Norma if they were up to it.

At the hospital, the doctor told us that Tom was still unconscious and they believed he was suffering from a concussion. Norma was in X-ray and would be out soon. He said that we could probably talk to her if we promised to keep it brief and not upset her.

"Damon, do you think the killer thinks that Norma or Tom is the contact person?"

"No, I don't think so. I think they decided that if anything happened to either of them it would bring Adam and Ellen out of hiding. It may even bring the contact person to the surface; cause them to make a mistake that would reveal their identity. Whoever is doing this is already responsible in one way or another for the deaths of five people. There remains only three of the treasure group still alive; I think this was an attempt to take a short cut to Adam."

"Damon, I wish I had never gotten involved in this. I should have listened to my first instinct and kept clear of this whole mess."

Nora had to remain at the hospital because her arm was broken and she had 3 fractured ribs. The nurses were casting her arm and getting her settled into a room so we decided to check on Tom first. Tom was now conscious and his vital signs where good; they expected him to recover completely in a matter of hours. It was going to be a while before we could talk to either Norma or Tom so Charley and I went back to the station.

I was concerned as to what other new twists this case would take. My only two possible suspects were Tom Knight and Charley Gant. Now I had eliminated both Tom and Charley as possible suspects. I was unsure which way I should turn or who to look at next.

I told Charley about my plans to rent a houseboat and take Lora to the lake for a weekend. He offered to let me use his cabin cruiser instead. I was surprised to find out that he not only had a very nice cabin cruiser, but he also had a speedboat and a house at the lake.

"How can you afford all that on a cop's salary, Charley?"

"I don't talk about it much, but my father was a very wealthy man. He died some years ago and of course left everything to my mother. My father hated the fact that I decided to join the police department instead of taking over his business, but I wanted to be a cop more than anything in the world. When my mother passed away a couple years ago, she left me everything."

"Charley, I have known you for years or at least I thought I did. First, I find out you are a member of this treasure group of the Mayors and now I find out you are a millionaire also. Is there anything else I should know about you?"

"No, I think that about covers it. Damon, please keep the millionaire thing private; I don't want it to get around the department. I think it would cause people to treat me differently and I wouldn't like that."

"Okay Charley, I will keep that to myself, except for Lora, of course. That leads me to another question. If you have all this money, why did you get involved in this treasure business?"

"I told you, because it was a mystery. I didn't even really believe in it, but the mystery of it intrigued me. Now it has become more of a mystery than I ever believed it could be and all I want is to get free of the whole nasty business."

"Wow, amazing. You think you know someone and you really don't know him or her at all. It is none of my business, but about how much are you worth Charley?"

"The estate was estimated at several million, but some of my father's collections haven't been liquidated yet. So depending on how much they bring it could change by a million, one way or the other."

"Are you kidding? I had no idea. How could you keep this a secret?"

"Other than the Lake House and boats, everything my father owned was in and around Washington. There was really no reason for anyone to know about it, other than a few close friends of mine. I hope I can consider you a close friend also now Damon. You and Lora are both wonderful people and I would consider it an honor to list you both among my friends."

"Thank you, Charley. Thank you for the offer to use your boat. I can't wait to tell Lora about it."

"You save my ass, kept me in one peace and alive. I might just give you the damn boat."

"I'll do my best. You are married aren't you, Charley?"

"No, divorced a few years ago. We weren't compatible, I guess you would say."

"Sorry to hear that. Did you have any kids?"

"No, we didn't have any children."

It had been a couple hours, so we headed back over to the hospital to see if we could at least talk to Norma, if not Tom. We went to see Norma first, hoping she could give us some useful information that we could compare to what Tom might tell us.

"Hi Norma, how are you feeling?"

"A little banged up, have you seen Tom?"

"No not yet. But they said he is doing fine."

"Oh, Thank God, I was so worried about him."

"Tell us what happened. Norma."

"We just pulled away from the house in the van. We where going to stop by the station and see you Damon, then go to lunch. We started down the hill at the house, when Tom realized the van had no brakes. Tom just blew the horn hoping that people would hear it and get out of our way. I guess the person in that delivery truck did not hear it. That is all I can tell you, except that the brakes were fine last night when we came home."

"The brake line was cut Norma. Did either of you see anyone around the van, during the time between when you got home last night and when you got in the van again today?"

"No, I didn't and I think if Tom had he would have mentioned it to me. This would happen now, just when everything seemed so perfect."

"Perfect, how do you figure everything is so perfect, Norma?"

"Tom asked me to marry him last night and I said yes. I love him so much Damon. This is my first real chance for happiness and I don't want anything to happen to mess it up."

"That is great; I know you will both be happy together. You are a perfect couple. You should get some rest now. So we will be going."

"You mean that, you really think we are a perfect couple?"

"Of course Norma, don't you agree?"

"Well yes, but sometimes Tom just seems like he is just tolerating me. In fact, I was very surprised when he asked me to marry him last night right after he came in from the van."

"Tom went to the van last night after you had gotten home."

"Yes, he said he had left something in the van, so he went to get it."

"Then he may have seen something suspicious, we won't know till we talk to him."

"Damon, do me a favor and catch this crazy son-of-bitch, before he kills anyone else."

"Believe me, Norma, that is number one on my list of priorities right now."

"Oh really, I thought Lora was number one on your list."

"You have me pegged, Norma. Talk to you later and take care of yourself. I'm looking forward to attending your wedding."

We went to the ward that Tom's room was in, but the nurse informed us that he had been taken to X-ray for a final once over prior to his release. As Charley and I left the hospital, Charley started laughing to himself, an almost girlish under his breath type laugh.

"What do you find so funny Charley?"

"Not really funny, just interesting how something good may come out of something so bad."

"What are you talking about?"

"Norma and Tom are getting married. They wouldn't have met if Ellen and Adam had not disappeared. Ellen being Norma's sister and Adam being Tom's brother. It is my opinion that when Adam and Ellen went into hiding they where very much in love also. I also understand that this case sort of brought you and Lora together as well."

"Yes, I guess you could say it did but I have had designs on Lora since High School. Charley how about you, is there anyone special in your life?"

"I guess you could say that I have someone special in my life. We met a few months ago and for the first time in my life, I feel that I am in love with the right person."

"That is great, I had wondered. I never see you with anyone and you never talk about anyone."

"Well Damon, My personal life is very personal to me and I don't talk about it much. I don't feel that my personal life should interfere with my work as a police officer."

"I don't understand why you would think it would, but I am sorry I didn't mean to be prying into it Charley. I was just interested because I would like to get to know you better. I thought that maybe we could all have dinner or something one night. Of course it will be my treat, sort of a repayment for the use of your boat."

"We don't go out much, but maybe you and Lora could come to dinner at the Lake House, sometime in the future, once you understand the need I have for total privacy."

"Charley is there anything about you that isn't a secret. You are the most secretive bastard I have ever known. I guess that is why I know so little about you, even though I work with you and see you every day."

"I'm sorry Damon, I really don't mean to be so secretive, but I have found that people can be very judgmental and cruel when they know too much about another person. So out of necessity I learned not to talk about my personal life to anyone except close friends and people outside the department.

Wow! Amazing I work with this man every day and know nothing about him. I didn't even know about him going through a divorce. Spending the day with Charley had been interesting to say the least. It also eliminated him from the ever shorter and now nonexistent list of suspects. Charley did not need the money from the treasure and I believed him when he said, "His only interest was the mystery involved in it".

When I got back to the office, I called a meeting with the entire squad, because of the importance of this investigation; I had put everyone to working on it. For their own protection, I had people keeping an eye on Nick Stevens and Ed Doorman. I did not feel that Charley needed nor wanted watching, I felt he could take care of himself. Kelly and Bill felt that Doorman might be preparing to leave town on an extended vacation. He had withdrawn a lot of money from his account and had taken it in traveler's checks. He had also been talking to a travel agency. This was good news as far as I was concerned; it would be one less person to worry about.

Jack Morris and Bob Leonard had been monitoring Nick Stevens. He seemed to be just plain scared. He had a security company estimate the cost of additional security for his home. He also purchased a couple weapons from one of the local gun stores. He was already having the security company recommendations added to his house.

This was not as acceptable an approach to the situation as leaving town. As afraid as he seemed to be for his family and his own safety, I was worried he might be too quick to shoot and maybe shoot the wrong person. I did not know Stevens very well, but what little I had seen of him, at his Drug Stores, he seemed like a very nervous and spontaneous person. He may act out of fear before he had considered everything or even given any thought to the consequences of his action.

In both cases, I realized the need to talk to both men as soon as possible. I called Charley Gant, and told him that I wanted to meet with each of these men right away. Charley had been with me since I had asked him to set up a meeting with Stevens and Doorman. I knew he had not had the chance to contact them for a meeting at two-o'clock; besides, it was already after two. He called me back in a few minutes and told me that they would all be in my office at four. That was fine with me, the sooner the better.

When Stevens, Doorman and Charley Gant all came filing through the squad room and into my office, it created a great deal of interest with all my detectives, so I closed the door behind them and pulled the blinds shut, to keep anything we said or did in total confidence. After they had all taken a seat, I began my questioning.

"Gentleman, first I would like to thank you all for coming. My first question is, which one of you is the contact person that keeps in touch with Adam?"

They just all looked at each other like each of them expected one of the others to speak up, but there was no response from any of them.

"In order to assist me in solving this case and catching the murderer, I need some answers, gentleman."

Again, they all remained silent. Then Charley Gant spoke up.

"Nick, Ed, I am sure we can trust Lieutenant Carter, so if you know anything at all, don't hesitate to tell him. Three of our friends are already dead and he is trying to help us. So if you do know something, please tell him."

Mr. Doorman, spoke up. "Lieutenant, I am not the contact person, but I am very concerned for my safety and that of my family. The Beale Treasure is no longer a concern of mine; I just want to remove my family from the path of this lunatic. I am leaving town tomorrow morning and I don't plan to return until this nightmare is over. I have spent most of my life looking for the Beale Treasure, but it is not worth my life or any member of my family's lives. Whoever wants it this bad can have it. Whoever it is obviously is insane to do what they have done, as far as I am concerned they are more than welcome to it. I just hope you catch them and give them what they deserve, what started out as more of a game has turned into my worst nightmare and I just want out of it."

"I am aware of your plans to leave town Mr. Doorman. I also think that is a wise choice on your part and I don't blame you one bit. I would advise you not to tell anyone, including a travel agent where you are planning to go. I would like you to keep in touch with me however, in case I need you for anything."

"It is nothing personal Lieutenant, but I don't trust anyone in this police department. Please don't worry about me; I am not taking any chances. I am not telling anyone my plans. I would like to know how you found out about them."

"For yours and Mr. Steven's protection we have been keeping you both under observation. Which brings me to you Mr. Stevens, you don't seem to be planning to leave town anytime soon, but instead are taking precautions to protect yourself and your family."

"I can't afford to leave town Lieutenant, I have six Drug Stores. I could lose everything if I run out on this mess."

"I understand that Mr. Stevens, but your recent purchase of a couple weapons concerns me a great deal. I am not only concerned for your safety, but also the safety of other innocent people. What exactly do you plan to do with these weapons?"

"Lieutenant, the weapons I purchased were purchased legally and I have a right to own them. I also have the right to protect my family and myself."

"I understand that Mr. Stevens and I know your rights. May I ask you how much training you have had in the proper use of these weapons?"

"The man at the store I bought them from showed me how to use them."

"I didn't ask if you knew how to use them, I was asking if you know the proper way to use them. I don't want you getting trigger-happy and shooting at shadows. I don't believe you to be a killer Mr. Stevens and I don't want you to become one either."

"I'll be honest with you Lieutenant, I am afraid. Not just afraid, I am scared to death."

"I'm aware of that Mr. Stevens and I don't want that fear to cause you to use one of those weapons and possibly kill someone or get yourself killed."

"I appreciate your concern, but I have to do what I feel best to protect myself and my family."

"Mr. Stevens, it is very important that I know if you are the person that Adam selected to keep in touch with?"

"No Lieutenant, believe me if I was I would tell you. I'm too afraid not to tell you."

"Okay Gentleman, is there anything else anyone can add to assist me in this investigation. If not, good luck to you Mr. Doorman. Please be very careful and use caution, Mr. Stevens. Charley, I would like a few words with you. Good day to you gentlemen, thank you all for coming and your time."

Mr. Stevens and Mr. Doorman left Charley Gant and I in my office as they each shook my hand and walked out.

I closed the door behind them, and then looked at Charley.

"What do you think Charley? You know these men better than I do."

"I think they are both being totally honest with you. I also know I am not Adam's contact person. So maybe your hunch was right, unless the contact person is already dead, he must have gone outside of the group. Right now, I haven't got the slightest idea who on earth it could be, how about you Damon?"

"Not a clue Charley, not a clue. Either the contact person is already dead, or they are a person outside the group. In either case, I feel that Adam and Ellen will be turning up soon. They will be coming back to find out why there contact is no longer contacting them. The other possible reason would be that the contact person notifies them about what has been happening here. Depending on where they are, they may even hear about it on the news or in the newspaper. Then they will return out of concern and in hopes of putting an end to this ungodly mess."

"I think I will go on up to the lake, and make sure the boat is ready for you to use. You and Lora want it for this weekend, don't you?"

"Yes, I think so. They are calling for good weather this weekend, pretty, sunny and warm. But don't go to any trouble Charley."

"It is no trouble; I just need to check a few things that I would have to check anyway."

Chapter 12

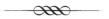

It seemed with every day that passed that it took me longer and longer to get home. Probably because now I felt that I had something more than Ranger to come home to. It felt good to know that Lora would be there waiting for me. I cannot ever imagine taking Lora for granted or our love making to ever become routine or lack excitement in any way. I was excited just thinking about her, so I stayed excited most of the day. There is not a minute of the day that she is not on my mind.

There was one thing about Lora that bothered me a great deal. She seemed to have something weighing on her mind very heavily. Something was bothering her and I had no idea what it could be. When I would ask her if anything was bothering her, she would just say. "No, not really" or "It isn't important". The last time I asked her she said, "I will be able to tell you soon I hope".

I was worried she may have a medical problem that she was concerned about and had not gotten the test results back yet. I knew she went to the doctor a few days ago. I wouldn't know what to do if something happened to her now. I don't think I would want to go on living without her. She has become such an important part of my life.

I could hear Ranger barking as I neared the front door. As I went into the house, Lora was not in the kitchen as usual. She was on the deck looking out over the valley. I came up behind her moved her hair gently away from her neck and kissed it. She responded with a little shiver of contentment, but made no effort to turn and face me. So I turned her toward me, but when I did, I could tell she had been crying. Her mascara had smeared and her eyes were red and still full of tears.

"What is the matter honey?"

"Oh, Damon, I wish I could tell you, but I just can't right now."

"Why, why can't you tell me? You are keeping secrets from me already?"

"No, Damon. But I just can't tell you yet."

"Is there something wrong with you Lora; are you sick or something?"

"No, Damon, Nothing like that. You have to trust me. I will tell you in due time. You just have to trust me just a little bit longer. If you love me and trust me, you will."

"I'm sorry Lora but it bothers me that something is bothering you. What kind of a husband would I be? If I wasn't concerned and wanted to know what the trouble was?"

Lora started to smile, than began to laugh.

"What is funny Lora?"

"You referred to yourself as my husband, Damon."

"I guess I shouldn't have done that, it just slipped out."

"That is okay Darling, I don't mind. I don't mind one little bit."

"Just tell me one thing, is it something that will affect our relationship?"

"I don't think so or at least I hope it won't."

"It better not, I like our relationship just like it is. The only addition I want to add to it is a ring."

"Daman, what ring are you referring to? Oh! You mean an engagement ring."

"Well yes, to be honest I have been thinking about it, but feel it is too soon. I don't want to frighten you away, with a commitment this early in the relationship."

"You won't frighten me away, but perhaps we should wait a little longer."

"Agreed; Now go get cleaned up and get a jacket if you want, I'm taking you to dinner at that new restaurant up the road. I don't want you wearing yourself out cooking tonight. Plus I have some good news for you."

"What is the good news?"

"I want to tell you about it over dinner."

"Okay, I'll go fix my face and I'll be ready to go in a few minutes."

At dinner, I told Lora of Charley Gant's offer to loan us his boat over the weekend. She was delighted at the offer and felt it was quite generous of Charley. We then discussed everything that had been going on in the case. I also told her all that I had learned about Charley and that I had no idea of any of it prior to him telling me during our time together today.

Lora had been to see Norma at the hospital, but she was unable to see Tom. She felt that both Norma and Tom were recovering nicely. Seemed their only concern was about each other. Lora's spirits seemed to improve as she told me how much Norma and Tom loved each other. She felt that they may even be planning to get married in the near future. That the only reason they were putting it off was because of all the problems that had arisen recently involving this treasure business.

I wanted to question Lora about what was bothering her, but she seemed to have put whatever it was out of her mind temporarily and I did not want to upset her again.

By bedtime, we were both exhausted and too tired too even consider making love. We just went to sleep with a good night kiss. This was the first night we had not made love since we had been together. One night was fine, but I didn't want it to become a habit, I enjoyed making love to Lora far too much for that to ever happen and I hoped she felt the same way.

The next day was quiet for a change. Jack and Bob informed me that Mr. Doorman and his family had left town early in the morning. They did not leave information with anyone as to any plans or destination.

As far as I was concerned, I was glad to see that he was leaving town and out of harms way. I was still hoping Mr. Stevens might follow Mr. Doorman's example and leave town as well.

I was able to visit Tom Knight at the hospital in the afternoon. He seemed distant from the case and the happenings regarding it. His only interest seemed to be Norma. He was concerned about how she was doing. When I left him, I asked to see his doctor. I told the doctor that I felt it would be the best thing for both Tom and Norma if arrangements could be made to allow the two of them to spend some time together. The doctor agreed and said he would see what he could work out.

I was glad it was a slow day. Mayor Caldwell and his wife's funeral were to be at two o'clock today and I wanted to be with Lora for it. There was a chance that Lora was going to have to take Carol as well. Seemed that her husband was not sure he could get to the funeral. He had an important meeting regarding the old textile mill, or so he said.

That was fine with me I would take both Lora and Carol. I could console Lora and Lora could console Carol. Most of the Police Department would be at the funeral anyway along with everyone connected to city government and a multitude of friends and family. There were over four-hundred people expected to attend the funeral. I expect that the funeral will take much longer than anyone anticipated.

I called Lora, so she could inform me as to what she wanted me to do.

"Of course Damon, I want you to be with me. But we need to take Carol also, seems her husband is too busy."

"Your kidding, he is too busy to go with his wife to her parent's funeral. What a jerk, I hope Carol soon gets wise to what an asshole this guy is and dumps him."

"I think this is the last straw with Carol. She told me this morning that she wanted to get that attorneys name and number that you thought would be a big help to her."

"That is great, I will be happy to give it to her. You know who would be a good man for Carol?"

"No who, Darling? Not you I hope."

"No, of course not, I'm your man and I intend to stay that way."

"Then who do you have in mind?"

"Charley Gant."

"But isn't Charley about our age?"

"He is a few years younger."

"Than that means he is about ten years older than Carol. Besides I thought you told me Charley was seeing someone."

"I don't consider the age to be a problem. Carol is very mature and Charley seems to be a wonderfully nice man, now that I have gotten to know him better. Also I don't think whoever Charley is seeing would be an issue either, he seemed very reluctant to even tell me he was seeing someone."

"That may all be true, but the fact remains. Carol is still married, Charley is still seeing someone, so I feel it will be a while before we can do any shooting of Cupids arrows in their direction."

"You're right, honey. Maybe we should wait a few days."

"Damon, what do you mean a few days? What about six months or a year?"

"Well Darling it didn't take us but a couple days."

"I think our situation is a little different. Neither of us was seeing any one and neither of us was married. Also neither of us had just lost both our mother and father."

"I was just kidding, Lora. I know it will take some time."

"I should hope so. Damon, I need to leave here in a few minutes to go to the Mayor's house to pick up Carol. We can just meet you at the church. I know you hadn't planned on going this early, but since I am taking Carol I need to be there early."

"Ok, I will just meet you at the church then, wear red so you will be easy to find."

"Oh, Damon, I never know when you are kidding and when you aren't."

"Who's kidding? There are going to be a lot of people there, I don't want to spend a lot of time finding you."

"Damon, I'm not wearing red, you will just have to work at finding me. I will be wearing black, as I should be out of respect. Like almost everyone else attending the funeral."

"I was kidding."

"It is a good thing I love you so much."

"Yes Darling, otherwise you wouldn't tolerate me."

When I got to the church, it was not hard to find Lora. She was very tall for a woman and that beautiful blonde hair stood out in a crowd. I joined Lora and Carol, and then rode with them in the limo to the cemetery. The whole time we were at the church and the cemetery I kept looking over the crowd, watching for anything out of the ordinary, suspicious or unusual from anyone there. I had a feeling that the murderer was there, pretending to be innocent and paying their last respects to the Mayor and his wife. I knew it was a real long shot; it could be any one of the hundreds of people there. This criminal was far too clever to give himself away that easily.

After the graveside service, I rode back to the church in the limo to get my car and Lora could pick hers up as well. The limo driver took Carol back to the Caldwell house, where we rejoined her.

"Damon, I have been thinking about what you said. That if I thought of anything else that I should let you know. My father did mention, that he had noticed having seen a police officer more frequently than normal in the last month. He said it seemed like he kept running into this man in places that he didn't feel was normal to see him at."

"Did he mention the officer's name, by any chance?"

"I don't think so. If he did, I'm afraid I don't recall it."

"Well thanks Carol. At this point in the case anything could be of help."

As I left Lora and Carol to head back to the station, I began thinking it would be nice to get a solid lead in this case. A name, description, physical evidence, or just about anything at this point. It was almost as if the criminal knew what we would be looking for and was especially cautious to be sure we did not find anything. He seemed to know our procedure as well as we did.

Doctor Kline and his wife's funeral were two days ago and Mr. Kent's funeral was tomorrow. Tom and Norma had barely escaped death and were in the hospital. Mr. Doorman had left town and Mr. Stevens had confined himself to his home, which was almost like a fortress now. Charley Gant was the only member of the group that did not seem to be panicking and nervous about anything.

Maybe I had been a little too hasty in thinking Charley should not be on my suspect list. Come to think of it. I was going by only what Charley had told me. Maybe I should verify some of the information he had given me. I think I will get Kelly and Bill to check out Charley's story.

Charley did act as if he was trying to keep something secret from me, but maybe that was just my imagination.

It would be extremely awkward, if it turned out that Charley had nothing to do with the killings and he found out that I was investigating him. Treating him as a criminal and suspect the same weekend he had loaned Lora and I his boat for a romantic weekend on the lake.

Maybe I should just try to rent a boat the way I had planned originally and not borrow Charley's boat.

I had become so involved in my thought process that I had allowed myself to slip a few miles over the speed limit. I heard a siren to my rear, I looked in my mirror and I saw an unmarked police car. Siren blaring, lights flashing, I pulled to the curb at the first opportunity. A man dressed in plain clothes got out of the car behind me. As he walked toward me, I could see it was Jack Morris.

"Jack, what do you think you are doing?"

"I wanted to talk to you, Lieutenant."

"Couldn't it have waited till we got to the station Jack?"

"I guess it could have waited."

"Then Jack would you mind, going back to your car. Turn off all you're flashing lights and allow me to proceed to the station where we can talk without drawing the attention of all the people passing by."

"Just wanted to know how you thought the funeral went?"

"Jack, you were there. It was a funeral; it went as well as funerals go. Is that it Jack? You humiliated me in front of all these people to ask me my opinion of the Mayor's funeral?"

"No, I also wanted to tell you what all Mr. Stevens is doing to his house. You wouldn't believe what all he is installing on it Lieutenant. He is making it into a security vault. Alarms, steel meshing on the windows, double and triple locks on all the doors and windows. No one could get in or out without a great deal of effort."

"Jack, would you mind if we continue this conversation at the office, we are beginning to draw a great deal of attention. What I mean is with all the flashing lights and everything."

"That is all I wanted to tell you, Lieutenant."

I was straining to control my aggravation about this unbelievably stupid act. "Thanks for the information Jack. May I go now?"

"Oh, yes go ahead; I will see you at the station."

I thought to myself, *"Not if I have any luck at all."*

When I got to the squad room, Kelly and Bill along with a couple other detectives seemed to be having a bullshit cession at Kelly's desk. I just went to the coffee room got a cup of freshly brewed Joe and headed to my office. Kelly and Bill were hot on my heels with big grins on their faces.

"Well Lieutenant, did Jack give you a ticket? We saw he had you pulled over on Fort Avenue."

"You saw what that idiot did."

"Lieutenant, half the people that attended the funeral saw what he did."

"Oh great, I wonder how long it is going to take me to live this one down?"

I was sure that the humiliation of Jacks, stupid act was going to follow me for at least a few days. The one thing that I have always hated about cops, is when they have the opportunity to poke fun at one of their own they take full advantage of it and get a great deal of pleasure doing just that.

I always figured it was like a comedian, only makes fun of his own religion or ethnic group. To make fun of another religious or ethnic group, that would be in bad taste.

Just then, I saw Charley Gant heading for his office. I felt this was as good a time as any to tell him, we wouldn't be using his boat this weekend. I took my coffee and headed to his office.

"Charley"

"Hey Damon, great I was coming over to talk to you in a few minutes anyway."

"What about, Charley?"

"I wanted to tell you about the boat and this weekend."

"That is what I came to talk to you about. I hate to put you to so much trouble, so I think I will just go with my original plan and rent a boat."

"Absolutely not Damon, I don't want you to do that. I have already cleaned the boat up and stocked the refrigerator with food and drinks for you and Lora. Everything is all ready for you, all you need to bring with you is, any clothes and toilet articles you might need."

"Oh, you shouldn't have gone to so much trouble."

"No trouble, we had a blast doing it. We have never invited anyone from the department up to the lake before; it is an exciting first for us."

"Wow, I don't know what to say."

"Say nothing, we are happy to do it and like I said, it was fun."

"Okay Charley."

"Great, here are the directions of how to get there. Just let me know when we can expect you and everything will be ready."

I left Charley's office feeling like a real heel. Here we are using his boat and excepting his gracious offer and hospitality. While at the same time, I planned to get Kelly to verify his story.

It was obvious that he was hoping to perpetuate a friendship between Lora and me, with him and his girlfriend. At the same time, I have a duty as a police officer to follow up on any leads I might have in this case. Surely as a fellow officer, Charley will understand that, if he ever finds out about it.

It had already been a rough day, so I decided to leave and go home a little early. When I got to the house, Lora's car was already there. She did not have to go to the office today due to the funeral. She had decided to lie out on the deck, in hopes of getting a suntan before the weekend.

I was excited to see her there and not just because she was all covered with oil and topless with only her bikini bottom on. I would have been glad to see her if she was covered from head to toe, with a flannel shirt and overalls. I must admit that seeing her as she was, added to my excitement a great deal, it also added to her desirability, if that was possible.

Lora appeared to be asleep when I came in, so I went straight to the bedroom and changed into a pair of shorts. In the bedroom, I found Ranger and Smoky on the bed also asleep. They just looked at me when I came in, then went back to sleep. After changing cloths, I went out on the deck to join Lora.

The sound of me opening the door woke her and she just looked up smiling. She rolled over on her back then just laid looking at me as I sat down beside her. Even though I knew it was dangerous under the circumstances, I leaned over to kiss her hello. Knowing that a kiss could lead to much more that would not allow her to get the suntan she wanted. After all, we had missed our love making the previous night.

As tempting as it was, I decided to pass on it, as least until tonight. I told Lora about Jack Morris pulling me over shortly after I had left her and Carol. How it seemed that everyone saw him do it and when I told her why he pulled me over. All she could say was, "What is wrong with that man is he nuts or is he that stupid?"

Then I continued to explain to her about Charley Gant and my fears concerning him. That I felt bad about using his boat, but that he had gone to so much trouble. I just could not refuse to accept the use of it for this weekend.

Whatever had been bothering Lora did not seem to be weighing quiet so heavily on her mind this evening? She seemed a bit more relaxed as she began telling me about what Carol and she had discussed after I left this afternoon.

Carol was planning to leave that jerk husband of hers. She planned to continue to stay at her parent's house. Then to file for divorce once things calmed down a little and returned to normal.

Then she started telling me all the things that Carol had told her about her life with her husband. He turned out to be more of an asshole, than I had thought he was. I could not believe some of the things he had done to Carol and how he treated her. I had told Lora to tell Carol, if there was anything we could do to help to feel free to ask.

We remained on the deck until after dark. Then we had a late dinner, so it was late by the time we settled into the hot tub to relax a little before going to bed.

After being in the tub for a while, something seemed to catch Lora's attention in the direction of town.

"Damon, what is that bright light over in town, I don't remember it being there before."

I turned to see what light she was referring too.

"I don't know Honey, looks like a fire. I will go get my scanner and see what we can pick up on it." I said as I got out of the hot tub to go into the house.

I turned on the scanner as soon as I got to it and put it on the fire department channel, I was just in time to hear a report on the fire. Having heard the report I didn't see any reason to take the scanner back out with me, so I turned it off and put it back on the night stand.

"It is a house fire on Oakmont Circle, Lora."

"Oakmont Circle?"

"Yes, Oakmont Circle."

"What address? What is the house number?"

"I don't recall what they said the number was."

"Was it twelve thousand twenty-two Oakmont?"

"Something like that I believe. Why?"

"Go find out Damon."

"Okay, I'll call the Desk Sergeant at headquarters and asked him."

I called the sergeant and got the address on Oakmont."

"Lora, yes it is twelve thousand twenty-two, Oakmont. How did you know that and who lives there?"

"That is Nick Stevens home, Damon."

"How do you know that?"

"What difference does it make how I know? It is his address."

"I have to go, Lora, if it is his house I need to be there."

At that moment, my pager went off so I called back down to the Desk Sergeant. He told me that Bob Leonard called in and he wanted me to come to the house fire on Oakmont. Also for the sergeant to tell me, it was Nick Steven's house.

I was dressed and headed back to town in a hurry. By the time, I got to the Stevens house it was just a pile burning where the house had once been. I located Bob Leonard that had been watching the house.

"What happened here? Bob?"

"I don't know Lieutenant. There was a flash on the backside of the house. I got out to investigate, then suddenly like it had been hit with a flamethrower, the whole house was on fire."

"Did you hear an explosion or anything Bob?"

"No, not explosions more like a firecracker going off. I ran over to the house and started firing my gun in the air, in hopes that the noise would wake up the people in the house."

"Are they still in there?"

"No, luckily they all got out. My shooting woke them up, and they managed to get out onto the porch roof just in time. Then they all jumped into the swimming pool."

"Any of them hurt."

"No, just some smoke inhalation and their nerves are pretty well shot."

"Where are they Bob?"

"The Rescue Squad took them all to the hospital to get them checked out."

"Bob, you remain here, get a fire investigator out here. Tell him we suspect arson; also get some more of our people out here. But don't interfere with the fire department investigators this is more in their line of investigation than it is ours."

"All right Lieutenant, I'll give Jack a call and get him over here also. I relieved him about three hours before the fire started." He had no sooner said that when Jack pulled up to our location.

"Jack, like I just told Bob don't mess with anything. Let the fire department investigate this. Do you understand Jack?"

"Yes Lieutenant, I understand. You just make sure that Kelly and Bill understand when they get here. I heard them on the radio and they are on their way also."

"I'm going to the hospital to talk to Mr. Steven's, so just convey my orders to them when they arrive. By the way Bob, good thinking firing you weapon to wake up the family. You probably saved all of their lives."

"Thanks Lieutenant."

"You did that Bob, Wow that was smart thinking. So everybody got out of the house that is amazing in itself. The way that Mr. Stevens had that place locked up. I wouldn't have thought they could have gotten out. You can just jerk my chain with surprise." Jack said.

"Neither did the Killer Jack. If it were not for Bob's quick thinking, they wouldn't have gotten out. From what I hear they didn't have a second to spare."

I went on to the hospital to see if Mr. Stevens or anyone in his family could add anything to what little I already knew. Mr. Stevens confirmed it was the gun shots that Bob fired that alerted them. That if it had not been for that and the fact that the workers had not finished with the upstairs windows yet, they wouldn't have escaped the fire.

By the time that I got back to the scene of the fire, the fire was completely out. There was nothing left of the house accept two chimneys still standing. They had cordoned off the area for the night. The fire investigators felt it would be better to wait until day light to begin searching through the rubble of the house looking for clues. After seeing what was left of the house, I did not really have much hope of them finding anything.

I told my people to go on and I headed back out to the house. Lora was asleep when I got home, but she woke up long enough to say good night in a very special way.

The next morning I joined the fire investigators at the Stevens house. They had determined that the fire started at the fuel tank in the rear of the house. Due to a leak in the tank or line causing the fuel to flow under the house, it spread rapidly through the first floor.

Not wanting to get in the fire departments way, I went down the road to a diner. While I looked over the morning paper, I had coffee and breakfast. Then I returned to the Stevens house to see if they had any more information that might be helpful.

The fire investigator explained to me that determining where the fire started was a big help in locating the cause. In this case the fire was started by an electrical short.

"So the fire was an accident?" I asked the firefighter.

"No, it was arson, look over here. Someone placed these two wires so that when they made contact they would make sparks and ignite the fuel that was running out of the fuel tank."

"Then they must have done it minutes before the fire started."

"Wrong again, Lieutenant. What they did was to fasten the wires with a rubber band to each side of something that would melt in air temperature. This would keep the wire separated until it melted. This may take two or three hours, but would slowly allow the wires to eventually come together to create the spark."

"What would they have used to separate the wires?"

"Ice more than likely, in the night temperatures the ice would melt very slowly. As the ice melted it would allow the wires to touch and of course leave no trace."

"How can you be so sure that is the way it was done?"

"Look over here at what is left of the wires near the fuel tank. These two wires see how they have been each stripped back then made to form a hoop. That is so they had a better chance of making contact with each other. Then there was a rag tied around both wires, most likely soaked with combustible liquid that would ignite easily. It is simple and effective, almost impossible to trace back to the arsonist. These people were lucky to get out alive."

"I will need a complete report on this as soon as possible."

"You will get it Lieutenant as soon as we finish our investigation and verify our findings. We also need to run some laboratory tests on a couple of things, which might give you something more solid to work with."

I went to the motel where Mr. Stevens and his family were staying to ask them if they had noticed anyone near that fuel tank. They had not and Mr. Stevens told me that he was taking his family and leaving town even if he had to close all his drug stores to do so.

With Stevens leaving town, that only left Charley Gant, all the other members of the treasure-hunting group were either dead or had gone into hiding.

Chapter 13

———— ◆◆◆ ————

What a week. I was looking forward to what I hoped would be a nice quiet romantic weekend on Charley's boat with Lora. I still felt a little bad about investigating Charley after he had been so nice and I had really gotten to know him better.

I was a little relieved when Kelly told me that Charley's parents had died and that they had left him a very large estate. Seems that everything she found out about Charley was exactly as he had explained it to me.

Kelly was amazed to find out how wealthy Charley was. He had been discrete about letting anyone in the department know anything about his personal life. I told Kelly to please, keep everything she had learned about Charley to herself. He had his reasons for keeping his wealth and life a secret and we should respect those reasons. I did not want Charley to find out that I had her look into his background.

The hospital had released Tom Knight, but they wanted to keep Norma for a couple more days. Tom came straight from the hospital to my office. He wanted me to bring him up to date on everything that had happened while he was in the hospital.

I could not tell a great deal about the case to Tom. I did tell him about Doorman and Stevens leaving town. Also about the fire and that it was arson and what method they used to start the fire. Sensing Tom's concern about the other killings and the fact that Adam and Ellen could also be dead,

Of course, he wanted to know how and why I thought this, but of course, I could not tell him. Then I told him that Lora and I were going to spend the weekend on Charley's boat.

"Getting awful friendly with Lieutenant Gant, aren't you Damon."

"No Tom. Not really, I had told him our plans to rent a boat and he offered to let me use his instead. I do consider Charley a friend and fellow officer."

"How much do you actually know about Gant?"

"Not a great deal, but I think enough. Why do you think you know something I don't Tom?"

"Do you know how wealthy he is and how he came to be that way? Do you know about his divorce and what the reasons were for it?"

"I know about his wealth. I don't think his divorce is really any of my business or yours. Does his divorce pertain to the case in any way, shape or form?"

"No, it doesn't. I did find it interesting and informative though. It is just something I would have never figured Gant doing."

"Well Tom if it isn't pertaining to the case, I don't really want to know about it."

"Okay Damon, suit yourself, you don't want to know, I won't tell you." He had a big smile on his face as he left my office and headed back to the hospital to see Norma.

I told everyone that I was going to the lake and I would prefer not to be bothered unless it was an extreme emergency. This case had taken its toll on all of us, so everyone understood my need to get away from it for a couple of days. Even the Captain and the Chief sent a memorandum around telling everyone to go through them if there was a need to contact me and they would make the determination if it was important enough to bother me.

Unlike Charley's life, my life seemed to be public knowledge. Far too many people knew too much about my personal life. They all seemed to know that I had come through a very disturbing divorce. That I had dated very little until I connected with Lora. I took very little time off and worked many nights and weekends. In short, I had very little life outside the department and everyone knew it. They were all glad that I had some outside interest now.

I was looking forward to this weekend like a kid toward Christmas. I wanted to be alone with Lora and out of contact with the world, somewhat. It was going to be sort of like a mini vacation, a break and a get away from this horror that had surrounded us the last couple weeks.

I did not know what all Charley had stocked the boat with, in the way of food and drinks. There where a few things that I wanted to be sure we had. I went by the store on my way home and picked up some champagne and a diamond ring. It was not an engagement ring, more of a dinner ring, because I did not know how Lora would feel about an engagement ring at this stage and so early in our relationship. It was more of a notification that I was interested in replacing it with the engagement ring in the near future. That this ring was to serve as a reminder in the mean time, that I was very serious and loved her very much.

When I arrived at home, Lora had already gotten our things together and was ready to go, so we headed out toward the lake as soon as I took a shower and changed cloths.

It was only about a forty-minute drive to Charley's house on the lake. The directions he had given me proved invaluable and very accurate as well as easy to follow.

As soon as we arrived and got out of the car, a man came out of the house to greet us.

"Hi you must be Damon and Lora. My name is Hank and I am Charley's friend. Charley will be here very soon, but he told me to tell you to go on down to the boat and start making yourself comfortable. I have another cooler still in the house full of more food and drinks that I will bring down with me when I come."

"Thank you Hank."

Lora and I got our things out of the car and went down the planked walkway to the boathouse. When we saw Charley's boat, we were dumbfounded. We thought it might be nice but nothing like this. It was not just a boat; it was a yacht with all the comforts of home on it. It was much nicer than the houseboat we had planned to rent and bigger.

I saw Hank coming down the hill pulling a very large ice chest, so I went up to meet him and give him a hand with it. We had just gotten it on the boat when we saw Charley heading down toward us carrying another bag.

"Damon, could you come here for a moment?" Charley yelled down to me.

"Sure Charley, I'll be right there."

When I reached him, he showed me what he had in the bag. It was two, one hundred dollar bottles of very good champagne. Made me feel kind of cheep, that I had only paid twelve dollars for the one bottle I bought.

"Damon, I thought Lora and you might have something special to celebrate this weekend so I went and got this just in case."

"This is too much Charley; you have gone to way too much trouble for us."

"Not at all Damon, Believe me it means as much to me and Hank as it does to you and Lora."

"We have met Hank; he seems like a really great guy."

"Oh he is, we really get along well."

I did not know what to think, Charley was talking about Hank more like a girlfriend than a friend. The thought that Charley might be gay had never entered my mind. Hank did seem a little on the feminine side in a very masculine way. I must be mistaken; there was no way that Charley was gay.

Charley was walking ahead of me as we headed toward the boat. He was telling me about different things.

"Damon, the gas tank is full and you feel free to use it as much as you want. There is a chart of the lake on the boat. I have marked a cove near the Dam that is a great place to spend the night. If you want, I will lead you to it in the speed boat, but it is easy to locate from here."

"Charley, you have already gone to enough trouble, I'm sure I can find the cove on my own."

When we got to the boat, Hank was busy showing Lora what all they had stocked the boat with and how to work different gadgets on the boat.

Then Charley showed me how to operate the boat and different accessories like the power anchor and lights. He told me he could get to the cove in his speed boat in about twelve minutes so if I had any question just radio or call him and he would be there quickly. Then we all settled down to have a drink together and talk before Lora and I headed off to the cove.

Charley and Hank were sitting together on the lounge. Charley's hand was on Hanks leg, and Hanks hand was on top of Charley's hand. I could not just come out and ask Charley if he was gay. My God, what if he was not, that would really be bad. I was thinking; maybe I should have let Tom tell me about the circumstances around Charley's divorce. Maybe that would have cleared up this whole matter for me and I wouldn't be in this awkward position of not knowing what to say or do.

We wanted to get to the cove with plenty of daylight left to settle in before dark, so we started up the engines while Charley and Hank were untying the boat from the dock. As we pulled away from the dock, they stood on the dock with their arms around each other's waist. They waved to us as we headed across the lake and out of sight of them. Just prior to that I had turned to look one last time, I saw them kissing each other. Well I guess that answers that question, Charley never said his girlfriend was a girl and he never referred to her or him as his girlfriend.

"Lora, can you believe that Charley is gay."

"Yes Damon, I know."

"What do you mean you know, how long have you known?"

"Oh, I have known that Charley was gay for a long time."

"Why didn't you tell me?"

"I thought you knew. After all you work with him and have known him a lot longer than I have."

"No, I had no idea. I don't think anyone at the department knows he is."

"I know the Mayor knew about it and Chief Lewis, I also believe that Captain Mirant knows. I just assumed you knew about it also, why is it important?"

"It just would have helped if I had known, I was very uncomfortable when I first suspected it and didn't know. I was afraid to ask questions or say anything that might hurt their feelings or embarrass either or both of them."

"Does it bother you that Charley is homosexual, Damon?"

"No, not too much, but I was riding around with him all over town in the last few days and spending some time in his office."

"So, you are worried that when people see you with Charley, they might think you are gay also."

"I don't know, Lora, maybe a little."

"First of all Damon, like you pointed out, very few people know. Secondly, you were two police officers doing your job. You weren't out on a date with him or anything like that."

"Well, what if he had done something?"

"Like what Damon?"

"You know something gay."

"Damon, what are you talking about? Do I have to worry about you doing something heterosexual when you are riding around with Kelly in the car with you?"

"No of course not, how could you even think I would ever do anything like that."

"That is because you love me and Charley loves Hank just as much. I think it is kind of nice that Charley found so much happiness after so many years of unhappiness."

"I guess you are right Lora, I shouldn't let it bother me. Let's just forget about it and enjoy the weekend."

"You wouldn't believe what all we have. We have crab legs, steak, and all kinds of wonderful food and drinks. I think they thought of everything that could make this weekend wonderful for us."

"Oh, that reminds me, get that bag that Charley brought and put it in the refrigerator."

"Wow, do you know what this cost a bottle?"

"Yes"

Finding the cove that Charley had recommended was no problem at all. We dropped the anchor and got settled for the evening. It was a warm night, great for sitting out on the deck under the stars. It was quiet except for an occasional boat passing further out in the lake. We put a romantic music tape on the stereo, as a background, making the mood perfect as we ate the dinner that we had prepared together.

I went down into the cabin to get the ring I had gotten for Lora and one of the bottles of champagne. There could not be a better time than now to give it to her. Then I rejoined Lora on the deck put my arm around her pulling her close to me and kissing her. Then I handed her the small velvet box from my pocket. She had the most wonderful smile on her face as she opened it.

"Oh Damon, It is beautiful." Lora seemed almost speechless as she looked at me with her tear filled eyes. She took the ring from the box placed it on her finger, and then kissed me with all the passion of a woman in love.

"Yes Darling! Oh, yes I will marry you." Lora said excitedly as she kissed me again.

This was not what I had expected, it was not intended to be an engagement ring, it was a dinner ring. A large diamond set in the middle with smaller diamonds around it. She had taken it as an engagement ring and I was not about to object. I can think of nothing that would make me happier than to marry Lora.

When we made love it was always spectacular, but that night it was even more special and spectacular than usual. We had bonded and had a formal commitment to our love.

We remained anchored in the cove and did not move the boat. We had everything we needed right there. We spent the day, swimming, fishing, eating and drinking. We made love a few times, it seemed we just could not get enough of each other.

A family had set up camp on a small beach about three hundred feet from where we were anchored but that did not bother us in the least. They built a fire and after dinner, we sat on the deck watching them as the children played and roasted marshmallows over the fire. They were a little noisy but far enough away that it did not bother us, not that anything would bother us. We were in our own little world and I don't think it would have bothered us if they had been setting off fireworks.

We sat out on the deck looking up at the stars that seemed brighter than usual. Occasionally we would see a shooting star as it zipped across the sky. We were comfortable happy and in love, it could not be anymore perfect. We turned in early, so we could make love, while we were not tired.

We had been in bed for a couple hours and almost asleep when there was a banging on the side of the boat, like someone hitting it with his or her hand. Then I heard someone say something that I could not make out. No boat had gotten near us or we would have heard the motor.

The first thing that occurred to me was that the anchor had come undone, we had drifted toward the campsite on the shore, and they were trying to alert us to it.

"What is that Damon, what is going on?"

"I don't know Darling; I will go check it out."

"Damon, I hear someone saying "Help Me" over and over."

Then Lora yelled, "Okay, we are coming."

I got up and put my shorts on and grabbed a flashlight, then ran up on the deck. I did not see anyone or anything. We had not drifted and the people in the camp seemed to all be asleep. Then I heard someone say, "Help me, please Damon, help me". It sounded like Charley. I shined the light around but saw nothing.

"Where are you?" I yelled

"Down here, I'm hurt." he replied.

I went to the stern of the boat and shined the flashlight over the back of the boat. There hanging onto a small float cushion with one hand and the swimming platform with the other, was Charley.

"Charley, what the hell are you doing and how did you get here? Where is your boat?"

"Help me, Damon, I'm hurt. I'm hurt real bad."

By then Lora had gotten dressed and had come up on the deck to join me.

"What is going on Damon? Who is it?"

I got out on the swimming platform located on the back of the boat, at water level.

I told her. "It's Charley, he says he is hurt. Go get a blanket and see if you can find a first aid kit. No, wait; give me a hand getting him into the boat first."

I dropped the ladder for him to climb up, but he did not seem able to use it. I grabbed his hands and pulled him up to his waist onto the swim platform. I tried with Lora's help, to get him up on his feet. It was then that I realized his left foot was gone, cut off at a little above the ankle.

"Oh my God Lora, his left foot is gone. Help me get him into the boat. Quick!"

Charley was not a small man and could do very little to help us. It took every ounce of strength that Lora and I had to get him off the swim platform and onto the deck of the boat. We laid him on the seat on the back of the boat. Then Lora went to get a blanket and look for the first aid kit.

He was suffering from shock, hypothermia and loss of blood. His leg was not even bleeding very much; I don't think he had much blood left.

"What happened Charley?"

"Damon, I was coming to find you. I went down to the boathouse. I was going to come here in the speedboat. Because of the phone call, I got. When I got to the boathouse, someone hit me on the head knocking me out.

"Who was it, Charley?"

"I don't know. When I woke up, I found myself with my left foot padlocked with a chain around my ankle which was locked to the boat. The steering wheel was tied down with a rope to keep the boat straight. The boat was going at full speed toward the dam and the mountains. I had just moments before the boat was to impact with the shore. I could not free myself or do anything to stop the boat. The boat went into the woods in the next cove over from here at high speed and with a great deal of force. I flew out of the boat and into the woods where I was again knocked unconscious when I hit a tree. When I regained conciseness, I realized that my left foot was gone, ripped from my ankle by the chain and violent impact when the boat hit the trees. I pulled myself through the woods, toward the waters edge. I came across a float cushion from the boat lying on the ground. I used it to keep me afloat long enough to swim here to the boat and you. I had to let you know about the phone call, I had to warn you."

"Charley what phone call are you talking about?" "Charley, tell us, who was the phone call from?" "Talk to me, Charley?" "Warn me about what, Charley?"

He kept slipping into unconsciousness. I had to know what he was trying to tell me. It has to have been important or he wouldn't have risked his life to get here to tell me. Charley then regained consciousness for a few minutes.

"Damon, I heard on the phone. They know who the contact person is. They also know that they have the last decoded cipher."

Charley was out again.

Lora had returned with the blanket and first aid kit. She wrapped Charley up in the blanket and put a tourniquet on his leg to stop the bleeding. While I called for help it occurred to me that, the killers might over hear me call on the CB radio and realize that Charley was not dead so I used the phone.

I got hold of the sheriff's office and they said they would send help. I did not know where I should go or even how to get there if I did. I also did not know the lake well enough to be wondering around in it at night. I told them the approximate location where my boat had anchored. That I was going to head toward what looked like the lights of a marina on the other side of the lake from my location. They told me that it was a marina and they would have the rescue squad meet me there. They also had a volunteer fireboat on its way to my location.

I started the engine, but forgot that our anchor was still out. I tried to raise the anchor, but it had caught on the bottom. I did not have time to try to free it. I just ran to the bow and cut the rope.

Once I got the boat moving, I asked Lora how Charley was doing. She told me he had lost consciousness, but seems okay.

I could see the flashing lights of the emergency vehicles ahead of me as I was going full speed across the lake toward the marina. Then I saw the fireboat coming, it pulled up beside me and I just told them to get in front of me and lead me to the marina. I was afraid I would hit a shoal or something, because I did not know the lake and could not see the markers in the dark.

By the time we reached the marina, the parking lot was full of police cars and ambulances all of which had all their lights flashing. There were also a number of people that had arrived to see what all the excitement was, that apparently either lived or where staying near there.

I helped them get Charley off the boat and onto a rescue squad's gurney to take him to the waiting ambulance. They told me they had a helicopter waiting just up the road in a field to take him to the hospital. That was good news; he needed immediate attention if he was going to make it.

This was the end of our quiet romantic weekend. The deputies wanted us to fill out reports; I knew that would take a good portion of the night. We were now at a marina full of people and could not take the chance of going back to our quiet cove. In addition, we no longer had an anchor, so we could not anchor back at the cove again anyway. Besides I was not about to take that boat out on the lake again tonight. I would probably run it aground or even worse.

"Damon, what about Hank, shouldn't we go check on him and make sure he is all right. We also need to tell him what happened to Charley and where he is."

I tried to call the lake house, but there was no answer. I got one of the deputies to drive us over there, in his car. We arrived and I rang the doorbell several times before Hank, finally answer the door.

"Hi Damon, what is going on, is there something wrong? I was asleep."

He had obviously been drinking heavily. His eyes where blood shot as if he had been crying, not sleeping just before we got there.

We told him what had happened to Charley. He became very emotional and start yelling, "God I hope he did not suffer"

We told Hank, Charley was alive, and is in route to the hospital by helicopter.

"Charley is alive?"

I told him we would drive him to the hospital. I was hoping to ask him some questions on the way. Like what was so important that Charley was coming out to see me at this time of night.

Under the circumstances, it was hard to get anything out of Hank. He told us that he thought that Charley had gone to bed early. That there had been no phone calls. He did hear the boat being started and heard it pull away from the dock. That is when he went to check to see if Charley was in the bedroom, he was not. Hank, then feeling the effects of the excess of alcohol he had drunk, just went on to bed.

"Hank, you did not think it was odd that Charley was taking the boat out so late and not tell you he was doing it."

"No, I had been drinking and I was not thinking straight."

"Hank, I don't mean to pry. I need to ask you these questions. Do you often drink as much as you did tonight and you appeared to have been crying when we arrived?"

"No Lieutenant I don't normally drink much and yes I do mind you prying into my business."

When we arrived at the hospital, they were still working to keep Charley alive. They told us that no one could see him and that it might be days before anyone could. They also told us that if he lived they would have to remove his left leg above the knee. That he was not strong enough to survive the operation at this time. However, he will need the operation as soon as he was strong enough. He had lost a great deal of blood and they were giving him transfusions of whole blood. That even if he lived there was a chance that he may have brain damage. His brain had been deprived of blood and oxygen for a period during his transport to the hospital.

All this was more than Hank could handle. He completely went to pieces there in the hospital to the extent they felt they should admit him also.

It was daylight by the time we left the hospital and we drove back up to the lake to find the marina where we had left the boat. I was going to drive the boat back to Charley's house and Lora was going to drive the car and meet me there. We would then unload the boat and return to town and our own house. Our romantic weekend had come to a horrifying end, but we had two wonderful evenings and a great day before it did. We were truly grateful for that.

We had gotten the key to Charley's house from the doctor.

We put everything away that would spoil. Then Lora tried to clean up the blood on the boat, while I looked around the house for any clues that might help.

Charley's speedboat was not in the boathouse of course I did not expect it to be. I assumed that that the boat was his that went into the mountain. That boat was capable of doing at least eighty miles an hour or more. Charley said it was going full speed when it hit the trees. I would call the different sheriff's offices around the lake to see if it they had found the boat yet.

The drive home was quiet. Nether of us had much to say to the other. We were both very tired and had a great deal on our minds. Lora seemed very upset, which was very understandable after what she had been through; she also seemed to be deeply involved in thought.

"Damon, when we went back to Charley's house, there was a mixed drink on the stand near the door. Did you happen to notice it?

"No I did not, why Lora."

"Because when we came back from the hospital the glass was still there."

"I'm sorry Honey; I'm not following what you are getting at."

"There was no ice in it when we came back from the hospital. When we first went to the house and woke up hank the drink was fresh, it had ice in it."

"So, Hank had fixed himself a drink."

"He said we woke him up from his sleep. You mean he stopped by the kitchen on his way to answer the door to fix a fresh drink."

"I don't know Honey; right now my mind is too tired to worry about what Hanks drinking habits are."

"Ok Damon, I just thought I would mention it. Also it appeared that he had been crying, not sleeping."

It was great to be back in the peace and quiet of our home again. Ranger and Smoky, both were very glad to see us. We had put them in the garage with plenty of food and water. Because we wanted to be alone all weekend, so we had decided not to take them with us

Lora was very exhausted as she took a shower before getting into bed. By the time I had taken my shower she was fast asleep. I took special effort not to awake her.

Chapter 14

T he next morning was Monday. When I arrived at the office, the news of Lieutenant Gant had already circulated around. I was instantly, bombarded with questions about what happened and how he was doing.

Kelly informed me that Chef Lewis and Captain Mirant both wanted to see me, the minute I got there.

There was little I could tell them; this case had been just one dead end after another. The mere lack of suspects and evidence, made me look like I had not been doing my job as well as I should have been. I was not looking forward to seeing either of them. I had no leads, no progress and no suspects. All I had was five dead people, one burned down house and three people hospitalized, without the first clue of who was responsible.

I made a quick call to the hospital to check on Charley's condition and progress. They informed me that there was little change. He was still on the critical condition list and was in intensive care. I asked about Hank and they informed me that he checked himself out of the hospital shortly after Lora and I had left. That he was unable or unwilling to give the hospital any information about himself. That they had been unable to obtain his medical records due to the fact he wouldn't even give them his social security number or date of birth.

Thinking that was a little odd and being concerned about Hanks well being and state of mind. I tried calling the lake house, but got no answer. I called the Sheriff's Office and asked if they would send a deputy by to check on him. I was afraid he might try to take his own life or something, because he was so upset over what had happened to Charley. I had no idea how gay men handled such a crisis. I think it would not be much different, if any, from a straight man. I know I would be a little suicidal if anything like this happened to Lora.

Reluctantly I left the peace and quiet of my office to go talk to the Chef and Captain Mirant. I was hoping I could see them both at the same time so I wouldn't have to go through this but once.

I got lucky for a change; Captain Mirant was in Chef Lewis's office when I got there. The Chief had his secretary bring us coffee, then I started trying to explain this completely bizarre case to them. It all made no sense, from Tom digging up the graves right up to someone trying to kill Charley. All about the treasure, the Mayor's treasure-group, Adam and Ellen's involvement, also Tom and Norma's roll in this whole mess. The only thing that was easy to explain was what all my effort and investigation had turned up on the killer or killers; which was absolutely nothing at all. I had no suspects and no leads to follow up on at this time. I had no idea where Adam was or who his contact was. I didn't even know if Adam or his contact person was still alive.

The only positive thing that I could tell them was that the killer or killers were very smart, very ruthless and where determined to be the ones to recover the treasure, if it even existed. There was one other thing; the killer seemed to know exactly what we were doing in the investigation at all times and was always one-step ahead of us.

After the meeting, which took over two hours, I headed back to my office with the satisfaction that I had told them everything I knew. The real satisfaction was they were both just as bewildered as I was about this case and had no suggestions to offer.

I met Kelly and Bill coming out on my way in.

"Lieutenant, the County Sheriff called, said you had asked if he would send a Deputy to Lieutenant Gant's house to check on someone. He just called to tell you that when the Deputy arrived at the house, he found it on fire. They seem to think that the cause of the fire was a skillet of grease left on the stove with the burner on high. That the fire was now under control but the house was a total mess. The area in and around the kitchen was destroyed by the fire. We were just on our way to tell you. Then we thought we would go up and see if we could find out anything else."

"What about Hank?"

"He didn't say anything about a person named Hank. He did say there was no one at the house when the Deputy arrived and a neighbor had already called the Fire Department. They arrived a couple minutes after the Deputy had gotten there."

"I don't think there will be anything there to find. Besides, I need the two of you here. I'll sent Jack and Bob instead."

"Jack called in sick this morning. He isn't here."

"Okay, I'll send Bob and Sara Johnson. Sara can use the experience and Bob is a much better person to learn from than Jack."

"I agree, I'll go tell Bob to get Sara and head up there. Can you give them directions on how to get to Lieutenant Gant's house?"

"Yes sure, I want to see you and Bill in my office. Bring everything you have on this case with you. There is something we are overlooking, something obvious I feel, but I can't put my finger on it."

We settled down in my office with all our stacks of files on the case to go over them carefully.

"Lieutenant, is Lieutenant Gant going to be all right?"

"No Kelly, at best he is going to lose most of his left leg. There is also a very good chance that he has suffered some brain damage. They aren't sure how much yet, but he could end up totally incapacitated for the rest of his life."

"Bill and I are a little ashamed. At one time, we felt that the man we are looking for might be Lieutenant Gant. He is so secretive about his life and everything. Also he was involved with this treasure group."

"Don't feel bad, I thought the same thing at one time also. Now let's get started going over this stuff and see if we can figure out who might really be the person we are looking for."

We spent the next four hours going over every little detail of the case. We examined each person involved individually and still came up with nothing to indicate who the killer might be. Yet all three of us felt the answer was right there in front of us, but we just were not seeing it.

It had been a hard day and I was more than happy to be heading home that night. I was thinking, *"I wonder what Thomas Beale would say if he knew that what he did in 1820 would have such devastating, consequences on so many people almost two hundred years later"*. If the whole treasure thing were some kind of sick hoax, he would probably be getting a big laugh out of it. There was that two hundred pounds of gold that Adam and Ellen found. If it were a hoax, why would that gold have been there?

Lora's car was not at the house when I arrived. When I went in, Ranger and Smoky did not come to greet me either. The house was empty, so I went to the kitchen to see if there was a note. I found a note on the kitchen counter from Lora. She had taken Ranger and Smoky and gone to her house for the day.

I called over to Lora's house to ask when she was coming home.

"Damon, I have to wait here for a phone call, but I need to talk to you. So why don't you just come over here and I will fix dinner for us here."

"Who are you expecting a phone call from Lora? Must be pretty important for you to wait all day for it?"

"It is Damon, very important. Come on over here and I will explain everything to you then."

"Okay Honey, I will get a shower and put on some fresh cloths and be there in about an hour."

"I'll have dinner waiting for you, and Damon I just want you to know how much I do love you and I would never do anything to hurt or upset you."

That was a strange way for her to say she loved me. I wondered why she did not just say, "I love you or Love you". I was also wondering what all this business about a phone call was. Lora sounded a little upset like the time she had been crying. With all these questions on my mind, I hurried and took a shower and changed clothes so I could get there as quickly as possible.

I arrived at Lora's a little sooner than I had told her. Lora almost had dinner ready anyway.

"Lora, what did you want to talk to me about and what is this phone call you are waiting for?

"I will tell you everything after dinner."

We both just picked and played with our food. Lora was in deep thought, as if she was trying to decide exactly how she was going to tell me whatever it was that she wanted to tell me. I was concerned about what it was also, so I did not have much of an appetite either.

After dinner, it was apparent she still had not received the call she was waiting for, so we went in and sat in the living room to talk, I was impatient to hear what the problem was.

"Damon, I am the person you have been looking for."

"Of course you are Sweetheart; I have been looking for you my whole life."

Lora started crying. "No Darling. I'm the person that you have been looking for in this whole horrible mess."

"What are you talking about Lora; I know you are not the killer?"

"No of course not, but I am the person that Adam and Ellen have kept in contact with all this time."

"What? Why haven't you told me this before?"

"Please understand Darling, I couldn't. I had given my word to Adam and Ellen that I wouldn't tell anyone."

"Lora, what you are telling me is that you have been deceiving me and basically lying to me the whole time we have been seeing each other."

"Yes, I know and it has been tearing me apart inside. I just could not tell anyone, there were lives at stake. I wanted to tell you and it was upsetting me that I couldn't. You would tell me about the case. You needed to know who all the members of the Mayor's treasure group had been and who the contact person was. I knew the answers and I could not tell you. Do you know how hard it has been for me to keep my promise to Adam and Ellen, when I knew I could help you if I told you what I knew?"

"I became good friends with Ellen about two years ago, about the same time that she started dating Adam. They both grew to trust me a great deal. Adam sat right here in this living room and told me all about the Beale Treasure and the Mayors group of friends. He also confided in me all about everything he found about decoding the cipher."

"After they found the gold they didn't want to see anyone. They especially didn't want to meet with the other members of the group. They had me meet them in Appomattox. That is when they told me that they were leaving town, but they needed a person that they could trust completely to remain in contact with."

"They told me about the danger involved, that there was someone that would do anything to get their hands on the treasure. That if anyone knew I was in contact with either him or her it could cost me my life. At first I didn't want to do it, but they told me they had no one else they could trust, so I finally agreed to do it."

"Adam explained to me what I was to do and how I was to do it. He told me that every two months I would get a letter telling me any information that needed to be passed along to the Mayor and his friends. There would also be a general delivery address, that I was to send newspapers to and any information about what was going on here. That I was to wear gloves and write to each member of the group anonymously telling the information Adam told me to tell them. Each time the general delivery address would be different. Adam and Ellen had bought a motor home and they kept moving all the time."

"I was the perfect person, because I was the Mayors secretary. Mayor Caldwell confided in me, almost everything that was going on in the group, as well as any suspicions he had toward anyone in the group. That is how I knew Charley was gay; I thought for sure you would notice that when I let it slip out. The fact that I knew Nick Stevens address by heart; I thought sure you would figure it out by then."

"Adam must be somewhere in the area. He has found out that the only member of the group still left was Charley Gant. He was unable to get in touch with me, so he must have called Charley and told him that I was the contact person and that he needed to talk with me in a hurry."

"One thing that leads me to believe he is here in the area is because I haven't gotten a letter from him, telling me where to send the papers. I should have gotten it weeks ago. It must have been Adam and Ellen that told Charley about me, they wouldn't have done that unless they were in the area or on their way back. Actually, I expected them to be back here a month ago, before any of this mess happened."

"I had been good friends with Norma in high school so it was easy for me to renew our friendship, which allowed me to keep Ellen informed of what was going on with her sister. Then when Tom showed up and contacted Norma that was a bonus. I did not tell Adam that his brother was here or that Tom and Norma where seeing each other. Adam had never mentioned his brother to me, so I didn't feel it was a good idea to tell him that his brother was in town."

"It was very hard for me to keep the fact that Adam and Ellen were alive and safe from Tom and Norma. Each time I met, with either or both of them I had to listen to their concerns in regard to Adam and Ellen."

"I know that had to be hard on you Lora. It must have been a great relief to you when the Mayor told Tom that they were alive and in hiding."

"We must be careful who we tell anything to, including Tom and Norma. We do not want this insane maniac to know that they are alive and most likely that they may be in the area. That is if he or she doesn't know already. Also Damon, if Adam and Ellen are back in the area, it probably means that Adam has decoded the last cipher that he found with the gold and now knows the exact location of the treasure."

"Lora, you could be in great danger, the killer has already killed five and maybe six people trying to eliminate Adams contact to draw him back or to get information."

"No, I don't think so, because if Adam is back, I have become insignificant."

"I'm afraid not. What are you doing right now?"

"Talking to you and waiting for Adam to call."

"Exactly, you are still his contact. The killer might not know that Adam might be back also."

"Oh God Damon, you're right, I'm still the best way to find Adam. The killer might not know that I am Adam's contact. There is also that book, I have no idea why I was sent it."

"What book, where is it?"

"A book Adam sent to me, I got it about a month ago. There was a note with it, said to enjoy reading it and that he would get it back from me when he got here in a few days. But that was almost a month ago and he is just now getting here."

"Where is this book now?"

"It is at your house. You don't really think I am in any real danger do you."

"That is a chance I'm not prepared to take. I need to get you out of here and to someplace safe."

"What about Adam, I need to wait for him to contact or call me?"

"Why do you have to wait? I want you out of this mess; you have done what you promised to do. Your part is finished. I don't care about the stupid treasure, you are my treasure and I don't want anything to happen to you."

"I don't care about the treasure either, I wish I had never heard of it or gotten involved in this."

"Get your things Honey; I'll put Ranger and Smoky in the car. We will just leave your car here for now."

"Where are we going?"

"I don't know. I just know we aren't staying here."

I just started driving, with no destination in mind. I turned frequently and kept a close eye on my rear view mirrors to make sure that no one was following us. The whole time I was trying to think of somewhere I could take Lora that she would be safe.

I pulled over at a pay phone, to call Norma. It had occurred to me that if Adam could not get hold of Lora, his next logical choice would be Norma.

"Tom, this is Damon. I don't have the time to go into detail with you about everything right now, but Adam and Ellen may be in the area and may try to get in touch with Norma."

"How can you be so sure? What is going on anyway?"

"I don't have time to explain everything to you right now, Tom. You just have to take my word for it. Where is Norma? Is she still in the hospital?"

"No, I picked her up yesterday; she is here at the house with me. She is asleep and cannot come to the phone. She is in a lot of pain and can not move around."

"Good, you both just stay there and be very careful. Whoever is doing this is starting to get panicky I think and may do anything at this point. Be sure that if Adam contacts Norma, that you also tell him to be very careful and to trust no one accept you, me, Norma and Lora."

"What if I need to get hold of you Damon?"

"Call Kelly Williams at the police department, tell her to try to reach me on the radio. Other wise I will call you every now and then. If an emergency comes up, call my house and leave a message on my answering machine; I will check my messages if I cannot reach you by phone. Right now I need to find a place for Lora to stay that she will be safe."

"Lora, why is Lora in danger? She is the contact person; I was right after all."

"That is part of what I don't have time to explain. I will tell you everything as soon as I have a chance. Just trust me for now and do what I am telling you to do. Tom, if Adam does call tell Adam that he needs to get in touch with me as soon as he can do it safely. What do you mean you were right after all?"

"Nothing, It just occurred to me yesterday that Lora might be Adams contact. Has she heard from Adam or received anything from him recently?"

"Not for about a month."

"Okay Damon. This is your town and your area of expertise, so for now I will do what you say with no questions asked. You are going to have a lot of explaining to do later."

"I know Tom I think everything is coming to a head, so maybe I won't have so much to explain after all."

While I was talking to Tom, I remembered that I had a cousin that lived in Nelson County. I would call him and see if Lora could stay with him and his family for a while. I remembered my family telling me they had a very secluded house up in the mountains and they had no direct connection to me. No one would ever think to look for Lora there. I changed phones, then called information and got his number. Once he figured out who I was and what my relationship was to him. He gladly agreed to allow Lora to stay with them for a while.

It was not far, but it was dark now and I did not feel comfortable trying to find the place in the dark. I felt it would be better if we stayed in a motel tonight then went up to my cousin the next day. That would also give them time to get to know Lora and I before I left her there with them.

He gave me directions that lead me from a four-lane highway to a two-lane, then a rural road, to a dirt road, to a cow path. We finally were able to find it. Lora was going to be safe there, I was not even sure I could find the place again.

We spent a few hours talking about family and just being acquainted. Then I explained our situation to them, that there was a very good chance that someone was out to kill Lora. My cousin showed me the small arsenal that he claimed was for hunting. However, some of the guns he had, only had one use and it was not hunting, not for animals or birds.

I stayed for dinner, so that Lora would feel comfortable being alone there. Then I headed back for town.

When I got back to my house, I called Kelly and asked her what had been going on. She told me that the County Sheriff had called for me. That they had found Charley Gants speedboat over on the mountain. That it was up in the woods about thirty feet from the edge of the water. The place it hit the mountain was straight across the lake from Charley's house. The fact that it had gone so far up into the woods was why it took them so long to find it.

The Sheriff also said there had been no sign of Hank Jones and wanted to know what you wanted to do about him.

"List him as missing or whatever you have to do?"

"Hanks last name is Jones."

"Sheriff said that is what he told the people at the hospital when they were trying to admit him."

"No, don't do anything about him right now. I don't know what we would do anyway we know nothing about him. Has Tom Knight called?"

"No, not that I know of."

I had left Smoky with Lora, but had brought Ranger back to the house with me. I was about to turn in for the night when Ranger started barking and going crazy to get out. The only time he ever acted like this was when someone was messing around outside. I let Ranger out and he went around to the lower side of the house and into the woods chasing something. Then I heard a pistol shot and Ranger stopped barking.

I had my gun and followed the direction that Ranger had taken into the woods. I was calling his name and looking around for any sign of him. Then I heard a noise off to my left. I found Ranger he had a gun shot wound in the shoulder. He would probably make it if I got him help quickly. I took him up and put him in the car, then locked the house and rushed him to the emergency animal hospital.

As soon as I arrived, they started working on him. I had to wait outside the operating room and had no idea how bad he was hurt or what they were doing to save him. It had been almost three hours when the doctor came out to talk to me. He handed me the slug that he had removed from Ranger and told me that he was going to make it and would be fine in a week or so. They needed to keep him there at least for a couple of days.

Ranger, was very important to me, I have raised him from a puppy. Up until Lora came into my life a few weeks ago, Ranger was the most important thing in my life, other than my family. I got up at sunrise even though I had only had a couple hours of sleep. To go out and look around to see if I could find anything that may give me a clue as to who may have shot him.

I got lucky for a change; I did find the shell casing that had ejected from the pistol when they shot Ranger. It was as I thought, it was a nine-millimeter automatic shell casing, the same as I use in my own gun. I was sure it must have been someone looking for Lora. I was so glad I had taken her to my cousins where she would be safe.

This case was becoming very personal to me now. Friends hurt or killed, people I knew murdered, Lora's life and safety placed in jeopardy and now my dog shot. Yes, it was getting very personal to me and I was determined to bring this person or people to justice. No, matter what I had to do to accomplish that.

I took the shell casing I had found and the slug that the vet had removed from Ranger to ballistics. I was hoping they could determine something from them that would help. Then I drove over to Norma's house, to see her and Tom. I knew they would be hungry for information as to what was going on and how I had come into possession of some of that information.

When I got there, I did not see Norma's car out front in its usual parking place. Of course Toms van was not there, it had been totaled in the accident. I knocked on the door hard enough to wake the dead. When no one came to the door, I knocked even harder. There was still no sign of anyone. I listened at the door and could here voices, it sounded like it may be the television.

I walked around to the rear of the house and went to the back door. It was wide open so I went on in to look around. The television was on in the bedroom and the volume turned up very loud. I could see nothing out of the ordinary about the house. It was a mess; it had also been a mess the last time I was there, when I had come to question Norma. Then as I was heading toward the back door through the kitchen, to leave; I noticed a couple wet looking spots on the floor in the kitchen. They could be blood, so I took a paper towel and soaked one up. They had just looked wet; they were actually dry and hard. If it was blood, it had been on the floor long enough to dry, at least several hours.

I felt the need to wash my hands after handling what ever that was on the floor. Afterward I grabbed another paper towel from the roll to dry my hands off. As I was about to throw the two in the waste can, I noticed a piece of paper with what appeared to be a phone number on it. I reached into the waste can and retrieved it. The number was familiar to me, I knew this number, I had seen it recently. I went over to the phone and dialed the number. I got a recording saying, "This number is out of order". I put the paper with the number on it in my pocket and left the house the same as I had found it, TV on loud and the back door wide open.

I got in my car and drove off, still thinking about where I knew that number. I had only driven a couple blocks before I pulled to the curb to look at the number again. I pulled it from my pocket and sat staring at it a minute. Then it hit me, the prefix was that of the lake area. I got the direction that Charley Gant had given me to the lake house out of the glove box. He had me write the phone number to the lake house on the directions. It was the same. Why would Norma or Tom have the number to Charley Gants lake house?

Maybe Lora gave it to them, in case they needed to get hold of us for some reason. Yes, that must be it. With my mind at ease, I pulled out and continued driving. Suddenly it hit, Lora could not have given either of them the number. I had not given it to Lora. Then how and why did they have it.

I was also very curious about Hank Jones, if that was really his name. I would also like to know what might have happened to him. It was strange that he apparently wanted to keep his identity a secret. What was even stranger was that he checked himself out of the hospital minutes after Lora and I had left the building. Then there was Charley Gants house catching fire. The smoke and water damage to the whole house had eliminated any chance of finding anything to lead to his identity had been destroyed. There were no personal items of his at the house and no photographs of him either.

He had made no effort to check on Charley's condition or try to see Charley. For a man that was suppose to be in love with someone. Hank was demonstrating a total lack of concern, so this all leads me to believe that someone had taken him or he had something to hide. In either case, I wanted to find Hank and ask him a few questions. Right now, we had him listed as a missing person, also as a person of interest, wanted for questioning.

I left Tom and Norma's house with more questions than I had when I got there. When I was thinking that, maybe some of my questions would have answers after talking to Tom and Norma. The fact that they where not there and the way the house was left open with the TV on, was also very strange. Then there were the drops of blood on the floor, if in fact it was blood. I just hope they are both all right and would be in touch with me soon. That seemed to be the nature of the case. Every time you found the answer to one question, it would just lead to more questions.

It was after lunch and I had not eaten much in the last two days. I would just pick at my food and eat a couple bites leaving the majority of it on my plate. I went to the dinner that Ellen had worked at and I first had lunch with Lora. It was not so much that I was hungry, but being their made me feel like I was a little closer to Lora. It ended up that I had a cup of coffee and a grilled cheese sandwich.

The server ask me how Norma and her boyfriend where getting along since the accident. I told her fine that they where back home. Then she said:

"Norma's boyfriend looks so much better since he shaved that beard off and much younger also. He did not have it when he first started coming in here. I don't know what possessed him to start grow it."

"I didn't know he ever had a beard."

"Yes he had it for a couple weeks a while back. I guess Norma must have objected to it, because he shaved it off after only having it about a week."

Chapter 15

I was afraid to trust anyone with Lora's location; I also did not trust using any phones other than pay phones. So a couple times a day, I would find a pay phone to call her on, never using the same one twice. I missed her a great deal; it just was not the same coming home without Lora there to great me. I missed her most at night; I had gotten use to feeling her body next to me and hearing the sound of her breathing.

She was very upset when I told her what had happened to Ranger, she had grown very attached to him and loved him almost as much as I did. She felt a little better when I told her that the doctor at the animal hospital had told me that Ranger was recovering nicely. That I could pick him up in a couple days, but to be sure he still took it easy.

Lora was concerned that Adam had made no effort to contact anyone that she was aware. She felt sure that he would make an effort to get in touch with Norma. As soon as he realized that, he was unable to contact her any longer.

The fact that Charley's friend Hank had apparently disappeared also bothered her a great deal. She was afraid that something terrible might have happened to him. That maybe he shared the fate that they intended for Charley and is now at the bottom of the lake. I told her that I did not think so, because his car was not at the house, only Charley's two cars were there.

So many people had been hurt, killed or their lives disrupted by the craziness that seemed to have no end. Anyone involved, automatically assumed the worst when anything out of the ordinary happened to anyone. I had decided not to tell Lora about my visit to Norma's house nor what I found there. I did ask her if I had given her Charley's lake house phone number. Her answer of course was no.

In all my years as a police officer, I have never had a case that had affected me so personally. Nor have I ever had a case that was so frustrating to me. I guess it could be because I was involved so closely in so many ways, too personally connected to see the obvious. Maybe I should turn it over to someone that is more distant and disconnected from it. The fact is that I want to be the one that brings this person or persons to justice. I want to be the one that is responsible for seeing that they pay for every ounce of misery, pain and heartache that they have caused for a great many people, me included. This was no longer just my job; it had become a personal vendetta. I don't like any criminal, but I never really hated one the way I hate this one. I have never been more determined to catch anyone before, as I am to catch these people.

The perpetrator of these crimes could be anyone. Fifty million is a big incentive to turn even an honest man or woman into a manic and killer. That was my dilemma; this killer could be virtually anyone. The only thing that set them aside was their uncanny ability to commit these crimes, leaving little to no evidence behind. They almost had to have some knowledge of criminal investigation as well as a working knowledge of explosives and human behavior. They also needed one more thing; they were getting inside information from right there in the police department.

There had to be a cop involved, more than once the statement surfaced in the investigation, that the police department could not be trusted. There was the theft of the C-4 from the property room. The security there might not be great, but only a cop could have gotten in there to steal it. I decided to try a long shot, at this point any shot was better than none.

I called Kelly, Bill, Bob and Sara into my office and told them to run a check on everyone in the department from the Chief down to the janitor. Look for education in criminal justice, psychology and demolitions. We were looking for someone with above average intelligence, which may have served in the military. Most importantly, the names of anyone that may have shown any interest in the Beale treasure.

"Lieutenant this is going to be hard to do without people in the department knowing about it and questioning us as to why we are doing it." Kelly stated.

"I know, but everything that we have, as little as it might be, leads me to believe that at least one of these killers is a cop and right here in our own department."

"We will do our best Lieutenant and try to keep what we are doing as quiet as possible."

"I'm sure you will Kelly." I said as I reached into my desk drawer and took out a box and an envelope.

"That is why your promotion to Sergeant was approved. Congratulation Sergeant Williams."

I handed her the box containing a gold Sergeants badge and the envelope with her confirmation in it. There were a few moments of jubilation from her fellow detectives as Kelly removed her old badge from her badge case and replaced it with the gold Detective Sergeants badge.

However, there were people in the room that had been with the department, much longer than Kelly. Everyone seemed to agree that she had earned the promotion and completely deserved it. There seemed to be no jealousy or resentment among her fellow detectives that where present anyway. I was sure that Jack Morris wouldn't be very happy about it, but Jack was seldom happy about anything.

That reminded me to ask Bob Leonard, how his partner was doing. If he was, still ill and when he expected to come back to work. As limp as Jack was, we still could use every available man on this case.

"Bob, how is Jack doing?"

"Not sure Lieutenant, it is hard to get him to answer his phone. I guess he is sleeping a lot with the medication he is taking for the flu."

"How are you and Sara getting along working together?"

Bob closed my office door. "Lieutenant, I've been meaning to ask you about that."

"Ask me what Bob?"

"I have been wondering if we could make it permanent."

"You mean you want to keep Sara as your partner, instead of Jack."

"Yes Lieutenant, I really prefer working with Sara. Jack is fine and a good cop, but to tell you the truth. Sometimes I wonder if his elevator goes all the way to the top. I don't mean to belittle him in anyway, but you have to admit Lieutenant that at times he seems a little screwy and doesn't use his head as he should always."

"I can't comment on that, but if you want to keep Sara as your partner. I don't see a problem with that. Consider it done."

"Thanks Lieutenant."

Bob left my office a much happier man. I went down to Ballistics Lab, to check on what they had found out on that slug and shell casing. My theories of the possibility of a bad cop in my own department; were calibrated and intensified by what I read in the ballistics report. The slug and casing were the same as we issued there at the department. Also by the hammer strike on the casing, the weapon that fired it was a standard police issue automatic.

For the first time since this case began. I felt we might be on the right track. As much as I hated the idea that we might have a bad cop among us, if we did we need to weed him out.

As I headed home, I could not get the thought out of my head. The words "Dirty Cop" left a bad taste in my mouth. I could not help but wonder who it might be. Fifty million was a big incentive to turn a good man bad, even a cop.

The house was ominously empty, no Lora or Ranger to greet me. I even missed that little fur ball of Lora's, Smoky. Not wanting to remain there alone, I decided to just take a shower and change cloths then head back to town. I would go back by Norma's and see if Tom and her were there or had been there. Then grab a bite to eat somewhere and go back to the office.

When I came out of the shower, the phone was ringing. It was Kelly.

"Lieutenant, we need to see you right away!"

"Okay, Kelly. I will be back at the office in about thirty minutes."

"Sir, if you don't mind I think it would be better if we came to your house."

"You and Bill have something."

"Possibly we do. On what you wanted us to check on. I don't think we should discuss it over the phone if you don't mind?"

"All right Kelly, you and Bill come on out to the house, I'll be waiting."

"Sara and Bob are coming also."

"Okay, that is fine, Bring them with you."

I finished getting dressed and put some coffee on. I was sure from the sound of Kelly's voice that we may need it or even something stronger. She seemed very distressed with their findings.

It was about fifteen minutes before the two cars pulled into the driveway. I went to the front door to greet them. Then we all got a cup of coffee and took seats in the living room, to discuss what they had found.

"Okay, what did you come up with?" I asked.

"Your not going to be happy about it, Lieutenant, you aren't going to like it at all in fact."

"Tell me, let me be the judge of whether I like it or not."

"Okay, we found one person in the whole department that fits what you told us to look for, to a tee."

"Who was that?"

"First let me explain why they fit, then we will tell you, who."

"Okay."

"This person was born and raised in Bedford County about two miles from the location of the old Buford's Inn. He wrote his senior paper in High School on the Beale Treasure. He was a Captain with an engineer battalion in the army. He was in charge of demolitions and was an expert in its usage. When he got out of the Army, he finished getting his masters degree in psychology but did not enter the field. He became interested in Law Enforcement while in college, so he also got a degree in Criminal Justice while he was on the Virginia Beach Police Department. He also has the IQ of a near genius. Also he has seen every report on this case, but hasn't shown the slightest interest in it even though he was acquainted with everyone involved and good friends to a couple of them. Like the Mayor, Dr. Kline and Mr. Doorman."

"Okay, Kelly. Who is this person?"

"Scott Barker."

"You are talking about the Police Commissioner!"

"Yes Sir. Scott Barker the Police Commissioner."

"Wow, I didn't expect this. He is the only one that you came up with and you checked every one in the department?"

"Yes Lieutenant. Everyone accept the members of our own squad."

"I said everyone."

"Yes, but most of the squad, was involved in doing the checking, so we didn't see the need."

"I wanted you all to check each other out also, but never mind that now. Looks as if we may have found our fish, I just was expecting it to be a shark, not a whale. Your right as big as this case is, he has not asked me a single question in reference to it."

"This came as a total shock to all of us, Lieutenant. That is why we felt the need to come out here and inform you right away and in person."

"Bob, you and Sara start keeping an eye on the Commissioner. However, for God's sake, don't let him find out you are doing it. Kelly, you and Bill see what else you can dig up on him. All of you keep in mind that if we are wrong, this man can put us all out to dry. So be very careful and discrete in doing anything. If it is Scott Barker and he finds out that we are onto him we will all be in a lot of danger. Remember he may have already been involved in the deaths of five people along with the attempted murder of Lieutenant Gant and the disappearance of this man Hank."

"Lieutenant"

"Yes Bob, you have something to add."

"No, I just wanted to inform you that I talked to Jack tonight and he is coming in to work tomorrow."

"Did you mention to him anything about you and Sara being partners now or that Kelly made Sergeant?"

"No Sir. I thought I would leave that honor up to you, Lieutenant."

"Thanks a lot Bob."

That ended the meeting on a lighter note, at least everyone left with a smile on his or her faces. Except me of course, I was the one that was going to have to tell Jack all the news in the morning.

I wanted to call Lora, to see if she could add anything to this new development with Scott Barker. I drove to a payphone up the road near a restaurant, where I figured on eating after I spoke with her. After a few minutes of saying how much we missed and loved each other I was able to get to the point of the call.

"Lora, What all can you tell me about Scott Barker?"

"Well, he is the Police Commissioner of course and he would come to the Mayor's office to talk with Caldwell often."

"What did they talk about?"

"Public officials always seem to lean their conversation to the same subjects City affairs, politics and police business."

"What about the Beale Treasure, did they ever talk about that?"

"Yes, Often. Mayor Caldwell knew that Mr. Barker had spent his young life in that area of Bedford County. So the Mayor was always asking him about something to do with the treasure or the geography of the area."

"So, the Commissioner was not a member of the Mayor's treasure group and had never been involved in it."

"No, In fact it always seemed to annoy him that the Mayor was asking him question all the time about it."

"You mean, like angry?"

"No Damon, More like he was disgusted with the idea of talking about it. That it was a total annoyance to him to answer the Mayors questions in regard to the treasure."

"Do you remember anything more about Barker or the treasure?"

"Only that he gave Mayor Caldwell a copy of a paper he had written in High School about the Beale Treasure."

"Did you read the paper Lora?"

"Yes, I did. I found it very interesting and well done. It did not surprise me that he had gotten an A plus- on it. He really is a very intelligent man. He stated in the paper that he felt that Thomas Beale was a jokester and that the whole thing was a hoax. Either that Beale was trying to play an elaborate joke on Robert Morris or he was trying to get even with him about something. He didn't believe that the treasure has ever existed."

"Really, that is interesting."

"Yes, In fact he was really shocked, when the Mayor hinted to him that a large deposit of gold had been discovered with another cipher with it."

"Mayor Caldwell told him that?"

"Yes, the Mayor was trying to convince the Commissioner that his interest in the treasure was not a waist of time. Because the Commissioner had made the comment that the Mayor and his friends were crazy for spending so much time and money looking for something that didn't exist."

"Holy Cow Lora! I wish you had told me this when this whole thing started. Of course there were several important things you neglected to tell me."

"Damon, I told you I was very sorry about that. You can't let that go and now why all these questions about Scott Barker?"

I spent the next few minutes explaining to Lora what we had found, and why the Commissioner was of great interest to us in this case. She was happy that we were making some progress in the investigation. She really liked my cousin and his family, but she felt out of place there. She wanted to come home and be with me. That was good news to me, because I wanted her home also but not until there was no longer a risk that any harm would come to her.

Reluctantly I said good night and hung up the phone. Then I went into the restaurant to get dinner. I was not able to eat much; I had far too much on my mind. I knew I would need to talk to Scott Barker the next day. I also knew I had to handle it very diplomatically. I would need to question him in a manner that didn't tip him off to the fact that I was questioning him. After all, he was my boss and I don't think he would take kindly to knowing he was a suspect in a murder investigation.

I also needed to keep in mind that everything we had on him was purely circumstantial; we had no hard evidence to link him to any of the crimes. In fact, if I were able to choose my suspects, he would be way down on the bottom of my list of choices.

Scott had never struck me as the greedy type. He was a public servant, drawing a meager salary in comparison to what he could be earning doing something else. He had the brains and education to get a much higher paying job than Police Commissioner.

The more I thought about it the more ridiculous it seemed that he would be involved in these crimes. That kind of money can make many people do things you would never think they were capable of. He was, as of right now, our prime suspect. He had the background and knowledge. The motive could be the money involved.

I did not relish the idea of going back to my lonely house. I knew I would need to try to get some sleep. The ordeal that I had to face in the morning was going to require a rested alert mind. If we were wrong I could find myself without a job.

The next morning I awakened abruptly from my restless sleep by the loud sound of a clap of thunder. What a gloomy rainy day, the kind of day that did not bring the best out in people. Bad weather had a tendency to make people more irritable and a lot less understanding. Not at all the type of day I would have preferred under the circumstances.

To add to my frustration and tension filled day, the first person I encountered as I got to the station was Jack Morris. He was in the coffee room pouring the last drop of coffee out of the pot and into his cup. Then he just stood starring at me with a defying look on his face, while I had to make more coffee. He did not say a word, just looked at me.

"Good morning, Jack. Good to see you back, over your illness and feeling much better."

"Thanks, Lieutenant, for your concern about my well being."

"Jack, I need to talk with you this morning, so as soon as I get a cup of coffee; would you mind joining me in my office for a few minutes?"

"Glad to Lieutenant, I need to be brought up to date about what has been going on while I was ill."

It was clear from Jack's tone of voice and his over all demeanor that he was already aware of some of the changes that had taken place in his absence.

With a fresh cup of coffee in hand, I went to my office. Where I found Jack seated just inside the door. Irritably he ran his finger around the top of his coffee cup. I closed the door behind me, and then took a seat at my desk.

"Well, Jack apparently from your attitude this morning you have already heard something?"

"Yes Lieutenant. If I'm not mistaken, I heard Sara refer to Kelly as Sergeant Williams this morning."

"That is correct Jack, Kelly was promoted to Sergeant."

"That is just wonderful, I am very happy for her. The fact is that I have been a detective for fifteen years and a patrol officer for ten years before that. These years have given me the opportunity to first see you, come in and get promoted over me, which pleases me to no end, and now I get to see Kelly, which has been with the department all of five years, promoted over me as well. Maybe if I'm really lucky I will still be a detective when they promote Bob or Sara also."

"Jack, I'm sorry that you had to learn about it in that manner. I was hoping I would have a chance to talk to you beforehand."

"Why would you want to talk to me Lieutenant? Just to tell me that I am going to be retiring on a detective's pension in a couple of years; rather than retiring on the pension of a Captain, Lieutenant or even a Sergeant, that I have not only earned but deserve."

"Jack, I understand how you feel."

"Do you Lieutenant? I don't think you do! How could you? You have received unearned citations and promotions on a silver platter, since you joined this Police Department. But you had a college degree that you got while I was already out here protecting your sorry ass!"

"Jack, I think you have said enough. I will do you the favor of forgetting about this. As far as I'm concerned this conversation is off the record and never took place."

"Frankly, Damon, I don't give a damn if this is on the record or not. I also hope you remember every word of it, because the day will come soon that you and this department will regret how I have been treated and screwed over."

"Jack, I suggest that you shut up right now while you still have a job and a pension. What you just said could constitute a threat to me as well as the department. This is a ground for dismissal, so I recommend that you just go back to your desk. You only have two more years to retirement, don't screw up now."

"Lieutenant, if you don't mind? I think I will get Bob and go out on the road and get away from this cesspool for a while."

"That sounds like a good idea Jack, why don't you do that? Go calm that temper of yours and maybe get some breakfast or something. Also, I have put Sara with Bob, so for right now you don't have a partner."

"That is fine with me. In fact it is better than fine, it is great. Maybe if I'm working alone, I will get credit for what I do and not have it given to some other idiot to get them a promotion instead of me."

"Okay Jack, I get the point. You are dismissed."

Wow, that was much worse than I thought it was going to be. I did not expect it to be pleasant but I was not expecting Jack to go off the deep end like that either. His reaction to Kelly's promotion gave me serious concerns about his mental stability. It is not as if he did not know that Kelly was up for Sergeant. Everyone in the department knew she was under consideration for promotion. Actually, I expected him to be more upset about the fact that I had put Bob and Sara together. He seemed almost happy about that.

I called Scott Barker's office to set up an appointment to see him. They told me that he was out of the office this morning, but that he could see me around two o'clock. That was fine with me, it would give me time to get over my run in with Jack and get my wits together again.

When two o'clock came, I took Kelly and Bill with me to the Commissioner's Office. I also posted a couple people outside the building. I did not know what to expect, if he was involved there was no telling what reaction he may have when and if he felt discovered. Of course, Kelly and Bill remained outside of Scott's office in the waiting area.

"To what do I owe this visit, Lieutenant Carter?"

"I wanted to discuss this case with you Commissioner. You either know or did know several of the people involved. Actually I'm a little surprised that you haven't gotten in contact with me about it."

"I've been keeping abreast of what is going on in the case, Lieutenant. You and your people have filed reports that are very accurate and informative. I really haven't seen the need to question you about it; although to my knowledge you don't have a suspect right now but I am not the least bit concerned. You and your team are on top of things and doing a good job of investigating it without my interference."

"Since you where friends with a couple of the victims, would you mind if I ask you a few questions, Commissioner?"

"Not at all Lieutenant ask me anything you want. I will be glad to answer any questions you may have if it will help bring this insanity to a quick end."

"Sir, I understand that Mayor Caldwell told you that they had found some gold in connection with the Beale Treasure. Is that correct, did the Mayor tell you that?"

"Yes he did, I was telling him that I felt that the Beale Treasure was an elaborate hoax and he told me that in an effort to convince me otherwise, but a little bit of gold does not constitute a treasures existence."

"Two hundred pounds of gold is not a little bit, Commissioner."

"Two hundred pounds Wow! Now that is a lot of gold. He did not tell me that they had recovered two hundred pounds. What is that worth today?"

"That would be worth about one million three-hundred-thousand dollars."

"Really, that much, I had no idea. Now if he had told me that, I would have been more interested. That much gold would draw a lot of attention. Where is it now and who has it?"

"Supposedly it is in Adam Knight's possession. He kept it to use to keep his location secret while he worked on deciphering the last cipher that was found with the gold."

"A find of that magnitude does add to the validity of the treasure considerably. I thought Adam was a missing person, he and his girlfriend."

"Not missing Commissioner, they are in hiding."

"I'm beginning to think the reports I read were not as complete as I thought they where."

"I understand that you where in the Army?"

"Yes, I was a Lieutenant. I was with an engineer battalion, I got out in 1966 but not before I served a tour in Vietnam."

"Really, I was in Vietnam also. What type of work did you do with the engineers?"

"Blew up bunkers and other things, I was in demolitions."

"Then you went to college again when you got out of the service, for psychology if I'm not mistaken and got your masters degree, right?"

"Yes, that is correct. Lieutenant, what has this line of questioning of my life got to do with the case you are working on solving?"

"Just interested sir, I don't really know much about you, but I will confine my line of questioning to the case at hand if you wish."

"Well, if I didn't know better, I would think you were questioning me as a suspect in the case."

"You, a suspect? Sir! No not you, not at all."

"Lieutenant, I might not call my officers in on a regular basis but that doesn't mean that I don't know what is going on in my own department. You had your people check the personal files on almost everyone in the Police Department, including me. You used certain keywords in your checking through the personal files. You used military service, demolitions, psychology, Beale treasure and Bedford County. I am sure I came up as one of your closest matches."

"You did this because you believe that someone inside our department is involved in this crime. There is the C-4 missing from the evidence room that was used to kill Dr. Kline. So whoever the killer is, has knowledge of demolitions. He must also have a real good knowledge of psychology to be able to convince and push the right button for Mr. Kent to kill himself. I'm also sure that the Mayor's secretary informed you that the Mayor talked to me often of his interest in finding the Beale Treasure."

"Well congratulations Lieutenant on a job well done."

"Commissioner, are you telling me you are the man I am looking for?"

"No of course not Lieutenant, I am congratulating you for the fine job you are doing on this case. You are not leaving any stone unturned and you are right I fit perfectly to your profile of the killer. I admire your investigative skills and techniques and the fact that you are taking nothing for granted.. I almost hate to tell you after you have gone to so much trouble, but I was in New York visiting my family when Dr. Kline's was murdered, also when the Mayor was murdered. In addition, while Mr. Kent was being convinced he had to shoot himself in order to save his family; I was in a City Council Meeting trying to get the Department a larger budget for next year so I can buy much needed equipment and give fine officers like yourself a raise in pay."

"I apologize, Commissioner if I was wrong. But in a case like this we have to follow up on any hunch or lead."

He started laughing and patted me on the back.

"No need to apologize Lieutenant, you are doing your job. That is exactly why I am not having you down here to explain to me every little thing you are doing. I know you are doing everything it takes to bring this case to a satisfactory-conclusion as soon as possible. I also have no reservation that you will do exactly that and apprehend these killers in the near future. You just keep up the good work Lieutenant and don't worry about stepping on toes. You just find out who is responsible for these crimes and put them away, one way or the other."

I left the Commissioners office, somewhat relieved, but also a little disappointed. Here we are right back to square one, with no leads and no suspects. Of course, I would check out the Commissioner's alibis, but I was certain they would prove to be valid.

Chapter 16

The uncertainties of this case seemed to be greatly abundant and were challenging to say the least. I could use a few less of them and a few more solid clues. The only thing I felt relatively certain about was that at least one of the criminals involved in this case was in my own Police Department. That was the only explanation for the theft of the C-4 from the department armory and the fact that the criminal seems to know exactly what we are doing at all times.

I took Kelly and Bill into my office when I returned.

"What happened with the Commissioner, Lieutenant?"

"Nothing, He was up front and honest about everything. He also has an alibi for the time that all the killings took place. We will confirm his alibis but I am reasonably confident that Scott Barker is not our man. But I'm almost certain that someone in this department is."

"We feel the same way Lieutenant, but who?"

"Who was the next logical suspect on your list after Commissioner Scott, Kelly?

"Not Chief Lewis, he came from Norfolk and hadn't been here long enough. Major Taylor was on vacation with his family in the Bahamas when the Mayor and Dr. Kline were murdered. I think you have already eliminated Captain Mirant and of course, we know Lieutenant Gant is above suspicion because he is a victim. That is the entire supervisory staff in the department that would have had access to all the files without us knowing about it."

"Who said it had to be a command officer, it could be anyone in the Detective Bureau? Anyone in the Bureau would have access to the information regarding this case?"

"For that matter, it could be Bill or I."

"Yes, it could be, but I hope not. You are two of the only officers I really feel I can trust with any certainty at this point."

"Why thank you, Lieutenant. I consider that a real compliment. So you don't mind telling us where you stashed Lora?"

"I said I trusted you with some certainty, not that I completely trusted you."

Kelly and Bill both started laughing aloud.

"Well so much for feeling honored. Kelly said laughing. I was just kidding Lieutenant. I knew you wouldn't tell us and frankly, I wouldn't want to know."

"I want the two of you to go back over the personnel files of everyone in the Detective Bureau and this time I want you to do everyone, even each other. Start with the files in our squad that you didn't do the last time."

Sara stuck her head in the door.

"Lieutenant, you have a call on line three, it is Tom Knight."

"Okay Sara, tell him I will be with him in a minute, to just hang on."

"Kelly, Bill, you have any questions?"

"No, Lieutenant."

"Then you know what to do, so go do it."

I took Tom's call after Kelly and Bill had left and closed the door to my office behind them.

"Damon, Adam just called."

"Great, where is he?"

"He wouldn't say, but it was great to hear his voice after thinking he was dead for so long."

"What did he say Tom?"

"He is in the area and he wants to meet with the three of us."

"Who is the three?"

"Lora, Norma, and of course myself are the three."

"What about me Tom?"

"I tried to talk to him about you, but he said that at least one of these people that have been killing off his associates is in the Police Department, he is not sure who it is. He is afraid there maybe more than one."

"Well, Lora is not going to meet anyone without me. You can tell Adam that, I want to solve this case but not at the risk of Lora. So if I don't come, neither does Lora."

"Okay Damon, I'll tell him. He is supposed to call me back in about ten minutes."

While I was waiting for Tom to talk to Adam and call me, back. I called my cousin from my office phone and told him to bring Lora down to a store about halfway to town. That I had stopped at while I was there, I wrote down the number of the pay phone. We planned for him to bring her to the store and wait by the phone for me to call so I could tell her that Adam wanted to meet with her.

When I hung up the phone, I noticed the light on that line did not go off immediately as it should have. I took a quick look around the squad room to see who might have been on the phone. Almost everybody there was on the phone, so it did not give me a clue as to who may have been listening. I knew I should not use my office phone to call up there, but I was waiting for Tom to call me back and I had no choice in the matter.

When Tom called back, he told me that Adam wanted to talk to me before he agreed to let me meet with him and Ellen. That he understood how I felt about Lora because he felt the same way about Ellen. He said that I should go to the pay phone at the diner where Ellen had worked and he would call me there in twenty minutes. That did not give me time to go pick up Lora.

I trusted Kelly and Bill, I could send the two of them to pick up Lora and have them take her to my house and stay there with her. I agreed to be at the phone at the diner.

I then told Kelly and Bill where to meet Lora and what they should do with her. That gave me just enough time to get to the diner to receive Adam's phone call.

When the man called saying he was Adam, his voice sounded vaguely familiar. I was able to convince him that I was on the level and my only interest in this whole matter was to put the people in prison that had been responsible for the murders and other crimes, I had no interest, what-so-ever in the Beale Treasure.

I told Adam, or whomever, I was talking to, that I had sent two detectives to pick up Lora and that she would be available in less than an hour.

He told me to get Lora and that he would tell Tom where to meet Ellen and him. That Tom would let me know. All this cloak-and-dagger business was beginning to get to me, but under the circumstances, I could understand the precautions he was taking.

I called Tom and told him to call me at my house and give me the information about the meeting and that Lora and I would be there.

I was on my way to the house, expecting Kelly and Bill to be there in a few minutes with Lora. When they did not show I called them on my car radio.

"Lieutenant, two men wearing ski masks and overalls where waiting here when Lora and your cousin arrived. They knocked your cousin unconscious and took Lora."

"What! They have Lora?"

"Yes Sir. I'm afraid so."

"What were they driving and which way were they headed?"

"No one seems to know their vehicle was behind the building and they had left by the time anyone realized what was going on."

"I'm on my way up there. How is my cousin?"

"He is fine but he is going to have a real headache for a while."

I turned on my red lights and headed toward the store as fast as I could. I kept my eye on the traffic while scanning everything else in hopes that I would see Lora.

I did not take the time to call Tom and tell him what was happening. I figured that when he could not reach me at the house that he and Adam would call off the meeting anyway.

When I reached the store, the rescue squad was there treating my cousin. The county Sheriff and a couple of his deputies were there along with Kelly and Bill.

The moment my cousin noticed me coming toward him, he started crying and said. "Damon, I'm so sorry, they took me by surprise, and then one of them hit me with his gun. They took Lora with them. Oh my God, I am so sorry I let you down Damon."

"You couldn't help it. I am sorry I put you in jeopardy. Did you see anything that could give us a clue as to who they were or where they might be heading with Lora?"

"No nothing. We pulled in near the pay phone. When we got out of the car, they came out of the bushes behind the phone. One grabbed Lora and the other hit me with his gun. I am so sorry Damon. You trusted me and I have let you down."

"Hey, you did me a big favor by protecting Lora like you did."

"Yes, I did a great job of protecting her, didn't I?"

My one and only concern was getting Lora back safe. I was not putting blame on anyone except the bastard's that took her. It occurred to me just then that the people that have Lora might contact Tom. I used the pay phone to call him.

"Tom, they got Lora."

"What, how did they manage that?"

"Right now that doesn't matter, the fact is they do have her and I want her back. They may contact you. If they do, you get in touch with me right away. They don't want her dead; if they did they would have killed her right here. So they are probably going to use her to make a trade."

"Trade for what Damon? Oh, I guess they want my brother."

"Probably, or they might want any information he can give them about that stupid treasure!"

"Forget it, Damon. I just got my brother back after thinking he was dead for a year. I am not about to turn him over to a couple crazed killers so they can torture him to get information."

"You think I'm going to let that happen?"

"You let them take Lora didn't you?"

"Listen Tom, if it wasn't for your brother and all his secrecy and cloak-and-dagger crap she wouldn't have been in danger. If he would have told me who the bad cop is and would have just come to the station; instead of all these secret meetings and going through six ways to Sunday to talk to anyone. Lora would still be safe where I had her hiding. It also wouldn't have been necessary if it wasn't for Adam that seems to have this need to keep everything so secretive."

"Don't blame my brother for your incompetence, Damon."

"All right Tom, this is getting us nowhere. The fact is that they do have Lora and I need you and Adam to help me get her away from them."

"You are right, Damon. I'm sorry. That should be our main concern at this point and I am sure Adam will be glad to help, if he can. There is one thing you should know about Adam. He got all the brains and I got all the nerve it seems. Adam is afraid of his own shadow Damon. What I'm telling you is that my brother is a devout coward."

"What you're telling me is that we can't depend on Adam. He won't put himself in any danger. Is that what you are saying Tom?"

"Yes, unfortunately that is what I'm saying. That is why he has been hiding and why all the secrecy. He is scared half to death."

"Tom, I'm going back to my office just in case they try to call me there. You stay at Norma's; they are bound to call one of us."

When I got back to the office there was a man waiting for me in Charley's office, with Kelly and Bill. Kelly was intent that I speak with him, but right now, my only concern was to find Lora and get her back.

"Kelly please just handle whatever problem he may have. I don't have time to deal with it right now."

Then Kelly told me he was from Langley, Virginia. He was there in response to my phone call the day before. She seemed to feel that it was important that I talk with him. I had called the CIA on a hunch but they gave me the run around and told me that they might have someone get back in touch with me. I cannot believe they sent someone down here. A phone call would have been adequate; I had one simple question to ask about Tom. I had to tell the man I talked to the whole story to get any response at all, which was very little. He did not tell me anything. He just said he would look into it and might have someone get back with me.

I called the police operator and told her to forward any phone calls for me to Charley's office. Then I went to talk to the person from Langley. He confirmed that Tom Knight was an undercover agent for the CIA.

Then the phone rang in Charley's office. It was Tom Knight; he told me that the men that had Lora had contacted him. They wanted to trade Lora for Adam. Adam wouldn't agree to it, that he knew that once they got the information from him he was a dead man. Adam and Ellen were leaving town again and going back into hiding.

"Tom, he can't do that. Doesn't he have any loyalty to Lora for everything she has done to protect him and Ellen?"

"Yes of course he does. That is why he wants to give these people what they want."

"So, Adam is going to give us the information, the cipher he recovered and the decoded message it contained. That would lead to the treasure."

"Yes, but Adam no longer has it. He sent it to Lora a month ago.

"Lora has the cipher and has had it for a month?"

"She didn't know she had it. Because it was concealed in a book that he gave her."

"What book, where is it?"

"You have the book, Damon. Lora took it to your house."

"How do you know that, Tom?"

"Oh, Adam told me."

"How did Adam know that she took it to my house?"

"I don't know Damon, what difference does it make?"

I looked at the man sitting across from me, he was able to here everything that was said. All he did was nod his head in agreement as if to say, just agree and go get the book.

"Okay Tom, I'll get the book and we will trade it for Lora."

I would have liked to spend more time with the man from Langley but I would have to leave him in the capable hands of Kelly and Bill. I needed to go to the house and get the book that Lora had told me that Adam had sent her.

After retrieving the book from the house, I took a razor and carefully opened the edge of the binding. Sure enough, hidden in the binding were three papers. Two very old and the third was the decoded message and an explanation of how it was decoded.

One of the old papers was just another cipher full of numbers. The other said:

> *To find the treasure, first you must know*
> *my associates and who their next of kin are.*

> *Thomas Beale 1820*

At first that made no sense to me. Then I read Adam's explanation of how he solved the cipher.

The key to the last cipher was the second cipher that Beale had left with Robert Morris in 1820. It contained the names of all Beale's associates and a list of their next of kin. Adam had to find the key and decipher the second original cipher before he could decode the fourth and last cipher. Then he numbered it backwards, not by words but by syllables skipping every other one. Now the end of the last cipher made perfect sense.

> *Now hold the secret of exactly were*
> *You must find our kin and give them their share*

> *Each number is a word but the words are not clear*
> *Perhaps to read it you must begin at the rear*

> *Each word in the key you cannot count*
> *You only need half of the total amount*

Adam really must be a genius to figure that out. I would have never come up with it.

I took the three papers and rushed back to the Police Station, to pick up a couple things. One was a second small pistol that I could conceal easier, along with a couple things that I had Kelly and Bill get for me while I was gone.

Then I headed over to Norma's to pick up Tom. He told me that the people that had Lora would exchange her for the ciphers and decoded message. He had the directions to the meeting place and that we were to go there and wait. They would contact us that we were to be unarmed. Then Tom asked me for my gun and asked if I had any other weapons on me.

"No, Tom, I don't carry a back up." I didn't want him to know about the second small gun I had concealed.

"Good, because if we want Lora back, we need to do exactly what these people want?"

"Where is Norma, Tom?"

"Oh, she won't be going with us."

"I didn't think she would be. I just ask where she was."

"She is out."

"Tom, I don't mind telling you that I don't like going to meet these people un-armed. What is to keep these people from killing all three of us once they have the information that they want?"

"I promise you Damon, that they won't kill all three of us."

I believed Tom when he said that. I felt certain that they wouldn't want to kill all three of us.

We stopped at a store near Montvale to wait at the payphone for a call as they had instructed Tom to do. When the phone rang, Tom wanted me to answer it. They want to meet in the vicinity of where the treasure had been, supposedly, hidden. They said they would have Lora with them and would make the exchange as soon as they had located the treasure. Once they had the treasure they would let the three of us go.

Of course, I did not believe that for a minute. Even if they got the treasure we posed a threat to them as long as we were alive. In order to conceal their escape long enough to get away they had to kill us.

I looked at the deciphered message and gave them the first landmark indicated on it. I told them that we would meet them there. From that point, they would be very close to the vault where the treasure was supposed to be.

The first landmark was an old Quaker meetinghouse and cemetery that had been located up near what is now the Jefferson National Forest.

We had to follow the road leading up toward the parkway near Montvale. The Quaker meetinghouse was no longer there, it burned around the time of the Civil War, only the stone foundation and cemetery was still there.

Tom and I arrived there first, so without Tom's knowledge I took the small gun I had and hid it near where I was sitting under a bushy plant. Soon we saw a large truck coming up the road, this was a very secluded location and few people ever used the old road. We were certain they must be the people we were waiting for.

The truck came to a stop, next to my car. Two men wearing ski masks and coveralls got out of the cab. There was no sign of Lora.

"Okay, give us the cipher."

"Not until I see Lora and make sure she is all right."

"She is tied up in the back of the truck. But before you see her, we need to search you for weapons."

Tom and I allowed them to pat us down for weapons, and then we sat back down while they went to get Lora out of the truck. She looked unharmed and was bound and gagged. They walked her over to our location.

"Okay, here is your girlfriend, now where is the cipher?"

I handed the papers to Tom; he looked at them, and then handed them to the two men.

There was an outcrop of rock on the nearby hillside so that when you stood at the south corner of the old Quaker meetinghouse it looked like the side view of the face and head dress of an Indian. Directly beneath it was a group of large rocks, which appeared to be a natural formation that was the location of the treasure. They would need to dig down a few feet on the southwest corner of the group of rocks. In order to gain access to the vault containing the treasure they would need to move a large rock away from the entrance.

The men seemed satisfied that they had the proper information, but wanted to see the treasure before they did anything with us. The two men walked to the back of the truck to get shovels, picks and digging bars. Leaving Lora, Tom and I unguarded which would have given me a chance to recover the gun I had hidden under the bush. I didn't do that for a very good reason.

They returned with the tools showing little concern that we might have gotten away. They no longer even had their weapons out and pointed at us. Then Tom walked over to the two men and turned to face Lora and I.

"I think it is about time that we end this little charade and introduce ourselves properly."

"You know, that might be a good idea, Tom. What is your real name?"

Lora looked at me in amazement. I am sure she wondered what was going on.

"I am Allen Morris, I believe you also know these other two gentleman."

The two men removed their ski masks.

"This is Jack Morris my uncle better known to you as detective Morris and this other gentleman is John Morris, my younger brother. I believe you know him as Hank. We are the descendants of Robert Morris the man that Thomas Beale left the box with the ciphers in the care of in 1820. Our relatives for generations have spent their lives and money to find this treasure. We are the only people that are really entitled to the treasure by our relationship. None of these other people were entitled to it. We had to take some rather drastic measures to ensure that the treasure ended up in the proper hands. I'm sure you can understand that, Damon."

I removed the gag from Lora's mouth, and then took her over to sit in the shade of a nearby tree near the bush I had hidden my gun under. Morris of course came with us, watching us both very carefully the entire time.

"They have a pile of gold bars in the back of that truck, Damon. It most be the gold that Adam and Ellen recovered a year ago."

"Is that right, Morris? Is that the gold that Adam found?"

"Yes, he didn't need it where he was going."

"What happened to him and Ellen?"

"They came back to town a little over a month ago for a meeting with the Mayor and his associates. They tried to contact Norma, but they got me instead. Of course Adam knew that I was not his brother Tom that had disappeared while on a covert mission for the CIA in Afghanistan two years ago. Adam of course knew this, but Norma did not. It was easy for me to pose as Tom Knight. I thought that Norma might be Adam and Ellen's contact person and would eventually lead me to him. I told them that I was Norma's boyfriend and that I would bring her to their location. So they told me where they where."

"Of course I didn't tell Norma that they called. They where out near that water filled rock quarry west of the town of Elon on route 130 where the highway nears the river. They could not have picked a better more secluded spot."

"What did you do with Adam and Ellen, you asshole?" Lora asked.

"Don't worry, lady. They are still together, in their RV at the bottom of the quarry in about two hundred feet of water. John got sort of carried away while questioning Adam. He accidently killed him in the process. Not before he told us he didn't have the cipher, that he had given it to the only person that he really trusted other than Norma. We figured it had to be the person that he trusted and was keeping in contact with the whole time. But unfortunately, Adam died before he disclosed to us the name of that person."

"What about Ellen?"

"Ellen, yes that was unfortunate, Jack hit her with his gun to keep her quiet. I guess he hit her a little too hard. She was dead before Adam. It would have been easier to get information out of Adam if Ellen had still been alive. We could have used her life to bargain with."

"So that is why you started killing off the Mayor and his friends?"

"Yes, we figured that would panic the person he had given the information to and cause them to reveal themselves. We had not figured on the person not knowing that they even had the information. Adam sent your girlfriend Lora the book but did not tell her what it contained. He did, however, tell us that it was in the book before John got carried away and killed him."

"Jack, how did you find out about Tom Knight?"

"After Adam and Ellen disappeared, we started checking his background for any clue that might reveal where he went. I found out about his brother Tom and decided that posing as Adam's brother Tom was a perfect in to Norma."

"How did you find out he was with the CIA?"

"The same way you did Damon. I tried to find information on him, the fact there was none was an indication that he was a spook for somebody. There was also no record of his death. No records for twenty years or more that the man even existed. This also meant, to me, that Norma had never met Tom and knew nothing about him. It really was too perfect to be real. I did not know he was with the CIA, I only assumed he was with one of those agencies. The CIA was as good as any, because I knew that it could not be verified."

While Morris was keeping Lora and I entertained with how clever he had been about everything he had done. Jack and John were busy digging at the stone vault. I knew that when they got to the treasure that they would kill both Lora and I. Then probably put our bodies in the treasure vault once they had removed the treasure. Morris was keeping a gun on us constantly as he talked. He only looked up toward Jack and John occasionally to check on their progress. The bush that concealed my gun was a couple feet away which made it difficult to get to my gun without him seeing me. I needed to keep him talking and hoped something would soon happen to distract him.

"What about the accident that you and Norma where in. Who cut your brake lines?"

"I did, it was supposed to be a staged accident. I knew you were suspicious of me, which prevented me from having the freedom I needed to do everything I needed to do. I cut my own brake line, but I wasn't planning on getting hit by a truck. I was going to flip the van over when I reached the playground in the next block. I damn near killed myself because of you."

"You almost killed Norma also."

"Yes, but I knew she was going to have to go soon anyway, so if she did get killed in the accident it was no big deal."

"What about Norma?"

"What about her? We arranged for her to find her sister and Adam. After the hair drier fell, into her bath water I am not sure if the electricity killed her or hitting her head on the toilet when she fell out of the bathtub.

"She is dead then also?"

"Yes, I'm afraid so. I really did like her, but I knew she would never forgive me for everything I had to do to find the treasure. Then there is the matter of killing her sister. So she had to go, I put her weighted body in the quarry with Adam and Ellen."

Lori was almost sick with grief and fear as she listened to Morris's morbid tail of how he had disposed of her friends. She did not know what my plan was or even if I had one. She knew that if she showed she was afraid we would both be dead in a short time. I did have a plan but my time was running out, I was beginning to get a little worried myself. I had to keep him bragging about how smart he was and how he had made fools of everyone.

"Jack was keeping you informed of everything at the police station and he also stole the C-4 that you used on Dr. Kline's car?"

"Yes, but of course he wasn't the only one keeping me informed."

"There was someone else."

"Who?"

"You Damon, you where giving me a lot of helpful information. After I showed you how Dr. Kline's car was booby trapped to explode. Which was no detective work, I blew it up so of course I knew exactly how the explosives were set to explode. That helped to gain your confidence, and then Lora here convinced you that I was sincere about finding Adam. The accident was a shear stroke of genius; that was the icing on the cake. After that you were sure I was on the level."

"What about the night at the lake? The night you tried to kill Charley. How did you know that Lora might be the person Adam had given the book to?"

"We didn't know for sure. Through the process of elimination, there was not anyone else left. We knew Charley did not have the book, so we decided to take the chance that it might be Lora. As it turned out we were right."

"Your brother John really had us fooled, he is a good actor."

"No, he wasn't acting. He is gay and really was in love with Gant. He was hoping that he and Gant could continue their relationship after we recover the treasure. Course John did not plan to reveal his roll in finding the treasure to Gant. He wouldn't have to; Gant had plenty of money that they could live on. It is Gant's fault, had he not listened in and overheard me talking to John over the phone then Gant would still be unharmed by this whole thing. He heard me tell John that I believed Lora to be the contact person and the person that had the book with the ciphers in it. After John hung up the phone, I heard the extension hang up. I knew that Gant had heard what I told John and he would want to get word to you as soon as he could do it without John knowing. Jack and I drove to the lake right away and were waiting for Gant at the boathouse. John, or Hank as you knew him, did not know that Gant had overheard the conversation. He also did not know we were at the boathouse waiting to kill his boyfriend. He was really upset when Gant did not die the painless death we told him he would. When he realized that Gant was still alive and crippled physically and maybe mentally for life, he was genuinely upset. After almost a year he and I, both, had become very involved with Charley and Norma."

Then Jack yelled and Allen looked in the direction of the vault in time to see John on the ground and Jack falling over. This held his attention long enough for me to get to my gun and had it pointed at his head when he turned back toward us.

"Drop the gun Morris, or I will blow your head off and enjoy doing it. This whole area is surrounded by police officers."

Morris had a shocked look on his face as he dropped his gun on the ground. Then he saw Kelly and Bill heading up toward where Jack and John were lying. They had shot both of them with tranquilizer guns that had knocked them out cold.

"How did you know, Damon?"

"You made a couple of small mistakes, just enough for me to be inquisitive enough to call the CIA. I wondered if it would be possible to get a message to Adams brother; if there was anyway to Contact Adam's Brother Tom in the event of a Family emergency. Of course, they told me nothing.

They wouldn't even admit to knowledge of or that they had ever heard of Tom Knight."

Then the man that had been in Charley's office from Langley came out of the bushes also.

"Allen Morris, I would like you to meet the real Tom Knight."

Other officers were now on the scene and with Allen, Jack and John all handcuffed and in custody. We finished the digging at the treasure vault.

Jack and John were now awake again. We decided to let them stay to see what they had given their lives and had sacrificed other innocent lives to obtain.

"Damon, how did you know?"

"Well to be honest Allen, you had me fooled. The one thing that bothered me was why wouldn't Adam tell his brother about what he was involved in and what was going on? After all his brother was a spook for a government agency, secrets were his business. If anyone could help him, protect him or keep a secret it was his brother. I just could not believe that he would allow his brother to think he was dead when he was not.

So yesterday I called Langley Virginia the CIA Headquarters and talked to a man, told him what all was going on here and asked if there was any way possible to give Tom Knight the message. He told me he would get back with me. This morning Tom Knight showed up at my office. He explained that he had been in Afghanistan for two years, the prisoner of terrorists. That Adam was lead to believe that he was dead, which explained why Adam had not tried to get in touch with him. In a covert raid on the terrorist camp where Tom was captive, Navy Seals rescued him. They flew him to a hospital in Germany where he has been until a couple weeks ago. He did not know anything about what was going on with his brother or here until I called yesterday.

He tried to get in touch with Adam, but was unable to find out where he was or what he was doing.

When the man I talked to told him everything, he drove down here today to find out what the heck was going on and what this was all about. He gave me a belt with a tracking device in it just in case but I also told them what the location was of the treasure, according to the information I found in the book.

We needed you to play out your hand, so we would know everyone that was involved in this with you. We also needed to know what happened to Adam and Ellen and where they were now. The belt also contains a wire and everything you said is on tape.

The Sheriff interrupted me as he approached our location.

"Lieutenant, we have completed digging and are about to open the vault. I thought you and Lora would want to be there when we open it."

"Most definitely Sheriff. Lora is over at the rescue squad being treated and resting from her ordeal. I will go get her and we will be there in a minute."

"Okay, we will wait for you. But hurry would you; we are all excited about seeing what, if anything, there is."

"Officer, take these three pieces of garbage up there also. I want them to see what they are going to death-row for."

With the large rock, covering the entrance rolled to the side, the entrance to the vault was now clear. I carefully entered what appeared to be a large hollow area under the rocks. I shined the light in not knowing what to expect.

As I moved the light around I got a reflection off something in the far corner of the cave-like vault in the rocks.

It was what appeared to be a brass trunk, half buried in the dirt. I moved toward it, followed by the Sheriff and a couple officers. We dug up the chest and took it out into the sunlight. It appeared to be the only thing in the vault. There was a very rusty Iron lock on it that had rusted to the point that it fell off the chest when we touched it.

The chest was heavy, but not heavy enough to be the treasure or even full of gold or gems.

When we opened it, there was a large ceramic jar in it, like an old milk jug. Someone had tightly sealed the jug to prevent moisture from getting in it. It took a few moments to get the top loose enough to open. We carefully opened the jug and removed its contents.

During the Civil War, anyone donated anything to the southern cause or property confiscated in the name of the Confederacy. Was reimbursed, in a matter of speaking, with bonds to the person making the donation or that had property confiscated. They were Confederate War Bonds that would only have a value if the south won the war. That is what the jar was filled with, a couple million-dollars worth of almost worthless Confederate War Bonds. From a historical aspect, they might be worth a couple thousand dollars, if that much.

Either Thomas Beale or some of his associates had returned and donated the treasure to the Southern cause or the treasure could have been discovered by Confederate solders, during the war and the treasure seized and replaced with these bonds.

Eight people had died, one crippled for life, property and lives destroyed, all over a bunch of worthless pieces of paper. The gold in the back of the truck that Adam had found was all of the treasure that remained.

I was happy to show the three men now in custody and their dreams of wealth now shattered, what they had done all this for. To watch them being taken away in handcuffs to prison filled me with satisfaction. I would be testifying at their trial and I hoped my testimony would be the cause of them all getting the death penalty.

I took Lora in my arms and we hugged each other so tightly that it hurt. Kelly and Bill following close behind us as we walked to my car. I was going to give them a ride back to their car, which they had parked about a mile down the road.

After we let Kelly and Bill out to go to their car, Lora turned to me and put her hand on my hand. "Damon is it all over? I pray it is over now."

"Yes Lora, I believe it's all over now."

"Damon what about Norma, Adam and Ellen? They are in that awful quarry."

"There bodies will be recovered by divers, along with the RV. Then after an autopsy and a check for any evidence. They will be given a proper burial, I promise."

"Oh Damon, what a nightmare this has all been. I could not have survived it without you. So many good people died and for what, a jar full of worthless paper."

All I wanted was to take Lora back to the house and be with her. When we got home, we sat on the deck watching the sunset. We would never look at the valley or the city in the same way that we had once looked at it. We had come to understand how important some things in life really were.

Material wealth could never be a substitute for the things that really mattered in life. Like love, happiness and people. Ranger was on his way to a full recovery, we had picked him up on our way home. We want the whole family together this evening. Fluffy and Ranger were lying on the deck near us. As we stood looking out over the valley as darkness began reducing our view. Lights started coming on in houses as families settled in for the night. I realized that there was no treasure greater or more valuable than the treasure I was holding in my arms at that very moment. The only treasure I ever needed or wanted.

The End